Under the Boardwalk

**Center Point
Large Print**

**This Large Print Book carries the
Seal of Approval of N.A.V.H.**

Under
the
Boardwalk

CARLY PHILLIPS

CENTER POINT PUBLISHING
THORNDIKE, MAINE

This Center Point Large Print edition
is published in the year 2004 by arrangement with
Warner Books.

The text of this Large Print edition is unabridged. In other
aspects, this book may vary from the original edition. Printed in
Thailand. Set in 16-point Times New Roman type.

ISBN 1-58547-499-1

Library of Congress Cataloging-in-Publication Data

Phillips, Carly.
    Under the boardwalk / Carly Phillips.--Center Point large print ed.
        p. cm.
    ISBN 1-58547-499-1 (lib. bdg. : alk. paper)
    1. Greek American women--Fiction. 2. Mistaken identity--Fiction. 3. Missing
persons--Fiction. 4. Sisters--Fiction. 5. Twins--Fiction. 6. Large type books. I. Title.

PS3616.H454U53 2004b
813'.6--dc22

                                                                        2004008038

As always, to the special people in my life:
Phil, Jackie, and Jennifer for your support,
understanding, and love.
And to Mom and Dad, for everything.

Acknowledgments

To Janelle Denison and Shannon Short for being my daily support group, best friends, and therapists all in one!

To Julie Leto, whose complicated mind gives me a plot in every book I write and whose friendship is invaluable.

To the Plotmonkeys—Janelle Denison, Julie Leto, and Leslie Kelly—without our Orlando trip, this book wouldn't have been written! We really need to do this again.

And to Lynda Sue Cooper, my special "cop" friend, and to Kathy Attalla, my first critique partner and close friend, whose knowledge in all areas far surpasses mine. THANK YOU for your help!

Under the Boardwalk

CHAPTER ONE

If walls could talk, the stories they'd tell. Especially *these* walls, Ariana Costas thought as she glanced at the rows and rows of pictures leading down the stairs of her family home. A true documentary of insanity if there ever was one—the infamous "wall of shame," as Ariana liked to call it—that portrayed her relatives at their conniving best.

Judging by the commotion she heard from the kitchen, her family was up to their usual tricks. Her heart skipped a beat as she realized that, sadly, nothing had changed in the five years she'd been gone. Apparently not even a missing daughter could deter them from their routine. Pulling her black suit jacket around her like armor, Ariana stepped inside the kitchen and into the fray.

Her mother's sister, who technically lived next door though you'd never know it with the amount of time she spent here, sat with the phone book, calling people at random.

"Hello? Do you need your chimneys cleaned?" Aunt Dee asked in her high-pitched voice. "Winter's around the corner and you can't be too careful. You wouldn't want to light a fire and discover there was an animal stuck inside, would you?" After a short conversation, she set up an appointment and marked it in her calendar.

Ariana was always amazed anyone fell for the scheme. "What are you and Uncle John going to milk these unsuspecting people for once you're inside?"

13

she asked as she walked over to the coffee machine.

Aunt Dee merely winked at her before moving on to the next number in the book.

In the meantime, her handsome father sat at the rectangular table drawing posters. A smile quirked at her lips as she took in his clean-shaven head. Prostate cancer seven years ago hadn't sidelined him. Instead, chemotherapy and her father's resulting baldness had started the family's biggest moneymaker, The Addams Family Act, derived from the old television show of the same name. Her father had taken on the persona of Uncle Fester, her beautiful mother with her raven hair was Morticia, while the rest of her relatives rallied around. Over the years the show had earned money at the local theater, and her family had become the pride of Ocean Isle, her small coastal hometown, fifteen minutes outside of Atlantic City, New Jersey.

Ariana was so grateful her father was healthy and still in remission, she kissed his bald head. Over his shoulder, she studied his poster. " 'Earn while you Eat! Join a weight study,' " Ariana read aloud. "And how much will this study cost each participant?" she asked her father.

"Only what they want to give. You know that," Nicholas said without glancing up from his work.

She rolled her eyes. Ariana had seen this scam and ones like it before. Every Costas relative conned their way through life with a wink, a smile, and legendary Greek charm. The only shocking thing was that her family members managed to avoid doing hard time, something Ariana chalked up to luck.

With a sigh, she took a cup from the pantry. She'd arrived at her parents' home late last night after being informed of her sister's disappearance, and she could barely keep her eyes open. The coffee was too dark and thick to look appealing, but then no one in her family claimed to be related to Martha Stewart or Chef Boyardee. Thank God.

She lifted the mug to her lips, breathed in deep, and choked on the fumes. She dropped the cup into the sink, her eyes watering. She tried to speak and coughed again. "What is this stuff?" she asked, wiping her mouth with the back of her hand.

Her mother breezed in, her long black hair flowing to her waist behind her, and kissed Ariana on the cheek. "It's brake fluid."

Ariana sighed. Yet another perfect example of why she'd avoided bringing friends home when she was a teenager.

Her mother patted her shoulder. "It wasn't meant to be tasted."

"Then what's it doing in the coffeepot?"

"We were out of Tupperware."

"Of course." Ariana's eyes began to tear again. "Give me a tissue, please."

A hand reached out and waved a handkerchief in front of her eyes.

"Thanks." As Ariana blotted the tears, she looked over her shoulder and into the eyes of a real, live monkey. In any other home, she'd have jumped back in fright. "Who does the chimp belong to?" she asked, resigned.

"Not a chimp, a capuchin," Aunt Dee explained as the small monkey jumped down from the counter and scampered to the middle of the room. "If you'll recall, Great-Aunt Deliria was engaged to a monkey. This could be a long-lost relative." She swept her hand wide in a grand gesture and pointed to the animal, who was now sitting on the kitchen floor and unceremoniously playing with both feet.

Ariana winced at the sight and didn't bother to remind her mother's sister that Aunt Deliria was an Addams family relative, not their own. The presence of the animal, who resembled the monkey on the television show *Friends*, spoke for itself.

Was it any wonder Ariana had escaped to Vermont and normalcy as soon as she was able?

And she'd stayed there until that phone call. The one telling her that her twin sister was missing.

"You people are insane! Aren't you worried about Zoe?" she asked.

Zoe, the vibrant, lively one. Ariana refused to believe her sister was dead. According to documented studies, Ariana should have felt her death the moment her twin left this earth. She'd known the moment Zoe broke her leg when they were seven. Surely Ariana would sense her death now. She didn't, and her heart insisted Zoe was still alive. She had to be or Ariana's chance to make amends would be gone along with her.

At the mention of Zoe's name, silence had descended in the kitchen and lasted long enough for Ariana to grow increasingly uncomfortable. And guilty. Of course they were worried. Despite the hustle of daily activity, Ariana had felt the pall of Zoe being missing, and when they thought no one was looking, she'd caught a look of sadness in each of her relatives' eyes.

Finally Nicholas rose from his seat and hugged Ariana. "It's okay," he said, his hold on her tight. "It is just that we agreed not to discuss Zoe until she walks in the door. Safe and well."

"And she will," her mother added with certainty. "Until then it's business as usual. And wait until you hear what new business we have planned."

Ariana wasn't interested in their newest scam, but those words of normalcy, at least by her family's standards, along with the scent of her father's aftershave, reassured Ariana as it had when she was a child.

Until he spoke. "Don't worry about your sister. Zoe's strong. After all, she's an Addams."

Which was enough for Ariana. "I need some air." She stepped outside and left behind the commotion, which had begun again.

Blocking out her family, Ariana started for Islet Pier. Though it was fall, she couldn't mistake the smell of the ocean, a part of living in a coastal town. And a part she missed when in the mountains of Vermont. Only after she'd walked far from her house did she realize she should have grabbed her coat. The cool breeze from the water and the fall temperatures combined to chill her skin. With home being the alternative, she shoved her hands into her front pants pockets and strode on.

Not surprisingly, Islet Pier and the stretch of beach

she and her sister used to frequent when they were kids were empty. Ariana recalled the many hours she and Zoe had played together here and the good times they'd shared, the pictures in her mind as vivid as if she and Zoe were together now. A lump rose to Ariana's throat along with the determination to find her twin and set things right between them.

A voice muffled by the sound of crashing waves interrupted her thoughts. Ariana believed she was imagining things brought on by her memories. Then she heard it again.

"Zoe!" the male voice yelled out more clearly.

Surprised, Ariana lifted her head and hoped that she'd see her sister, alive and well and as real as the sand surrounding her. She stepped out from the covering of Islet Pier and looked into the glare of the sun. At the same moment a shot rang out and a hard body threw Ariana to the ground.

"Hey, mister!"

Quinn Donovan stepped out of the South Side Center, a town-run facility for down-on-their-luck kids. He glanced at the gangly street urchin on the corner, all long limbs and wise-cracking smile. "Hey, Sam. How you doing today?"

"Not bad. Bet I can tell you where you got them shoes."

Quinn looked down at his scuffed loafers. "Where'd I get my shoes?" he asked, playing along.

The teen paused a beat before continuing. "You got 'em on your feet." "Sam" was Samantha, and she burst into belly-aching laughter at the same joke Quinn heard from her every time he volunteered. Quinn came by often to help, playing basketball with the kids or cleaning or doing whatever else was necessary.

He glanced at Sam and chuckled. Sam and the other kids reminded Quinn of his real life and prevented him from losing touch with who he really was. He'd pulled strings to get Sam placed in a decent foster home, and he refused to put up with any shit that would jeopardize her placement there.

"Shouldn't you be in school?" he asked her.

"Shouldn't you mind your own business?" The laughter quickly died as her huge green eyes flashed with defiant, angry sparks.

Quinn had been the same rebellious pain in the ass at that age. Stepping closer, he pulled the Yankees cap off her head and a mass of tangled blonde hair fell over her shoulders. Without the disguise she appeared younger and more vulnerable. Smart foster kids like Sam tried to beat the system by making themselves invisible in the mistaken belief they'd have a better chance at remaining in one home.

Shut up and don't cause trouble was the mantra repeated by caseworkers. Quinn ought to know. But even Quinn with all his experience hadn't known the kid was a girl until the third time they met. He hoped that once she adjusted, she'd trust her new foster family and revert to looking like what she was, a feminine young teen.

"They don't let you wear hats in school. Go now or I'm calling Aaron and Felice," he told her.

Sam's bravado crumbled and tears welled in her huge eyes. "They won't care, Quinn. Felice is pregnant and they don't need me around anymore."

Before Quinn could react, Sam took off in the direction of school. "Oh hell," he muttered.

Aaron and Felice were a young couple who'd failed at adoption too many times. They'd turned to foster care and requested a girl, even accepting a teenager, something few families willingly did. A hardass by nature, Quinn still had faith in Sam's foster parents.

He ran his hand through his already windblown hair and made a mental note to check in with Felice before pushing his thoughts toward *his* problems.

His Chevy Blazer sat parked across the street, but the crisp fall air, combined with the possibility of being alone, called to him. He had time before he had to return to the charade he was currently living, and damned if he wasn't going to make the most of it. He headed for the boardwalk and Islet Pier, the place that had been his refuge for as long as he could remember.

At this time of year the beach was deserted, the snack shacks were empty, and all would remain that way till spring. He breathed in the salty air and a sense of peace filled him—until his serenity was broken.

A jet black–haired woman strode down the steps, onto the sand, and toward the pier, beneath where Quinn stood. Her long dark hair blew around her shoulders in wild disarray, and the classic profile was unmistakable. A jolt of familiarity kicked him in the gut.

"No frigging way," he muttered aloud. Hadn't he taken care of Zoe Costas himself?

He calmed his thoughts and suddenly the other possibility dawned, this one more frightening than the last. If it wasn't Zoe he was watching beneath Islet Pier, it was her twin, Ari, the college psychology professor who Zoe had sworn was safely in Vermont. Who Zoe had promised wouldn't return to Ocean Isle and get in the way. Not on a bet. No matter how grief stricken Ari would have been when she heard of her twin's presumed death, Ari wouldn't desert her students mid-semester and fly home. She'd grieve in her own world, the *sane* world she'd escaped to years before. *Zoe had promised.*

Shit, he thought, shaking his head. Obviously, because of their estrangement, Zoe had no idea what her twin would or wouldn't do. Because Ari was here.

And Quinn had a problem.

Before he could decide what to do about it, the distinct sound of a male voice yelled above the crashing waves. A split second later, a shot rang out. Acting on instinct, Quinn jumped from the pier and tackled Ari to the ground.

Ariana hit the sand hard, grunting on impact. Pain shot through her chest. But even with the wind knocked out of her, she was keenly aware of the hard male above her and the too real knowledge that someone had taken a shot.

At her.

Waves beat against the shore and seagulls screeched

in the air, but in her ear, she felt hot, heavy breath. Every last nerve ending came alive with a female awareness she hadn't felt in so long.

Seconds passed in which neither of them moved. Not only was Ariana covered by a heavy male body, but he smelled extremely good. He was a combination of muscle and determination. And he'd either saved her life or fired that gunshot. She wasn't about to wait around to find out which.

As soon as he rolled away from her, she rose to her feet and took off at a run, zigzagging across the beach. The sand slowed her effort and she hadn't made it more than halfway to the main road before he grabbed her around the waist. Hauling her into his arms, he pulled her behind a vacant snack shack.

"What the hell kind of run was that?" he asked, breathing too easily considering she was huffing and puffing.

"Serpentine," she managed to explain, through her wheezing and fear.

Behind her, she thought she heard him laugh. "From *The In-Laws*?" His amused voice held utter disbelief.

But Ariana wasn't laughing. She had escaped into old movies to get away from her family's antics, and she'd obviously learned something. "If you ask me, you ought to be applauding my ability to think on my feet. When someone shoots at you, you don't give them a straight place to aim. You give them a moving target instead. It makes sense to me."

He obviously didn't agree with her thinking,

because he burst into a full-blown laugh. She tried to wriggle forward and out of his grasp, but he merely tightened his grip. He yanked her against him, pressing her solidly against his back.

Panic started to take hold, but before she could fight, he spoke. "I'm not going to hurt you," he said, his voice strangely reassuring despite their circumstances.

"Then let me go." While he debated, she used the time to draw deep, even breaths and regain her equilibrium.

He twisted around, pulling her with him to scan their surroundings. "It looks like our gunman's gone," he said at last.

She could have told him they were alone. No sound of footsteps, nothing disrupted the heady masculine breathing in her ear and against her neck, making her tingle.

"If I let you go, do you promise not to run?"

"Not that I have to answer to you, but I won't run." Because he'd promised not to hurt her and because she wanted to get her first glimpse at the man with the silken voice.

"Good." He loosened his hold, then grabbed for her hand instead. "Let's get out of sight." He turned and, after kicking the shack door open with his foot, tugged her inside.

To her surprise, she wasn't afraid to be alone with him. He turned on the light in the old building and she finally looked at him straight on. Sandy blond hair, cropped short yet still slightly messy from the wind, framed a deeply chiseled face. Dimples curved either side of his lips, and a day's razor stubble covered his cheeks.

He looked as good as he sounded. He was temptation in a black leather jacket as Ariana was now all too aware. And he was studying her with the same intensity she'd been giving him.

She should focus. She had more pressing concerns than whether his hazel eyes were more green than brown, or whether his lips were hard . . . or tender and soft when he kissed . . .

"You're not Zoe."

That broke her fantasies about the man. "What makes you so sure?"

"That's easy, sweetheart." He chuckled, his gaze raking her over head to toe. "You're dressed like a nun."

She'd always disdained her sister's flashy, sexy wardrobe, but at the moment, she'd give anything to be dressed more like her. The pantsuit Ariana had considered her armor earlier suddenly felt stifling and uncomfortable.

He shrugged. "Not to mention you're missing the second hole in your right ear."

She narrowed her gaze. He'd noticed little details about Zoe others might have missed, and she could have kissed his razor-stubbled cheeks. Ariana had found someone she could question about her sister's disappearance, and she was nearly giddy with relief.

But when he reached out and toyed with the single pearl in her ear, relief turned to desire. His calloused skin rasped over hers. Her body trembled, and it wasn't the cool air causing the sensation. "I'm glad to see you're observant."

"I'm also persistent," he said in a cocky voice that seemed to suit him.

A combination of arrogance, certainty, and suave charm, he was the complete opposite of any man she'd been with in the past. He definitely was a marked contrast from Jeffrey Boyd, the man who'd given her a taste of young love, then betrayed her by demanding she choose between him and her unconventional family. Ariana had done the only sensible thing. She'd left them all behind in search of her own life.

Unlike the men she dated in Vermont, this man was a package of pure testosterone and all-male sexuality, which probably explained the liquid rush of desire and the sudden attraction she felt for a perfect stranger. Though she sensed his need to be in control, the distinctive trait seemed to suit him. Whereas Jeffrey, she'd come to realize, had just been a pompous ass.

"If you're not Zoe, you must be—"

"Ariana." She licked her dry lips, her breath finally coming in even cadence. Gut instinct told her he wasn't a killer. He'd also been close to Zoe. Both factors tipped in his favor. "And you are?"

"Quinn." He extended his hand for a shake, holding on to her fingers for a few seconds too long to be considered polite. His thumb caressed the pulse point in her wrist before he lowered his arm to his side.

She tipped her head, ignoring the cascading sensations he'd inspired. "Quinn what?"

He shrugged. "Donovan."

"So tell me, how *do* you know Zoe?"

His gaze locked with hers. "We worked together at Damon's."

The casino. Ariana winced at the reminder of her sister's life as a sometimes showgirl, sometimes dancer, too-often con artist. "Let me guess. You were the bartender where she stripped? Her escort for ballroom dancing classes? Or her partner in bed?"

"Zoe never mentioned you were a smartass."

The chuckle in his voice cheered her. His hand came to rest on her shoulder, strong and comforting. She swallowed hard, angry at herself for her conflicted emotions when it came to her sister's choices.

She sniffed and wiped her damp eyes with the back of her sleeve. "I'm surprised she mentioned me at all."

"Actually she spoke of you often, Ari," he said gruffly, using her name for the first time.

Only her family called her Ari. This man knew that. But to the rest of the world, she was Professor Ariana Costas, proper and dignified. She'd come home to face her crazy family and she'd needed the conservative facade she'd built around herself to get through it.

But her normal camouflage wasn't helping. She hadn't been home five minutes and the insanity had begun again. Only this time she was embroiled in her sister's life, someone was taking potshots at her, and the sexiest man she'd ever seen was her only link to Zoe. Normalcy was nowhere to be found.

She met his gaze, the one that seemed to see inside her and read her emotions. "Whatever Zoe said about me, it couldn't have been pleasant."

He laughed. "Zoe does speak her mind," he said without directly replying to her statement.

"And she's cautious about trusting people." Ariana narrowed her gaze. "Yet she mentioned me to you." A fact that gave her another reason to get closer to him.

To this intense, sexy man.

CHAPTER TWO

Detective Quinn Donovan didn't break eye contact with Ariana Costas. That jet black hair framed a gorgeous face with glowing olive skin and sea green eyes befitting her Mediterranean roots. At a glance, she was identical to her sister. But her beauty wasn't what drew him. He'd worked with Zoe and *she* hadn't affected him at all sexually—though he acknowledged she was an attractive woman—and certainly not emotionally.

Yet in one meeting, Quinn had been sucker punched by Zoe's twin. There was much more to Ari Costas than good looks. In those deep green eyes, he saw a depth of character sadly lacking in his world. Even her federal-agent sister, who knew how to turn off her emotions, had softened when she spoke about her twin. Seeing Ari in person, Quinn understood why. Damned if she didn't get to him, too.

Despite the rift between the sisters, Ari seemed to know Zoe well. Quinn said, "Zoe's got good reason not to trust people." No cop or agent did. But, respecting Zoe's privacy and cover, he didn't reveal more.

"Especially me." Ari glanced away, with seeming sadness and regret.

Quinn hadn't anticipated Ari's reaction to her sister's disappearance or his response to it. He hadn't meant to hurt her, and guilt over his role in this charade hit him hard. As a child, he'd trained himself to experience no pain, yet he felt hers now.

"Aw hell." Reaching out, he massaged her shoulder, having a damned hard time ignoring the scent of her shampoo and the feel of her feminine softness beneath the suit jacket.

She shivered. For the first time, he realized she wasn't dressed for the weather. Shrugging off his jacket, he covered her shoulders with the heavy leather, all the while reminding himself he couldn't afford to let down his guard.

He didn't know who'd taken the shot or where the triggerman had gone to, but he didn't want Ari making herself an easy target. Which reminded him of her earlier attempt at saving her delectable behind. *Serpentine my ass,* Quinn thought. Didn't the woman know the old Alan Arkin and Peter Falk movie had been a comedy, not a lesson in sniper avoidance?

Another difference between Ari and her twin. If not for the outward resemblance to her experienced sister, Quinn would doubt they were even related. But they were.

And now Ari was here, getting herself mistaken for Zoe, and threatening to blow two years of painfully laid groundwork to take down a drug operation whose money was being laundered through Damon's new casino. Because Quinn had already ingratiated himself with Damon, the local division of Alcohol, Tobacco, Firearms and Explosives had agreed to take Quinn and his partner on loan from their police department. One group was working the drug sting, while Quinn was *this* close to substantiating the money-laundering accusation.

But as long as Ari stayed near Atlantic City, she was in danger and so was the op he'd spent two years setting up. Both Zoe and his superiors were going to be royally pissed at this turn of events, no more than Quinn himself.

He wanted Ari, her soft body, fragrant scent, and the feelings she aroused in him, gone. "Let me take you home."

She shook her head. "I'll be fine."

"Because if the sniper comes back, you'll *serpentine?*"

She scowled at him. "I hadn't thought about him returning," she admitted.

"Is your car around here?" he asked, even though he'd seen her walk to the beach and knew just how close her parents' house was located.

She shook her head.

He placed a hand on the small of her back and steered her toward his truck. Once they were seated inside, Quinn laid an arm over the back of her headrest and turned her way. "I assume you'll be going back to Vermont soon?"

29

Now that she'd been shot at and scared half to death, he was sure she'd leave New Jersey far behind. She'd damn well better, because until Ari was on a plane out of here, she was a walking target and was Quinn's problem.

"I'm not leaving until Zoe comes home," she said.

He clenched his jaw. "I thought the police said . . ."

"The police said she's *missing*," Ari said sharply.

"Missing with little likelihood of being found. No clues, no body," he said, softening his voice when he ought to be hammering the point home. When was the last time he'd tempered his words or his tone for anybody?

"Exactly." Her body shook with pent-up emotion. "And until I *see* her body, I will believe she's very much alive." Wrapping her arms around herself, Ari curled into the passenger seat beside him. "I'm staying right here and waiting until she walks in the door."

"Good God," Quinn muttered, running a frustrated hand through his hair. "Does stubbornness run in your family or what?"

She tilted her head toward him. "Why? Do you have a problem with stubborn females?" she asked, a small smile tilting her lips.

He groaned, then leaned so close he saw light freckles on her nose. "Listen very carefully to what I'm going to tell you, because I only intend to say this once."

Her eyes grew wide with anticipation.

"Your sister's alive."

She sucked in a deep breath but before she could interrupt, Quinn continued. "I can't tell you how I know or why I know, and you can't reveal what I just said to another living, breathing person on this earth."

And she'd better follow his instructions. Ari had caused enough trouble already. Just by showing up in Ocean Isle, she'd not only made herself a walking target, but she'd raised the notion that Zoe might not be dead after all.

"But—"

"Just listen." He placed a finger over her damp lips. The electrical connection pulsed directly to his groin. A damned inconvenient reaction, Quinn thought, and gritted his teeth. "Zoe will contact you when she can. In the meantime, you get on a plane to Vermont and do not under any circumstances come back until your sister tells you it's safe."

The entire operation depended on her cooperation. Damon needed to believe that Zoe was dead and that Quinn had done the deed. To maintain the charade, Ari needed to take herself home. It was the only way to keep her safe. "Do you promise?"

She met his gaze, her eyes damp with gratitude as she nodded.

"You'll leave town?" He needed to hear her promise.

"Yes."

Quinn exhaled hard and sat up, turning the key in the ignition. A glance over his shoulder told him Ari was trembling with relief. And since she wasn't Zoe, he trusted her to do exactly as she promised.

31

Professor Ariana Costas would return to her safe life in Vermont. And Quinn would never see her again.

Like hell she'd leave town. Even after a fitful night's sleep, Ariana had a hard time believing Quinn could suggest such a thing.

He possessed nerve and arrogance in abundance, not to mention a hefty dose of sex appeal. But no matter how attractive she found him, she wasn't sure how much she could trust him. She'd dealt with a domineering man before, and lying to Quinn hadn't been as difficult as it once would have been.

Ariana had come from a family of con artists, and she'd definitely learned a trick or two. The ability to fib convincingly had quickly returned, even if she wasn't all that comfortable with the act. But Quinn had boldly stated that he knew for certain her sister was alive, then refused to elaborate. Not even the police could say for sure what had happened to Zoe, yet Quinn, a man she barely knew, expected her to take his word at face value.

She couldn't give in to fear—her sister's life was too important. So was making amends and repairing their relationship. When the twins should have been each other's best friends and confidantes, they'd been each other's judgmental opposition instead. Zoe had disappeared not knowing Ariana cared.

Obviously Quinn didn't know the Costas determination very well. Ariana understood the danger was as real as the bullet she'd dodged yesterday, but she was staying.

To start, Ariana needed to get information from people at Damon's Casino, where her sister had worked. Since there was a strong possibility that the person who had shot at Ariana would be there and possibly mistake her for her twin again, Ariana would take a few necessary precautions beforehand. She needed to look different enough from Zoe that the shooter wouldn't confuse them again.

To accomplish that purpose, she'd made an appointment at a hair salon for later on that day, to change her haircut and color, but the external differences could only go so far. In order to fit in with Zoe's friends and coworkers and coax them to trust her with whatever they knew, Ariana needed to dress like her twin. The dark suits and long-sleeved outfits she'd brought with her were useless for this kind of fishing expedition. She needed to shed her Professor Costas demeanor in favor of a more relaxed, Jersey-girl image.

She rifled through her sister's closet, searching for something to wear. She pulled out a black miniskirt and red leather bustier from the closet. Lordy, her sister actually *wore* these clothes?

Ariana held both up in front of the mirror and turned from side to side. How ironic that she now had to take on the look and persona of the person she'd always chided her sister for becoming.

"Barbie with a black wig," she said, frowning at the sight. She had to make the huge transition from professor to vamp in one night, and she wondered how she'd ever pull it off.

"Looks more like a Halloween costume than something my Ari would wear," her mother said from the doorway to Zoe's room.

Ariana blew out a puff of air in frustrated agreement. "Tell me something I don't know." She looked over her shoulder at her mother.

Elena wore a long black dress that matched her raven hair, which cascaded down her back. Lace sleeves covered her arms to the elbows and then trailed to the floor. Her mother was wearing her Morticia outfit.

"You know when I first saw you standing there, I had a sense of déjà vu." Elena curled her fingers around the molding in the doorway as she spoke. "I felt an immediate rush of relief that Zoe was really home."

Ariana understood her mother's feelings. For all her eccentricity, Elena adored her daughters. "Come here, Mom." With a smile that didn't come easily with Zoe missing, Ariana extended her hand, needing her mother's hug as much as she sensed Elena needed hers.

Elena shuffled across the room with tiny steps. Beneath the dress, she twisted her ankles in a practiced move that would put Angelica Huston or Carolyn Jones to shame. "Show season's over," Ariana reminded her mother.

"All the more reason to keep my skills highly polished. Although things may change soon." Before Ariana could question her, Elena finally reached her daughter and pulled Ariana into her arms.

Closing her eyes, Ariana breathed in deep and, for a

moment, immersed herself in her mother's love. She soaked in the warmth and caring, then pulled herself together. She needed to be the strong one and help her mother through this hard time.

"Mom, Zoe will be fine." Ariana counted on Quinn's words as she reassured her mother. She was putting her faith in a man she'd just met and a story he refused to tell.

She straightened and tossed the clothing onto the bed behind her. "I need something more middle-of-the-road," she murmured, speaking of clothing. "What do *you* suggest I wear to Damon's?" she asked her mother.

The normally unflappable Elena stiffened suddenly. "Damon's?" she asked, her voice rising. "Why on earth would you want to go to the casino?"

Ariana lowered herself onto the bed and urged her mother down beside her. Since she already had one daughter missing, Ariana hadn't told her mother she'd been shot at yesterday, and she understood Elena's worry now.

She squeezed her mother's soft hand. "You aren't going to lose me, too. I just want to ask some questions and find out if anyone knows where Zoe went."

Elena's gaze remained downward, studying the patchwork quilt on Zoe's bed. "But the police already questioned people," she said, urgency in her voice.

"I know but it can't hurt for me to poke around some more. I owe it to my sister." And if she wanted to be able to face herself in the mirror ever again, she owed it to herself, too.

Elena shook her head vehemently. "You can't go there. It's not safe. And I can't be responsible for anything happening to you, too."

Ariana raised an eyebrow at her mother's words. "Who said you were *responsible* for anything? Is someone blaming you for Zoe's disappearance?" But even as Ariana asked, her mother's shenanigans came back to her in living color and a sick feeling settled in Ariana's stomach. "You were involved in a con, weren't you? You and Zoe. And now she's disappeared."

"Now darling . . ."

"Do *not* patronize me." Ariana rose and began pacing the floor. "For years you've been playing people and now you finally got into something dangerous!"

"Not exactly." Elena stood and glided slowly across the room, Morticia-style, until she came up beside Ariana. "It wasn't a con. At least not in the traditional sense."

"I didn't know there were *traditional* cons," Ariana said, disgusted. She tipped her head to the side. "Okay, tell me what happened."

Elena twisted her hands in front of her. "If only you two weren't so independent! So strong-willed. If only you'd find a good man like your papa and get married . . ."

Elena always rambled when explaining, and even more so when she was upset or nervous, but Ariana wasn't in the mood to hear her mother extol the virtues of having a man by her side. "What does this have to do with Zoe's disappearance?"

"Alec Damon opened the casino a few years ago. His pictures were splashed across the newspaper. What can I say? He seemed like a good catch. He was handsome. He looked just like your dear papa when he had hair. He was wealthy—not that Zoe cares about money now, but once she gets older, trust me, she'll want security."

Her mother's eyes glazed over as she recounted the casino owner's attributes. "And he's a complete gentleman with his dancers at the casino. He seemed perfect, even if he wasn't Greek." Elena nodded in satisfaction.

Ariana pinched the bridge of her nose hard and counted to ten. She and Zoe were old enough to pick their own men, but it didn't matter now. "So you took a job as a showgirl at Damon's and cozied up to the owner?"

She bit her tongue to keep from mentioning that her mother was getting too old to continue her dance routine. The truth was Elena didn't look a day over twenty and worked hard to keep it that way.

Elena nodded. "Of course I danced. And flirted. All with your papa's approval, I want you to know. He came to every performance."

Ariana wondered how many pockets he'd picked along the way. "Mom, please. What does this have to do with Zoe's disappearance?"

"I told your sister that I borrowed money from Mr. Damon and lost it gambling. I said if she didn't do something to help me, his men would come after me and—" Elena made a distinct slicing motion across her neck with her hand, the black scarf draped from her sleeve billowing in the air.

"And did you borrow the money?"

Elena nodded. "Well, yes. I told Mr. Damon that we couldn't afford to feed the newest member of the family, and he advanced me money on my salary."

"What new family member?" Ariana asked, now completely befuddled.

Elena blinked. "Why, Spank, of course!"

"Spank who?"

"Spank the monkey!" she said as if the answer were obvious. "You two met in the kitchen earlier."

A lewd monkey with a crude name. Oh, this was so typical of her family, Ariana thought, rolling her eyes. "I'm sorry I asked. So Zoe was concerned about you, and she went to the casino to . . . what?" she asked her mother.

"To get a job and help work off my debt. Two dancers would pay off five thousand dollars much faster than one. That's what I told your sister. But there really was no debt. Not one that would have me killed, anyway." Elena's eyes filled with remorse. "In reality it was a legitimate loan for a noble purpose."

"Marrying your daughter off to a rich man isn't exactly noble. How did I come from this family?" she asked for the millionth time in her nearly thirty years.

"It wasn't just his money that made him a good prospect. Honestly, I thought he was decent and honorable and would make a good husband for your sister. Not to mention, he's sexy, which you'd see for

yourself if you went there. But you won't. I forbid it."
Elena perched her hands on her hips and glared at
Ariana.

Her expression would have worked—if Ariana were
a child and not an adult who had been living on her
own for years now.

"I just thought if Mr. Damon got a look at your
sister, he'd fall head over heels." Elena made this last
pronouncement with a plea for understanding in her
voice.

"What world do you live in?" Ariana asked, in shock
at her mother's way of thinking, although considering
everything, she really shouldn't be.

"I beg your pardon, young lady, but what's so wrong
with believing in love at first sight? I know I felt it for
your father and him for me. And Zoe thought Alec
Damon was a handsome scoundrel." Elena scowled a
bit. "I'm not sure I liked the idea of a scoundrel, but
then the right woman can always train a man."

Ariana ignored her mother's philosophical musings.
Love at first sight didn't happen to most people, or the
divorce rate wouldn't be as high as it was. "Do you
think Alec Damon had something to do with Zoe's
disappearance? Is that why you don't want me to go to
the casino?"

Elena shrugged. "I really don't know what happened
to your sister." She swallowed as her voice cracked
with emotion. "Zoe had worked at Damon's for about
five weeks. Between the two of us, we'd paid off the
loan. Zoe knew that but continued to go there every
day, so I thought my plan was working and she *liked*

39

this Mr. Damon. Not that she ever admitted as much to me. No, my Zoe wouldn't give me the satisfaction of discussing her social life."

Ariana nodded. "Zoe kept to herself. She valued her privacy."

"As do you, moving so far away." Elena shook her head, obviously frustrated. "Anyway, she went to work one day and no one's story is consistent after that. Her car was left in the parking lot and she's been missing," Elena said on a wail of despair. "And I don't want to see my other daughter walk into danger."

Since Ariana couldn't promise her mother she wouldn't be doing just that, she settled for calming her. "I want you to go lie down. Don't worry yourself sick. I'll just see what I can find out and I'll be careful doing it." Ariana placed a hand around her mother's shoulders and led her out of Zoe's room, which had too many memories and was only upsetting her.

"Exactly what are you going to do?" her mother asked.

Ariana forced a smile. "Nothing for you to worry about, I promise."

"But Zoe was the tougher twin, the one who could handle herself in most any situation, and even she obviously couldn't best this Mr. Damon. What makes you think you can, my sweet Ari?" Elena lifted her gaze, concern and the worry lines in her forehead making her seem older than usual, someone carrying more of a burden than her normal, carefree self.

Elena's distinction between the twins merely strengthened Ariana's resolve not to let her sister

40

down. "Because you need me to handle him and so does Zoe. If I can hold my own with a roomful of cocky college students, I'm sure I can deal with Mr. Damon, too."

She wasn't as certain about Quinn, the sexy man with many secrets who believed she was on her way back to Vermont. She'd just have to do her best to stay under his radar during her trip to Damon's tomorrow night.

CHAPTER THREE

Quinn had agreed to meet his partner at a Dunkin' Donuts an hour outside of Ocean Isle. Connor Brennan took a bite of a donut and chased it down with a swig of coffee before wiping the sugar off his mouth with the back of his hand.

Watching Connor chow down on donuts, Quinn groaned. "You do realize you're reinforcing a bad cliché about cops?"

Connor balled the napkin he hadn't used and tossed it into the trash, then shrugged. "Who cares? As long as my stomach's happy, I'm happy."

Quinn leaned back against the sticky seat and laughed. "You always did make your stomach a priority." He'd met Connor when they were seventeen, two unwanted boys sharing their last foster home.

"And you were always willing to help me."

Connor, with Quinn as lookout, had stolen food, not for himself and Quinn, but for the younger kids in the house. Quinn, Connor, and a revolving door of other kids had all lived under strict and irrational rules. While watching the clock tick down toward their eighteenth birthdays and freedom, the two older boys had done what they could for the younger ones before getting out.

"We make a damn good team. Then and now." Connor grinned, flashing the killer smile women loved and the one that covered all the pain he didn't want the world to see.

Quinn agreed. The other man was the brother Quinn never had.

"So you had a close call today, huh?" Connor asked.

Just thinking about Ari being shot at made Quinn break into a sweat. He nodded. "The twins looked enough alike to nearly give me a heart attack. And apparently someone else thought they'd seen Zoe, too."

Connor muttered a curse. "Well, we'd better make sure Zoe doesn't find out about her twin's arrival and do something to complicate this mess even more."

"Agreed." Quinn wrapped his hands around the warm coffee cup. "So what'd you find at the pier?"

Connor's dark gaze settled on Quinn. "Right after your call, I sent a team to the area of the shooting. They came up empty. The wind and sand blew away any evidence."

"Damn." Quinn curled his hand around a plastic fork and twirled it in his palms. "Then we just assume it was one of Damon's men who thought they saw Zoe and took a shot."

"But once he saw you tackling her, he probably realized something was off and ran."

Quinn nodded. "Damon believed I followed orders and killed Zoe. He still believes it."

Which was why Ari's presence in town was so dangerous to her and to the investigation. "I assume you covered your ass with Damon today?" Connor asked.

Quinn nodded. "First thing I did after driving Ari home was to let Damon know Zoe's twin paid her family a visit—and left again. So if someone who answers to Damon made the same mistake I did and thinks Zoe's alive, Damon will correct them."

Connor let out a slow whistle. "The good professor nearly tossed two years' worth of undercover work down the drain." He shook his head. "So tell me," he said, the laughter in his voice signaling a fast change of subject, "is Ari as sweet looking as her sister?"

"She's sweeter." The words slipped out before Quinn could censor them.

"In what way? Sweet ass? Sweet cheeks?"

"Sweet Lord," Quinn said, rolling his eyes. He hated hearing Ariana Costas reduced to a piece of eye candy, but damned if he'd give Connor the ammunition to rib him for the duration of this case. "She's exactly like Zoe," he lied.

Connor's fathomless stare told Quinn he didn't believe him for a second.

"And I made her swear she'd go home."

"Think she'll listen?" Connor asked.

Quinn nodded. "Without a doubt. She didn't strike

43

me as headstrong like Zoe." Instead she was softer and more vulnerable.

And the fact that Zoe had faked her death, no matter how noble the reason, would hurt Ari. Normally Quinn lied without blinking, but he hadn't been able to forget the pain in Ari's eyes or the hope he'd seen when he'd admitted her sister was alive. He didn't want to be around when Ari found out the disappearance was a deliberate hoax. Ari would probably want to kill her sister all over again, unlike the rest of her eccentric family, who'd probably applaud the charade.

Zoe had once regaled him with stories and just the thought of their strange, large family made Quinn, the poster child for dysfunctional childhood and solitary living, break out in hives.

He shuddered and, after a quick glance at his watch, turned his attention back to Connor. "So what's happening on your end?"

"Just some basic bartending. Nothing out of the ordinary. Unless you count one pain-in-the-ass waitress," Connor muttered.

"Is Maria still busting your balls?"

"*No* woman busts them unless I let her."

Quinn raised an eyebrow. "Did I hit a soft spot? For a *woman?*" he asked in disbelief.

"You mention Maria, I push harder on the subject of how Ariana Costas got to you, my friend. The choice is yours." His partner leaned across the table, a menacing look crossing his face.

Too bad for Connor, that expression only worked on

the criminals and coworkers who didn't know him as well as Quinn. Quinn rubbed his hands together in anticipation of ribbing Connor further. Until his friend's words sank in. Under threat of having his sudden, unexpected feelings for Ari uncovered and dissected, Quinn would have to back off.

"I've gotta go." He stood and pulled his keys from his jacket pocket.

"Glad we understand each other," Connor said, his shoulders more relaxed now that Maria's name was out of the discussion.

Quinn shook his head and stifled a laugh. He consoled himself with the notion that by tomorrow, Maria would still be around making Connor squirm, while for Quinn, Ari would be a distant memory.

The next night, Connor stood behind the bar at Damon's mixing cocktails. The drink, a Cosmo in a brandy snifter with extra ice, ordered by a man in a large black cowboy hat, had him preoccupied until a sixth sense prickled the back of his neck.

Not one to ignore his gut, since it had kept him alive when he was a kid and again on the force, he raised his gaze. Taking in the sight of the woman who had to be Zoe's twin, Connor let out a slow whistle. Quinn was going to be pissed as hell, Connor thought.

He served the cowboy with the New York accent his drink along with a glass of ice water, no lemon, for the man's wife, before turning his attention to Ariana. She wore tight-fitting black leather pants and a bright red sweater that would be conservative if not for the low-cut V-neck that showed off her ample cleavage and a hint of white lace.

Instead of Zoe's jet black hair, hers had an auburn tint, and where her sister's flowed down her back, Ariana's brushed her shoulders in a chic cut that emphasized her olive skin and intense green eyes.

He could see why his best friend had fallen for her at a glance. Even if Quinn wasn't ready to admit it just yet. "What can I get you?" Connor asked, making a show of wiping down a bar glass as he spoke.

"Gray Goose on the rocks with a lime." She pursed her lips together in thought. "And information."

Because Connor was a trained professional, he caught the nearly imperceptible tremor in her voice. Still, he got to work on her request and mulled over her statement. Though he didn't know why she was here, he expected her to get the lay of the land and ask subtle questions. The kind he'd have no trouble accommodating. He needed to get a solid handle on her, since Quinn had already proven himself less than able to predict this woman's actions, Connor thought, holding back a chuckle.

"So how long have you been working here?" she asked.

"About a year and a half. Why?" He slid the drink across the bar on a cocktail napkin.

She shrugged. "Because my sister used to serve drinks here. I'm looking for people who saw her before she disappeared."

So much for anticipating her behavior. The only expected thing so far had been her quivering voice.

But despite her nerves, she'd gone right for the killer question.

He kept his tone casual as he asked, "What's your sister's name? There's plenty of babes who work here and move on."

"But only one who disappeared, I assume."

Before Connor could reply, Maria sauntered over and placed her tray down on the counter. Connor didn't need a distraction, and Maria, with those eyes that saw too much and who got to him in a way no woman ever had, diverted his attention too easily. She'd also been ducking his come-ons in a way he wasn't used to.

"Why don't I refresh your memory," Ariana said. "My sister's name is Zoe. That's a pretty unusual name and she's my twin. Another reason I'd think you'd remember her," Ariana said, forcing Quinn to tear his gaze from Maria.

Maria, meanwhile, glanced back and forth between Connor and Ariana and a scowl crossed her luscious lips. Lips he fantasized about in his sleep, drifting across his body and giving him immense pleasure.

Her displeased expression was the first indication Connor had ever had that Maria reciprocated his interest. Suddenly stringing Ariana along took on greater appeal, and he bit back a grin.

He leaned across the bar, closer to Zoe's twin. "Is your sister a beautiful redhead like you?" he asked in a deliberately husky voice.

"Okay, assuming my face isn't ringing any bells, no, she doesn't have red hair," Ariana said, her exasperation obvious. "She has long black hair. At least she did the last time I saw her."

Was it Connor's imagination or had a fleeting frown crossed her face?

He had no time to think further because she continued speaking. "But as I said, we're twins, so thank you for the compliment." She fluttered heavily made-up lashes and shot him a wide smile, no evidence of sadness at all. He wasn't sure which was the act and which was forced, nor did he care to figure her out. He just needed to keep her in the dark.

Without warning, Maria lifted her tray and smashed it down on the counter, clearing her throat at the same time. "Some of us are here to work, not pick up women. Think you can take my order sometime today?" Maria asked.

Ariana jumped, while Connor bit the inside of his cheek to keep from laughing. He'd busted his ass to get through Maria's reserve, and all it took was another woman's interest to light a fire beneath her. Hot damn.

He let his gaze slide provocatively over Maria's tight black miniskirt and tight white stretch tee. "Green's an awfully pretty color on you, sweetstuff. I'll be with you in a second."

He turned to Ariana, though he watched Maria from the corner of his eye. A red flush stained her cheeks, making her hotter and sexier than usual. Damned if he didn't want to get in on all that pent-up passion.

But first he had business to deal with. "I remember her now. Your sister hasn't been around here in a while," he said to Ariana, finally acknowledging the truth. Maybe Ari would accept surface answers, but Connor doubted it. "The police stopped by asking questions, but from what I heard, they came up empty, too." He tilted his head toward her. "My condolences though."

Her eyes glazed but to her credit, she recovered with a swing of her shiny hair. "None necessary. Zoe'll come home soon." Rising from her seat, she slid twenty dollars across the wood countertop, waited for him to make change, then left him a nice tip.

"Where are you off to?" he asked.

She shrugged, drink in hand. "Maybe I'll check out the slots."

Bullshit, Connor thought, but he just didn't know exactly what Ariana Costas had in mind. And *that* made him nervous.

"If you hear anything about my sister, I'd appreciate it if you'd give me a call." Her gaze held his a few seconds too long, and he saw the desperation in her eyes.

He'd been in this business long enough not to fall into the trap of guilt. He only hoped his buddy Quinn could hold out, too.

"Bye," she said with a wave.

"See ya." He glanced down. Only then did he notice she'd left a card with her handwritten phone number on it along with the gratuity. He pocketed the paper in his back jeans pocket.

Across from him, Maria seethed with jealousy, and Connor wondered how to best use this unexpected show of emotion to his advantage.

With full appreciation of what fate had shown him, he turned his attention to Maria. "I'm all yours, sweet-stuff. What can I do for you?"

Quinn stretched out at a booth in the lounge across from the baccarat tables, Damon beside him. His boss liked to monitor the big gamblers, and this view gave him ample opportunity. Damon's woman of the week, this time a busty blonde, hung on to every word he said, but all the while Damon surveyed his domain. And Quinn watched Damon. It was a scene Quinn had repeated nightly since being let into the casino owner's inner circle.

He hoped it wouldn't last much longer. Quinn was sick of living out of a hotel room. He missed his small house on the beach and the freedom to do what he wanted, when he wanted, without people looking over his shoulder. Most of all, he missed Dozer, his mixed breed who was currently residing with Al Wolf, director of the youth center. He hoped Dozer was behaving himself and not slobbering all over the kids, or else Wolf would . . . *Holy shit.*

Quinn's thoughts trailed off as the woman who'd promised him she'd return to Vermont strode into the room. Even with some outward changes, Quinn would recognize her in a heartbeat. She made her way into the casino, hips swaying, newly cut hair bouncing against her shoulders, and those green eyes darting around the room, something he recognized as pure nerves showing through.

Since tackling the professor in her dark suit two

days ago, he'd bet she wasn't used to her new look or sexy clothing. Neither was he. Under any other circumstances, he'd enjoy the view, but not tonight. He was furious, and when her gaze met his and remained, he refused to look away, forcing her to hold his stare or blink first.

She held her own.

She'd promised to get her ass on a plane. She hadn't. By walking in here, she'd shown she wasn't scared of the repercussions. She should be, Quinn thought as he rose from his seat.

But before he could intercept Ari and prevent Damon from seeing Zoe's twin, Damon put a hand on Quinn's shoulder. "Is that the woman you were talking about?" Damon nodded toward Ari.

"That's her," Quinn muttered.

As if Damon's date sensed competition, she hung on more tightly to his arm.

The fact comforted Quinn, while he tried to figure out what to do about this newest complication. "I thought she was leaving, but don't worry. I'll get rid of her."

"Let's see what she wants first," Damon suggested.

Quinn watched through gritted teeth as Ari strode up the three steps to the bar and greeted them with a wide smile. Thank God Damon preferred blondes, Quinn thought.

"Hi." Her gaze encompassed both men and Damon's date.

"What are you doing here?" Quinn asked, to hell with preliminary niceties.

She shrugged but didn't flinch at his angry tone. "I thought I'd check out where my sister works." She motioned around the room with one elegant sweep.

"Worked," Quinn reminded her. "You wanted to see where your sister worked."

She lowered her gaze, the confidence in her demeanor not as strong now. "I'm just not used to thinking of Zoe in the past tense." She drew a deep breath. "But you're right. I wanted to see where my sister *worked*." When she looked up, her grin was nowhere to be found.

A punch in the gut would have been a gentler way of hurting her, Quinn thought. But if she trusted him at all, which she had no reason to do, she'd play this game through. In the end, she would see her sister again.

"So now you've seen. Don't you have a plane to catch?"

Damon stepped forward. "Tsk, tsk, Quinn. That's no way to speak to a beautiful lady."

Damon's arm candy started to whine, but Damon cut her off by pulling cash out of his pocket. "Go play," he ordered his companion.

The blonde whose name Quinn hadn't bothered to learn treated Damon to a kiss on the cheek and sashayed off.

Ari raised an eyebrow Quinn's way. "I'd appreciate an introduction to your friend." Her sultry gaze settled on Damon.

Unlike when she'd convincingly lied to Quinn, now he detected traces of nervous energy as Ari made a show of fingering her purse and tapping her foot.

She was scared. Of Damon, he hoped, because that would mean the professor did indeed have the brain Zoe credited her with. And then Quinn could count on her to behave, at least while she was in the casino.

"Yes," Damon said from beside him. "I believe introductions are in order." He oozed charm. Slimy, not-to-be-trusted charm.

"Ariana Costas, I'd like you to meet Alec Damon. Mr. Damon owns this casino, in case you've been living under a rock for the last two years." Or in Vermont. "Damon, this is Zoe Costas's twin," Quinn said pointedly.

Damon smiled. "I thought I noticed the resemblance. Nice to meet you, Ariana."

"Same here." She swallowed hard. "I've heard so much about you, Mr. Damon. Not from my sister, since we . . . we hadn't been in touch in a while, but my mother talks about you often."

"Only good things, I hope?"

She nodded. "That's another reason I came by. I wanted to meet you. To thank you in person for lending my mother money when she was in need." Ari held out her hand and Damon took it.

"My pleasure." He released his grasp, his astute gaze raking over Ariana's body. "Your mother was a hard worker and a very talented dancer." He inclined his head. "Do you share her ability?"

She laughed. A full-blown, light and airy sound. Quinn's groin immediately tightened. Damn the woman, anyway.

"No. I'm sorry to say I have two left feet."

"Somehow I doubt that." His gaze traveled the length of her body, beginning with her long legs and remaining on her cleavage before finally landing on her face.

She did her best not to squirm, but failed. Still she faced Damon head on. "Thank you again for helping my family. And it was nice meeting you," Ari said, all but ignoring Quinn.

"The feeling's mutual. And . . ." Damon paused. "I'm sorry about your sister. Zoe was beautiful inside and out. She worked hard and we at Damon's valued her."

Ari tipped her head. "That means so much."

"Quinn, why don't you show Ms. Costas around the casino." The suggestion was nothing short of an order.

Despite Damon's civil veneer, Quinn didn't want her staying around unchaperoned. Quinn would follow his order with pleasure. Not just to find out what the hell was behind Ari's agenda, but to get closer to the sultry beauty for reasons he didn't want to name.

Putting his arm around her waist, he led her down the stairs and away from Damon. She was smaller than she looked, and her waist fit snugly against his body, feeling too good considering he wanted to throttle her.

He left the casino behind, entered the hotel lobby, and steered her directly to the office area and a vacant hallway. He paused only long enough to unlock the door and nudge her in. Entering his private domain, he slammed the door shut behind him and locked them inside.

He turned on the light before folding his arms across his chest and facing Ariana. "Well?"

"Well what?" She batted her eyes and forced the most innocent look she could manage.

It had to be forced considering she must be quaking in her stiletto pumps. "Does this look like Vermont to you?" He gestured around the state-of-the-art office, with its new computer, expensive desk, sophisticated phone system, and both audio and video bugs recording everything that was said.

She shrugged, taking in the sterile environment where he spent many of his days. "Not particularly. My office is a lot more musty and not as bright."

He closed his eyes and counted to ten. She was baiting him on purpose, and she was more like Zoe than he'd given her credit for. He wouldn't make the same mistake twice.

"Where's my sister?" she asked.

"She's missing. I thought the police told you that."

"But you—"

"Told you to get on a plane and go home." Quinn needed this record of their conversation for Damon's viewing later, but he'd never consider any place in this casino a safe place to talk freely.

His room upstairs was different, since he swept it regularly for bugs. He refused to be watched when he was alone, and Damon knew it. But Quinn was smart enough not to take Ari anywhere near his bed.

Stepping forward, he backed her against the wall,

bracing his hands over her head. Ariana sucked in a shallow breath, but her gaze never left his.

He bent his head close. Almost cheek to cheek, he inhaled her fragrant scent and felt the womanly heat emanating from her body. Apparently Ari was on edge, because she trembled and a faint sigh reverberated from her throat. He feathered his lips over the exposed skin on her neck, and that little taste made him hungry for more. Shifting his attention to her mouth, he touched his lips to hers. Their chemistry exploded.

He kissed her and she kissed him back, proving she was as greedy as he for intimate contact. Knowing she wanted him, too, he slipped his hands to her waist, holding her in place against the wall. And when she didn't fight that move, he slid his thigh between her legs, bracketing her in place. All the while his tongue tangled with hers and he learned the depth of the hidden fieriness she kept inside.

This woman excited him on many levels. She was complex and intelligent, with equal parts spunk, attitude, and vulnerability. It was the vulnerability that had driven her away from her family, and it was a part of what enticed Quinn so much now. He wanted to know her, contradictions and all.

Temptation beckoned. No one would blame him if he tossed her on the desk and acted out the fantasy replaying in his mind since the moment they'd met. Even Damon would merely applaud. But Quinn would blame himself. And she deserved better.

He swirled his tongue inside her mouth one last

time, let himself feel her fingers tugging at his hair and in his scalp, before breaking the kiss. His breathing came in shallow gasps. Desire clawed at him, begging him to continue what he'd started, but he lifted his head and looked into her heavy-lidded eyes.

He swallowed hard. "We can't talk here," he whispered. "This place is bugged," he said in a murmur nobody else listening could possibly detect.

"So unless you're interested in finishing what we started, you don't belong here." This time he spoke loud enough for anyone to hear, for the benefit of Damon's hidden bugs.

She ducked out from under his arms and glared at him with wounded eyes. But he could see from the almost imperceptible nod of her head that she got his message and his act for the camera.

"I don't answer to you," she said.

"Maybe you should."

She bit down on her well-kissed lower lip, pausing in thought. "I think you've got a point."

The hair on the back of his neck prickled in unease. "In what way?"

She leaned against the wall, her pose all the more seductive thanks to that hot kiss and the need still pulsing inside him. "Hire me," she said.

"Repeat that?"

"I said, hire me. Give me a job here."

Quinn couldn't believe she'd ask for something so stupid. "Why the hell would I want to do that?"

"Because I want to get closer to people who knew my

sister." Her voice softened and her gaze grew moist.

Too bad for her, he couldn't afford to give in to emotional blackmail. Besides, only a chump wouldn't figure out that she wanted entry into the casino so she could snoop around. "Sorry, but no."

She shrugged, which had the effect of lifting her glimmering cleavage for view. He wondered if the skin there tasted as good as her neck and lips just had.

"I'll just ask Damon, then," Ari said. "He seems like an agreeable enough guy. He hired my mother and my sister, and he did tell you to show me around. Besides, I think he liked me."

"Your boobs aren't big enough for him to like you," Quinn muttered under his breath.

"What?"

"Nothing," he said through clenched teeth. He wasn't thinking with his head. Not the right head, anyway. Those breasts might not be big enough for Damon, but they made Quinn's mouth water and his hands tingle with longing. She was a distraction he didn't need.

He didn't want her anywhere near the casino, Damon's operation, or him. Which meant he had a problem, since she'd already proven she'd do as she pleased. But Quinn hated being backed into a wall and he continued to grind his teeth in frustration. "What are you good at?"

"What do you want me to be good at?" she asked him.

He stepped forward, stopping until they were inches apart again. He already knew how well she kissed, how hot she made him, and how perfectly her body fit against his. The woman was playing with a man on fire. "You already told Damon you can't dance."

"There's plenty of other things I'm good at." Her eyes flashed determined sparks.

"Name one."

"I already proved I'm a good kisser, but I don't think that's what you had in mind." She cocked her head to one side, as she continued to tease and test his restraint. "I also have decent moves with my hands." She waved her delicate fingers in front of his face.

Visions of those hands roaming over his body caused an intense burning in his stomach. "Such as?"

"I waited tables in college and I can serve a mean drink."

"And what about your job, *Professor?*"

"I already took a leave." She placed her hands on her hips, as if daring him to argue.

And when her eyes darted from his for a split second, long enough to convince him she wasn't being completely honest, he wanted to. But since this damned independent woman would do what she wanted, he had no choice except to go along. "Fine. Your shift will be seven to midnight. I'll pick you up tomorrow night around six. Be ready."

"I can drive—"

He shook his head. "I plan to keep an eye on you. In fact, expect to have me by your side the entire time."

She opened her mouth to argue, then closed it again.

"Good thinking. Because I'll be watching you. And *that* is nonnegotiable."

CHAPTER FOUR

Ariana paced the floor while watching the street from the bay window in her family home. She didn't want Quinn coming here any more than she wanted him watching every move she made. He made her nervous. Not to mention his kiss was so potent it ought to be illegal.

She lifted her fingers to her lips. They'd continued to tingle all last night and through this morning. The memory of his mouth on hers and his strong thighs between her legs kept her aroused. They'd been combustible together, Ariana thought. No man had ever made her want with such ferocious intensity. And the heat in his gaze when he broke the kiss told her he'd wanted her, too. Unfortunately, he had an iron will and his desire wasn't quite as strong as his need to have her gone.

She was lucky he'd agreed to give her a job—a spur-of-the-moment idea on her part because she could think of no other way to return to the casino. Of course she intended to find Zoe, but there was more calling her back to Damon's than the mystery surrounding her twin.

Her first night there had been enlightening. Despite the fact that she'd been uncomfortable in the tight clothes and the emboldened persona she'd adopted, Ariana had been given a glimpse of her twin's more exciting life. From how men looked at her, to Quinn's

60

intense sexual reaction, Ariana had slowly discovered what it felt like to be bolder and untamed. And although she hadn't expected it, she'd enjoyed the experience too much to just walk away. Especially since she'd found a way to get information as well as an understanding of all she'd missed out on in her past.

Demanding a job from Quinn had been a spontaneous idea born of necessity—even if it meant following Quinn's rules.

She could have defied him and shown up at the casino, but he'd threatened to take her keys if she did. She believed him, which made no sense. How could she trust anything he said or did when his office was bugged, her sister was missing, and Quinn, who claimed to know the truth, wasn't talking?

At least not yet. Ariana needed time to work on him some more. So she waited for him to arrive and instead of focusing on how she'd accomplish that task, she was bothered by a more nagging question. One instilled by her past. What would this enigmatic man think of her strange family, all of whom were holed up in the kitchen, huddled over floor plans, conspiring to . . . Lord only knew what.

The answer to that question hit on a deep, raw insecurity she'd lived with since childhood, when children—girls especially—were cruel. She'd sought her escape in college and then in Jeffrey, hoping that if he fell for her first, he'd accept her family later. She'd been wrong.

She thought she'd buried those memories when she

moved away. Funny how quickly they came back now. The sight of a black truck pulling up to the curb cut off her thoughts. She ran for the door, intending to meet Quinn outside and avoid a family meeting completely.

"Ari, wait." Her mother's voice stopped her from leaving the house unseen.

Drat. "Can it wait? I'm on my way out now."

Elena shook her head. "The family's about to make a huge investment and we'd like you to approve. Besides, I want to know all about your trip to Damon's. You were so busy on the phone all day, we had no time to talk."

Ariana was too used to the Greek guilt to take her mother's words to heart. Today Ariana had a genuine excuse, since she'd been busy arranging the leave of absence she'd already told Quinn she'd taken. She'd also had to explain her sudden disappearance to her friends and colleagues, all things she wasn't ready to discuss with her mother.

Ariana glanced out the window. Quinn was on his way to the front door. "I promise I'll look at the family's plans in the morning, okay?" Though why they needed Ariana's approval when they'd never had it before was beyond her.

Disappointment flickered in her mother's eyes at the same time the doorbell rang.

"I've got to go. We'll talk in the morning?" Ariana kissed her mother on the cheek.

"Of course we'll talk in the morning." Elena strode around her and grabbed the door handle, taking control. "But I want to meet your friend before you go."

Ariana let out an exasperated sigh. "I'm over eighteen."

But it was too late. Elena opened the door and came face-to-face with Quinn. "I remember you," she said, a welcoming smile taking hold.

Quinn grinned right back. A warm greeting that, for Ariana, was devastating in its intensity. Heaven help her if he ever turned that warmth and happiness her way, and her stomach did a triple flip at the thought.

"And I remember you. How has Damon's best dancer been?" Quinn asked Elena.

"You flatter me." Her mother bought into his charm and actually blushed. "I'd be fine if it weren't for Zoe's situation. But you know that."

Quinn winced, his discomfort over the mention of her missing sister obvious.

"Come in from the cold." Grabbing Quinn's hand, Elena pulled him inside.

Ariana glanced at her mother and, for the first time, realized that Elena wasn't dressed as Morticia. Instead she wore black pants and a black turtleneck sweater. Relief washed over Ariana.

Her mother wagged a scolding finger her way. "Ari, you didn't tell me you met Quinn. Shame on you."

Unsure what to say, Ariana merely shrugged, and over Elena's continued chatter about how she, Zoe, and Quinn knew one another, Ariana met Quinn's gaze. His eyes appeared darker, his expression upset. Obviously he was uncomfortable with conversation that included talk of her sister.

Well, damn him, if he could ease her mother's pain and chose not to, he *should* be uncomfortable. If Ariana had proof to back up his claim, she'd tell her mother that Zoe was alive herself.

"Come inside," Elena said to Quinn, finally changing the subject.

Ariana shook her head. "We need to go or we'll be late for our *reservation*," she said pointedly. Her mom didn't need to know she'd taken a job at Damon's and have reason to worry about another daughter's safety.

"We have a few minutes to catch up," Quinn said.

Ariana shot him a dirty look.

"I always liked you," Elena said to Quinn.

"The feeling's mutual." He clasped her hand, the genuineness in his gaze all too real.

He obviously liked her mother, which didn't surprise her. With her warmth and effusive personality, everyone loved Elena. It was the family's overall dynamic that Ariana wanted to avoid.

As if reading Ariana's thoughts, her mother said, "Come meet the family."

Ariana cringed, but nobody seemed to notice as Quinn allowed himself be led into the kitchen. Ariana followed behind them, the dread in her stomach reminiscent of the times she'd brought friends home. Their laughter and snide comments would linger in her heart and mind long after the girls had left. Not for Zoe, who seemed both oblivious to her family's idiosyncrasies and untouched by teen angst. She'd always envied her twin that ability.

The chatter got louder as they approached the kitchen. The family remained huddled around the table, looking at plans. Aunt Dee had a book open in front of her, but Ariana couldn't see what she was reading.

Elena clapped her hands to get everyone's attention. "I'd like you all to meet our guest. Everyone, this is Quinn, a friend of Ariana's," she said, pointedly omitting her own connection to Quinn. "Isn't he gorgeous?"

Since she'd kissed that gorgeous face, Ariana was doubly mortified. She glanced at Quinn, who stood beside her, and realized he'd turned red in a full-blown blush. Ariana would take gratification where she could find it. At least she wasn't alone in her embarrassment.

Quinn waved a general greeting and glanced around at the people in the kitchen. He'd obviously intruded on a family gathering, and an uncomfortable edge gnawed at his stomach. He glanced at Ari, who didn't appear particularly thrilled either. His attention was divided between the people around him and the woman he'd kissed. He had spent long hours last night reliving that kiss and deciding how to deal with Ari. Around dawn, he'd decided that keeping her off balance and aggravated was his best plan. Anything to prevent her from getting too close—or *him* from wanting to get even closer.

Before turning his attention to meeting each person individually, he leaned closer to Ari and put his plan into action. "Miss me, babe?"

"Like a bad habit," she muttered.

He grinned. "For a college professor, you've got a lot of spunk."

Before she could reply, her family pushed her out of the way. They all gathered close, speaking to him at the same time. He couldn't hear their names, which was fine since it wasn't likely he'd remember even if they'd all been individually introduced.

Despite Zoe's preparing him, Quinn was shook up now. Coming from foster homes where no one gave a damn who came or went, he found this huge conglomeration of interested faces was disconcerting. He glanced at Ariana for reassurance, but she'd been moved to the outside of the group, and damned if she didn't look more uncomfortable than he felt.

Then again, she was the twin who'd hightailed it to Vermont and hadn't looked back until now. Though a part of him could understand the need for space, a bigger part of him wondered why she didn't value this family unit she was so lucky to have.

"Quinn." A large, bald man stepped toward him. "Irish?" he asked.

"Oh, for heaven's sake, Dad, leave him alone," Ari said.

"That's okay." Quinn turned to the older man he'd met once or twice before at the casino when Elena was dancing there. "I'm honestly not sure. I don't know much about my heritage."

His mother had been the quintessential cliché, a drug addict whose bed had been a revolving door for men who paid for her services, which supported her

66

habit. He supposed his father had been one of her paying clients, with no name, no forwarding address. His mother had OD'd one day, which came as no surprise to Quinn, considering the life she'd lived.

Ari's father shook his head. "A damn shame, not knowing your roots. But lack of knowledge means there might just be Greek blood in you yet." Hope and pride infused his tone. "What's your last name?"

"Donovan." At least that's what his mother claimed on his birth certificate.

"Good to meet you, Quinn Donovan. I'm Nicholas. Ariana's father. Welcome to my home." He slapped Quinn on the back in a way that made him feel accepted, especially since the rest of the family looked on, nodding their approval.

All except Ariana, who shook her head and shuffled uncomfortably from foot to foot.

An unfamiliar lump of emotion welled in the back of his throat. "Thank you, sir."

In reply, Nicholas pulled him into a bear hug. Another gesture so different from any Quinn knew well. Before he could become too complacent, he felt a tingle in the area of his back pocket, and a sense of disappointment pricked him deep inside, in his heart. Though he'd been forewarned of their tendencies, he still couldn't believe they'd turn their tricks on an unsuspecting guest of their daughter's.

Once Nicholas released him, Quinn stepped back and studied the family, wondering how to confront them. With a shrug, he opted for the direct approach. "Whoever took my wallet, I'd appreciate it if you'd give it back now." Quinn held out his hand and waited.

Elena sighed. "I told you it was too soon, Nicky."

A woman with her dark hair in long braids shrugged and said, "Back to the drawing board."

But no one seemed as upset at being caught as they were by the fact that whoever'd done the deed still hadn't perfected their technique.

"Well?" Quinn asked. "My wallet?"

Ari moaned. "Turn around, Quinn," she said, her voice dull and resigned.

He turned and came face-to-face with a grinning monkey holding his leather billfold in its hand.

"I don't know why they insist on saying men are descended from apes." Uncle John, another man who'd crowded Quinn earlier, spoke up. "This one's not the brightest bulb in the box."

Quinn shook his head in disbelief. He'd had his pocket picked by a monkey that resembled Marcel on *Friends*. Quinn wondered if it was possible to arrest the animal or if Ari's family had managed to pull the ultimate con. He wondered what they'd say if they knew he was a cop. And then he pondered what the hell he was doing analyzing so much when he was having such a damn good time watching these people in action.

He accepted the wallet and slipped it into his front jeans pocket. "Don't try reaching in there," he warned the smiling monkey.

"We really should go," Ari said, her eagerness to leave almost palpable.

He wasn't in any rush himself, but she was so mortified, he decided she deserved a break. "We do have to get going."

"But Ari hasn't seen our plans for the new family business yet," Elena said.

"There's always tomorrow, Mom."

Her mother shook her head, all that long hair whipping around her. "I'm sure your sister thought the same thing and where is she now?"

Quinn shut his eyes. He didn't know how much longer he could take lying to Ari's entire family when he could so easily put them out of their misery. But then he'd jeopardize two years' worth of carefully laid undercover work. He'd already been stupid enough to confide in Ari enough to ease her suspicions.

He reminded himself that his reasons for keeping silent were just. If he could hold out a little longer . . . He opened his eyes in time to see Ari hugging her mother tight.

"Tomorrow's Friday," Elena said. "I'm planning a big meal and I expect you here with the family. We'll talk, fill you in on our project . . . it'll be like old times."

Ari nodded. "I'll be here."

Quinn, feeling like an outsider, took a step back toward the door. Then another, and another. He was used to being on his own, but being alone in a close-knit crowd reminded him too much of all he'd missed out on in life. Finally he reached the door.

"And Quinn, you be here at four, too," Elena called out. "Living at the hotel, you could use a good home-cooked meal."

He raised an eyebrow. "I have a business meeting." He refused to accept their pity.

"So cancel it," Nicholas ordered. "When Elena speaks, people listen. And when she cooks, they eat," he added, laughing.

"You'd better listen or else Yiayia will put a spell on you," Ari whispered, coming up beside him.

"Who?"

"That's Greek for Grandma."

"Can I take that as an indication *you* want me here, too?" he asked.

She shook her head, the newly cut strands swaying sassily around her cheeks. "I'm just looking out for my mother. She's had more than her share of disappointment lately. For reasons I can't seem to fathom, she likes you and wants you around."

Her glossed lips glistened and his body tightened, yearning for another taste. "I think her daughter does, too."

"Arrogant man."

He chuckled, then turned to the family. "Thanks, Elena. I'll be here. Nice meeting you all." He followed Ari into the living room and back out the front door.

A stubborn woman with her own share of secret pain, a bizarre family of con artists, and a pickpocket monkey. And he thought his life had become routine.

Ariana awoke, stretched, and every muscle screamed in protest. If this morning was painful, last night had been no better. Her first shift at Damon's had been a crash course in hell instigated by one angry coworker named Maria. Quinn had put the experienced cocktail waitress in charge of teaching Ariana the ropes, then left her under both Connor and Maria's watch. It didn't take long for Ariana to pick up the sexual undercurrents between the two of them and realize she was a point of contention between them. Connor's constant flirting with Ariana didn't help the other woman's attitude, even if Ariana did suspect he was doing it on purpose, to aggravate Maria.

And speaking of aggravating, Quinn had made himself suspiciously scarce last night. Though Ariana should be grateful he wasn't underfoot as he'd threatened, she'd found herself watching for him all evening and was disappointed he hadn't shown up, except to drive her home. She suspected he'd tapped Connor as his eyes in the casino while Quinn himself made sure she didn't snoop around before or after her shift.

Which left her with only one way to get information about her sister. She needed to make friends with Maria. Ariana had an idea or two about how to take care of the other woman's sour opinion of Ariana, and it involved using Quinn. Quinn, who'd tried to maintain distance by not talking during the trip to and from the casino. Quinn, who'd walked her to the door, and whose hazel eyes had golden sparks as they'd stared into hers beneath the porch light.

He'd leaned forward, coming close. She'd seen the conflicting struggle going on in his mind, the desire to kiss her again as all-consuming for him as it was for her. He'd been about to give in. She *knew* it, and then the damn monkey had tapped on the window and waved, a big grin on his ugly face.

Aunt Dee had pulled him away, but the damage had been done. The moment had passed. Quinn had had time to think and regain control, while Ariana realized her family had been spying on them the entire time. Déjà vu all over again, she thought wryly.

Rolling to her side now, Ariana checked the clock on the nightstand, shocked to discover it was almost noon. She hadn't slept so late since . . . well, since the last time she'd pulled cocktail waitress duty back in college. But she didn't have all day to luxuriate, because some shopping was definitely in order. Though Damon's had a uniform, she needed a comfortable pair of shoes or she'd never make it through her second shift.

The buzz coming from downstairs told her that her nosy family was already up and about. She wasn't anywhere near ready to deal with them yet. She had no idea what they had planned, but she'd find out soon enough.

Ariana showered and slipped out the door before her mother could interrogate her about the trip to Damon's, or worse, her daughter's dealings with or feelings for Quinn.

So maybe she was a coward but Ariana stayed out all afternoon, coming home close enough to four o'clock that she didn't have time to talk to anyone before

Quinn's arrival. After a quick change of clothes, she packed up her uniform in an overly large handbag, smoothed her black skirt, took a deep breath, and headed down the stairs to face the troops, only to find out someone had already let Quinn inside and led him to the kitchen.

Ariana joined them, watching as each family member welcomed Quinn as if he were an old friend, which he might well be, since he'd apparently worked with Zoe at the casino. Despite the warmth flowing through the room, Zoe's absence was obvious to Ariana, not just physically, but in the forced way her family pushed themselves through their day.

As for Quinn, though he seemed wary about the family at first, he warmed up quickly, and it was obvious her relatives liked what they saw. So did Ariana. Faded denim molded over his behind, and his broad shoulders were covered by the same leather jacket he'd worn last night. His hair was just long enough to skim the collar and make her fingers itch to run through it. He was a man comfortable in his own skin, while in contrast, here she was in her parents' house, uncomfortable in hers.

"Hi." She spoke over the loud voices.

Quinn's gaze met hers. Pleasure and happiness flickered in his normally dark gaze. It lasted a second, but long enough to fill her heart before her mother pulled her into her family's midst. "Ariana, we have a surprise for you. Look at what we've got planned."

Feeling off balance from Quinn's reaction, she focused on the table where the plans she'd seen the

73

other day had been unrolled again. "What is this?" she asked.

"A day spa," Aunt Dee answered. Today Ariana's aunt was wearing a brightly colored kimono. Unlike Elena, when Aunt Dee wasn't in character as Wednesday Addams, she refused to wear the color black. Waving her hand toward the plans, Aunt Dee asked, "So, what do you think?"

Ariana thought she was in another dimension. "What do you all know about running a spa?"

"Nothing we can't figure out from some good old-fashioned research. See?" Uncle John pulled a book from beneath Aunt Dee's hands.

"The Complete Idiot's Guide to Self-Healing with Spas and Retreats," Ariana read aloud. "Oh Lord."

Quinn's chuckle reverberated around the room but no one seemed to notice. They were too preoccupied to care about his reaction.

"What we don't know, we'll learn," Elena said, joining in. "We'll join the Day Spa Association. Did you know it's located in Union City, New Jersey?"

Ariana assumed that was a rhetorical question, and said nothing.

Aunt Dee picked up where Elena left off. "We'll research and decorate. Oh, and we'll hire only appropriately credentialed employees, of course."

"Like Spank here?" Ariana pointed to the monkey, who today wore a sundress.

Ariana hadn't realized *he* was a she. And *she* reached for and kissed Ariana's hand. Ariana tried to pull her fingers free, but the monkey held on tight.

Elena shook her head. "Be serious, Ari, will you?"

Ariana blinked at the absurdity and looked to Quinn for backup. Surely any sane man would be looking for an escape, and she'd be happy to give it to him.

But he was studying the plans with concerted interest. "This looks like a workable option," he said, glancing up from the table.

A closer look told Ariana the plans were of this house, which sat on over two acres of unused property. Both the land and the building had been in the family for generations, though nobody knew how Ariana's great-great-grandfather had acquired enough money to purchase it and Aunt Dee's lot across the street.

Ariana suspected he'd won the land gambling, and nobody had ever disagreed with her notion. "You're expanding?"

"Yes. We need to make sure we have enough room for clients," her father said. "You really think it'll work, Quinn?"

Hands in his back jeans pocket, Quinn squinted as he studied the papers. The most adorable creases formed at the corners of his eyes as he nodded slowly. "Assuming you get the appropriate paperwork and town approval, the addition will fit in nicely with the rest of the house. I think it's a great idea."

Nicholas nodded. His smile told Ariana in no uncertain terms that he was happy with Quinn. "The architect we hired already filed for permits."

"Are you going legit?" Ariana asked and immediately winced.

"Way to impress your date, Ari," Aunt Dee said under her breath.

"He's not my date," she hissed. Yet she wanted him to like her family as much as she expected him to leave screaming. She didn't understand why she cared either way.

"Tell it to someone who believes you," her aunt said in a voice filled with glee.

But Ariana was still thinking about and regretting her comment. After all, not everything the Costas family did was a con. The Addams Family show, for example. Now that was real. It was just the other 99 percent of their activities that Ariana worried over.

Quinn's expression revealed nothing about his feelings. He probably thought Ariana had been kidding, since what people in their right minds operated a scam a day?

She glanced at her father, who also seemed unfazed by her comment. He was used to her expressing her emotions. It was the Greek in her, he always said.

And he continued after Aunt Dee hushed up. "Well, I'm certainly not going to spend our hard-earned money on something the cops can come in and close down. I want you and Zoe to have something meaningful from your parents. And I know Zoe will approve when she comes home." He paused, emotion clogging his words. He glanced up at the ceiling and everyone grew silent.

Ariana knew they were thinking of Zoe. She was too. And more than ever, she prayed Quinn was an honorable man.

Nicholas cleared his throat. "This spa will give us a feeling of security—we won't have to rely only on the show from year to year," he said as he ran a hand over his bald head.

Ariana looked at him, surprised. She'd thought the show was doing well, but then, she didn't live at home nor did she visit. How would she really know what was going on? she thought with a twist of guilt in her heart.

"With this layout, we can keep our family's privacy. We wouldn't want our personal moments exposed for public view, now would we?" Elena asked.

They had before, Ariana thought, immediately recalling the *National Enquirer* article from years past, but she decided not to mention that embarrassing time.

"Quinn, would you like a drink?" Elena switched from giving her opinion to playing hostess. "I mixed up a mango-and-papaya-smoothie. Of course, I added my Yiayia's secret ingredient."

Quinn raised an eyebrow, obviously unsure whether or not to accept. Ariana helped him out with a subtle shake *no* of her head. Though Yiayia still lived in Greece, like Elena, she didn't cook.

"There's no more," Nicholas said, sparing Quinn from having to answer.

"That's impossible." Elena started for the refrigerator. "Just this morning there was an entire pitcherful."

Nicholas sighed, then placed a hand on Quinn's shoulder. "Never anger your woman, Quinn. That's what my father told me, God rest his soul. But sometimes they just put you in a place where it can't be helped. The drink tasted like crap, Elena. It wasn't fit for a guest."

She narrowed her gaze and started muttering in Greek.

Ariana knew the signs of a storm brewing, as did Aunt Dee, who buried her nose in the Idiot book while Uncle John began whistling quietly and gathered together the floor plans for the house.

Ariana had watched this scene play out many times since she was a child. "I can sleep on the couch if you need my bed, Dad."

Quinn chuckled.

"Laugh now, but a Greek woman's anger knows no bounds." Nicholas imparted those words of wisdom, patted Quinn on the back, and then turned his attention to his wife, who'd folded her arms across her chest. "Aah, *agape mou.*"

He murmured the term of endearment but Elena wasn't buying it and she slapped his hand. "Don't try to sweet-talk me. What did you do with my drink? You didn't pour it down the sink, did you?" She shook her head. "No, because that would be a waste when there are starving people in the world." She pulled open the refrigerator door.

"It's going to get worse before it gets better," Nicholas said, warning Quinn.

"There's none here," Elena said.

Nicholas sighed. "I gave it to Spank," he admitted.

"Oh, for the love of . . ." Elena trailed off. All traces

of elegance gone in the face of her anger, she slammed the appliance door closed and stomped over to the monkey. "So tell me, did *you* like my drink? The secret ingredient is one my ancestors swore would restore youth and vitality. I plan to use it in some version at the spa."

Spank bared her teeth in an ugly smile, then smacked her lips together and blew Elena a raspberry.

"*She* liked it," Elena said, obviously feeling validated.

"Actually she felt much better after I gave her some Pepto," Aunt Dee said.

"Traitor," Elena muttered.

Aunt Dee waved away her sister's words. "Kiss and make up," she ordered, pushing Nicholas and Elena together.

From past experience, Ariana knew things could go one of two ways. Her mother would either turn and walk out, leaving her father on the couch for the night, or they'd retreat to the bedroom, everyone and everything else forgotten, and stay there for hours.

Personally, Ariana had never met a man whose company she wanted in her bed for all that long. In hindsight not even she and Jeffrey had shared the passion her parents still did, leaving her to wonder if she'd find it with any man.

Her gaze fell on Quinn and electricity crackled inside her.

At the same time, her father's hand came around her mother's back, pulling her close. He whispered in Elena's ear, something only she could hear.

The next few seconds were critical, so Ariana held her breath and counted to three. Elena whirled around, but instead of storming out, she touched Nicholas's hand. "If you're serious, you can make it up to me. Come. Now." She turned, head held high, and walked out of the kitchen and stormed up the stairs.

Nicholas grinned. "It's the best part of fighting, is it not?" Then, not caring that they had an audience, or perhaps performing for them, Nicholas headed out the door, following in his wife's footsteps.

Embarrassed as she always was at their display, Ariana turned around for sympathetic nods from Aunt Dee and Uncle John, but sometime during her parents' show, they'd disappeared, leaving Ariana alone. With Quinn.

The one man she could see keeping in her bed for a long time to come.

CHAPTER FIVE

"I thought we were having dinner with your parents," Quinn said as he started the truck outside Ari's house. "Elena said she was cooking." Much as he hated to admit it, he'd been looking forward to a home-cooked meal.

"You actually sound disappointed." Ari shook her head in obvious amazement. "I'm sorry, Quinn, but my mother had you fooled. She's not a traditional Greek woman."

"I never mistook Elena for traditional. I just thought

when she said she'd cook, she meant it."

"Obviously you don't know my mother's version of cooking."

"Any version of home cooking would be a damn sight more appetizing than the stuff that any of my foster mothers used to serve." Realizing how much he'd given away, Quinn quickly shifted topics. "So tell me what Elena meant."

Ari rolled her head to the side, meeting his gaze. In her eyes, Quinn saw questions. He clenched the steering wheel tight. No matter that he'd brought up the subject, it wasn't one he wanted to get into.

"My mother makes a phone call and dinner is delivered from the Greek diner in town," she explained.

Whether Ari read his mind or simply skimmed the topic of his past on purpose, he didn't know. But he was grateful. "Greek diner. Why am I not surprised?" he asked, laughing.

She chuckled. "Aunt Kassie owns the diner."

"I'll have to check it out one day."

"Be nice to me and maybe I'll take you." She not so subtly walked her fingers across the back of his seat until she reached his collar and dipped her hand into his shirt.

His neck tingled and he liked the sensation. "Define nice."

"Where's my sister?" she asked, not missing a beat.

He let out a groan and, unwilling to fall prey to her feminine wiles, volleyed the next change of subject right back at her. "I didn't meet your Aunt Kassie, did I?"

81

"I'll take that as a sign you aren't ready to play nice." She blew out a frustrated puff of air. "No, you haven't met Aunt Kassie. Her work at the diner keeps her busy and out of family trouble."

"Just like your work keeps you away and out of family trouble?"

She tilted her head to the side. "Don't bother asking questions when you won't answer mine. And don't pretend to know me."

"I'm not pretending. I know a little, and by the time we're through with each other, I have a hunch I'll know a lot more." But more intimate knowledge wouldn't come now. She was angry that he wouldn't answer her questions, so instead he decided to hit on a lighter topic. "Tell me about the monkey."

A reluctant smile pulled at her lips and she shook her head. "I don't know. I came home and there he . . . I mean *she* was. The dress was something new."

He chuckled. "Your family's a riot."

She turned her gaze his way. "Not many people think so," she murmured. "But they obviously like to take in strays."

The word "stray" distracted his thoughts from Ari's relationship with her family to his own problems and triggered a reminder of Sam. "Oh shit." He glanced at the street sign and took the nearest right.

"Where are we going?"

"We have to make a stop first. I have to talk to some friends. It's important or I wouldn't take the time." He drove through the side streets, winding his way toward Sam's foster parents' house.

"What about my job?" Ari asked, though from the way she'd folded her arms across her chest and leaned back against the car seat, she was resigned to whatever errand he had to run.

"It'll be there when you get back." He glanced at his watch. "Besides, we were planning on having dinner at your parents'. It's not like you're going to be late."

But he was days overdue checking on Sam and talking to Aaron and Felice. Quinn couldn't believe he'd forgotten about Sam's problems, but between Ariana and Damon, Quinn had his hands full.

Especially since two years of cultivating Damon's trust was about to come to fruition. Damon had just asked Quinn to oversee operations this weekend so he could get away with his most recent bimbo. Quinn would be able to compare the videotapes of the counting room with the books Damon turned over to the IRS. With a little luck, he'd also find the *real* books that documented the actual take from the casino. He was so close to the end he could actually taste it.

But that didn't mean Quinn could let Sam's problems get lost. The system did that too often. She had to know there was one person she could count on.

He pulled the car to a halt in front of a pretty house, yellow clapboard with white trim and black shutters. The kind of house Quinn had dreamed of growing up in with two parents, brothers, sisters, and a pet inside. He slipped the gearshift into park.

"Can we get something to eat in the casino before my shift?" Ari asked.

"Behave now and I'll consider feeding you. Wait here. This shouldn't take long." On impulse, he touched her nose with his fingertip before turning and climbing out of the truck, leaving one problem and heading for another.

After watching Quinn walk into the house and the door shut behind him, Ariana realized he wouldn't be right back. She grabbed her bag and moved into the back seat of his truck. Blocked by tinted windows, she quickly changed into her work uniform. The short black skirt and tight white T-shirt with "Damon's" scrawled across her breasts was a sight she hadn't wanted her family to see.

She planned on telling them about her new job at the same time she told them she wasn't leaving again for Vermont soon, as originally planned. Any sooner and they'd be meddling in her life, something neither she nor Zoe could afford.

She tied her last sneaker and glanced out the window. Still no sign of Quinn. "Damn the man." As long as she was early for work, she'd hoped she could implement her plan to convince Maria she had no interest in Connor. But if Quinn didn't hurry up, she was out of time and luck.

Another five minutes passed and Ariana ran out of patience. She grabbed her purse, left the truck and walked up the driveway to the house, then followed the bluestone steps that led to the front door.

"Who are you?" a voice coming from the bushes to her right asked. A young, female voice.

"That depends on who's asking." Ariana glanced around, but didn't see anyone.

"I'm back here. Behind the big bush and in front of the prickly ones."

Ariana followed the direction and caught sight of a baseball cap peeking out from between the surrounding greenery. "Well, show yourself. I'm not coming in to find you."

"Not a nature girl, huh?" the young voice asked.

"Not when I can avoid it," Ariana answered.

"Can't say I blame you." A teenage girl popped out of the landscaping, a hunter-green cap on her head and blonde hair hanging down her back. "I didn't think Quinn would go for the preppy type either. You look okay though." She had huge, sad eyes that seemed to see and know too much, and she stared at Ariana. And she couldn't be any more than thirteen.

"I'm glad I have your seal of approval."

The girl crossed her arms over her chest. "I haven't decided that yet."

"Well, I'm Ariana and I'm a friend of Quinn's. Who are you?" Who was this child to Quinn? Ariana wondered.

The girl came up beside Ariana. "Nobody important."

Ariana's heart squeezed tight in her chest. "You're wrong or you wouldn't know Quinn." She didn't know how or why she knew that to be true. She just did.

"He's okay," the kid said, grudgingly.

"Okay" seemed to be the operative word of the

85

moment. Before they could continue their conversation, Quinn stormed out of the house, slamming the screen door behind him. He ran down the steps, nearly barreling into Ariana. "Ari," he said, surprised.

She felt Sam bump her from the other side, then Quinn's hands came out and grabbed her forearms tightly. "What the hell are you doing here? I told you to wait in the car." His eyes appeared darker than before, as if a black cloud had settled over him.

"I needed fresh air and I was just talking to—" Ariana glanced around, but the teenager had disappeared. No sign of the baseball hat in the bushes, either. "Someone," she muttered.

"Well, let's get the hell out of here." Obviously upset, he led her to the car and headed out of the neighborhood and back toward Atlantic City and the casino.

"I met a friend of yours," Ariana said into the oppressive silence. He hadn't even turned on the car radio. "But she wouldn't give me her name."

"It's Sam." His fingers clenched the steering wheel tighter.

"Your sister?" she hazarded a guess, though she hadn't noticed a resemblance between Quinn and the young girl beyond the sandy hair color.

He shook his head. "McDonald's okay with you?"

"It's fine. Look, I don't want to pry into your private life—"

"Then don't."

"But she was upset and so are you. And I'm a good listener."

Quinn pulled into the drive-through of a McDonald's rest stop off the Garden State Parkway, then leaned one arm over the back of her seat and glanced her way. "If you miss psychology so much, why don't you go back to teaching and leave me alone?" he asked without much heat in his voice.

"Because it's so much more fun bothering you."

"Can I help you?" a voice asked through the microphone.

Quinn placed their orders without asking her preference, drove around to the window, and took the bags, handing them to Ariana to sort through. She didn't think it was wise to argue with him right now, so she let him pay.

She bit into her hamburger and watched as he did the same. He'd been distracted since leaving the house and she wanted to know why. More, she wanted to help him deal with what was bothering him. Not just because it would be a good distraction from her own problems, but because she liked him better when he was smiling. But she couldn't figure out a way to get him to open up, so she munched on a french fry in silence.

Since she obviously wasn't going to get any information out of Quinn by pumping him, she remained quiet the rest of the way to Damon's, and five minutes later the glittering lights of the casino came into view.

Instead of leaving the truck with the doormen at the front, Quinn pulled around back and into the garage, circling around till he reached his reserved spot in the back. Ariana crumpled her wrapper and put all her garbage into the bag, then reached for the door handle.

"Sam's in foster care."

Ariana swallowed hard. "It looks like a nice house. Is she with a good family?" She pivoted back to look at Quinn, holding her breath.

His brows furrowed over and he shook his head. "I thought so."

"But?"

"The wife's pregnant and they aren't sure they want to keep a troubled kid around now."

Ariana thought back on her initial exchange with the young girl. Who are you? Ariana had asked. *Nobody important.* Ariana winced. "That's . . . that's . . ." she sputtered, unable to come up with an appropriate comment to something so unspeakably sad.

"Exactly." Quinn shut the car down. "I knew this family. I handpicked them. I introduced them to Sam and I fought to get her placed there." He slammed his fist on the steering wheel in obvious frustration.

She covered his hand with hers, offering comfort the only way she could. "What's your relationship to Sam? To the family?"

He met her gaze and slowly started to reveal more. "Sam's a kid I met at the rec center downtown. Felice and Aaron are a couple I met over at Ocean Isle Medical," he said, naming the town's main hospital. "They couldn't have kids and Sam needed a stable family before her petty stealing and antics for attention ended with her in a juvenile detention center. I thought it was a good mix."

Damon's right-hand man, hanging out at the youth

center? Ariana desperately wanted insight into this man, but the more he revealed, the less she seemed to understand. She couldn't connect the dots. "What were you doing at the rec center?" she asked.

"Trying to give something to kids who feel like the whole world's against them." He spoke as if he knew the feeling.

And then she recalled his comment about his foster mothers and home cooking. Ariana's heart filled as she realized just why Quinn cared so much. He'd once been the scared, lonely child Sam was now.

A lock of hair had fallen over his forehead. She wanted to touch yet was afraid to destroy the moment. "Nobody can fault you for trying, Quinn."

"No, but I sure as hell can fault myself for screwing up at Sam's expense." He jerked his hand out of her grasp. "Let's go." He withdrew not just his hand but the fragile connection they'd started to share.

Quinn rushed through the back entrance to the casino with Ari on his heels. The faster he put her in Connor's hands, the faster he could get back to his undercover reality. A reality that was jeopardized by the woman with the big green eyes, who looked at him with compassion and understanding, not pity.

One simple touch and she had him spilling his guts. If he slept with her, he'd probably admit he was a cop and give her directions to Zoe. She lowered his defenses *that* much. Damn.

"It's a good thing I changed into sneakers," she said, running up behind him. "Where's the fire?"

"You're the one who was worried about getting to your job." But as they reached the bar, he slowed his step because there was safety in a crowd. With Connor behind the bar, Maria and a few other waitresses serving customers, and the beginnings of the dinner crowd filling the chairs, Quinn didn't have to worry about being alone with Ari and revealing secrets he didn't want her to know.

"Looking mighty fine tonight, Ariana." Connor's gaze raked over Ari in a way much too possessive for Quinn's liking.

She glanced nervously over her shoulder to where Maria was waiting on a table, before turning back to Connor with a smile. "Thanks." She reached for an apron behind the bar and tied the knot behind her back.

Obviously she'd figured out there was something between Connor and Maria—or at least that Connor wanted there to be. Or maybe she was just having problems with the other waitress. It didn't matter and it wasn't Quinn's problem. Better she get frustrated and quit, he told himself.

Now that he had Ari settled, it was time to go. He leaned close to Connor. "She's all yours, buddy."

His friend raised an eyebrow. "If you say so."

"I have business to take care of, so I'm outta here." Quinn turned and bumped into Ari.

She'd placed herself there deliberately, he'd bet, and they now stood chest to chest, their faces inches apart. She wasn't moving out of his way, almost daring him to face her or duck around.

"What are you doing?" he asked.

She shook her hair out behind her, the act bringing a whiff of fragrance to the air and a gut-clenching tightening in his belly.

"Just thanking you properly for the ride." She reached out and wrapped her arms around his waist, fingers laced at his back, which had the effect of rocking her hips against him.

"Ari," he said in warning.

"Quinn," she mimicked in reply, a calculating, mischievous look in her eyes as she rose onto her tiptoes. If she was nervous, she hid it better than the other night, and before he could object, she sealed her mouth over his.

His body recognized hers, molding perfectly. He fit into the cradle of her hips while she kissed him and he responded, their mouths in a moist, heated, synchronized rhythm. As if they'd done this many times before. Many, many times before. And damn but she was good. He cupped his hand around her neck, angled his head and thrust his tongue deeper into her mouth until she moaned from deep in her chest.

The rumbling reverberated inside him and desire flooded through his overheated body. But the sudden sound of clapping penetrated his need-fogged brain and reminded him that they had an audience—something Ari knew when she'd started kissing him. The woman had an agenda. *She* had the ability to play him, while *he'd* gotten lost in anything she offered.

Damn. He had to get himself back under control and fast. They stepped apart at the same time, with Quinn completely conscious of the stares of those around him—of the employees who answered to Quinn, and of Connor, who'd never let him live this down.

"Don't work too hard," Ari said, flicking a speck of lint off his shirt. "I'll see you when I'm off the clock." With a sassy wave of her hand, she turned, picked a drink tray off the bar, and walked over to the nearest table. The college professor was nowhere in sight.

"I didn't know they were an item," Quinn heard Maria say to Connor.

"You learn something new every day."

Quinn didn't have to turn to see the killer grin Connor was probably flashing the waitresses' way. Instead he watched Ari smile and flirt with a table of businessmen, then turn the same charm on the guys in T-shirts and grungy jeans. Once she set her mind on something, Ari had an ease about her and an ability to handle anything. She impressed him. A lot.

"Seems like you owe me an apology, sweetstuff," Quinn heard Connor say to Maria. "All I was doing was trying to relax the new employee, not pick her up. Though why you care now when you refused any date I ever suggested is beyond me."

"You're an arrogant male who thinks he's God's gift to women. *That* I can live without."

Connor chuckled. "Go ahead and try."

Quinn left the bickering duo behind. He had work to do. And Ari with the wandering hands and powerful kiss would be here when he was done.

Quinn leaned back in a plush leather chair in Damon's

inner office and watched the bank of screens monitoring tables in the casino. He forcibly kept his gaze from the monitor covering the bar where Ari worked. He felt her presence anyway. Real or imagined, her scent clung to his clothing and hours later he still tasted her on his lips. But slowly the night crept by and soon he'd be driving her home.

By meeting her both before and after her shift, he minimized her ability to walk around and talk to people, asking questions about her missing sister. He didn't know how long she'd put up with his presence, but once Quinn got his first look at the books this weekend, the entire operation might actually be over. Thank God. He ran a hand through his hair and shut his eyes, when a door slamming told him he had company.

"Slacking off on the job, Quinn?" Damon asked, his chuckle low and deep.

Quinn shook his head. "I'm just resting up before the long weekend."

"That's what I wanted to discuss with you." Damon slung his jacket over the desk and began a methodic unbuttoning and rolling up of his sleeves. His gold Rolex gleamed under the fluorescent lighting. "I've had to rearrange my plans."

Quinn's gut warned him he wasn't going to like the change. "I'm flexible," he said. He rocked back and forth in the chair as if years of planning weren't on the line.

"Roxanne can't get away, so we'll hit Palm Springs next weekend instead." Damon took a seat on the corner of the desk, unconcerned. "I'll just spend this weekend here." His arm made a sweeping motion in the direction of the monitors, which flickered behind him, showing his domain in all its full-Technicolored glory.

"Whatever works for you, boss. You know that."

Damon reached for the remote control and pulled the bar up onto the main television screen. "How's our newest employee?" he asked, bringing Ari into full view.

"She's settling in."

"And you're keeping an eye on her. I think that's a good idea, considering." Damon tapped his fingers on the desk, watching Ari as she worked. "She doesn't suspect you in her sister's disappearance?"

Quinn raised an eyebrow. "Hell no. I'm a charming guy and she likes me."

"From the videos I've seen, I'd say she likes you a lot." Damon tipped his head back and laughed aloud.

He'd obviously seen the kiss. Probably both of them, Quinn thought, and his skin crawled at the notion of Ari being watched.

"I don't want to find her going through my books. Her sister came too damn close. I don't intend a repeat performance." Damon's voice sobered. "Keep her busy," he ordered.

"Sure thing. It's not like being with her is a hardship," Quinn joked.

Damon inclined his head. "Good. Do whatever you have to. Even at the expense of being in the hotel. If I know she's occupied and in your capable hands, I

94

have no problem covering for you here."

Quinn forced a nod. "You got it, boss." He didn't ask what these new orders meant for Damon's trip next weekend. Whether Quinn would still be in charge.

Seven days from now was a long way off. He had another seven days to live out of a hotel, on edge, and undercover. He had seven more days of keeping Ariana as close as his shadow.

CHAPTER SIX

Ready to face a new day, Ariana walked into the kitchen. She had a full agenda, including filling her parents in on her plans to stay here for a while, though as soon as her sister came home safe, Ari would be on her way. In the meantime, she was adapting to living with her family again. The carafe in the coffeemaker was full, but having learned her lesson, she sniffed before pouring herself a steaming hot cup.

She sat down at the table and immediately saw a note propped on the centerpiece. Her aunt and uncle had gone out for the day, her father was at the diner, and her mother, the note said, was outside gardening. Without warning, memories assaulted her. Of the hectic breakfasts before the rush to school, when Ari would choose yogurt and Zoe would pick Froot Loops. Their differences were apparent even in such a trivial decision, she thought, smiling at the memory.

The peace and quiet she felt now was an unusual phenomenon, one that emphasized Zoe's absence. But this being her parents' home, of course it didn't last. Before Ariana could settle in, she heard the sound of voices and the subsequent slam of the front door.

"Ari?" her mother called out.

"In the kitchen." Ariana cupped her hands around her coffee mug and waited.

"You have company," Elena's voice came closer. "But you were in the shower so I had your friend wait with me." She walked into the room, holding hands with Spank on one side and, to Ariana's shock, the young girl she'd met yesterday on the other.

Ariana jumped up from her seat. "What are you doing here?" She started toward the girl. "Better yet, how did you know where to find me?"

Her mother prodded Sam into one of the kitchen chairs. "Relax, Ari. Let her have a drink first." As Elena got busy pouring Sam a glass of juice, she continued to speak. "She's wonderful company—"

"Sam, you need to tell me what's going on."

Elena placed the glass in Sam's hands, then gestured toward Ariana. "Go on," she prodded the girl. "Tell her the truth." Apparently her mother had formed a fast bond with Sam if she'd already uncovered answers.

The teen met Ariana's gaze briefly, guilt etching her features as her eyes darted away. "I got your address from here." She pulled Ariana's day planner from the plastic bag she was carrying.

"You took this?" Ariana grabbed the leather-bound

planner, which also acted as her wallet, out of Sam's hands.

Sam nodded. "Yesterday, when you were arguing with Quinn. I bumped into you and snagged it."

"See? That wasn't so hard." Elena praised Sam's truth-telling. "But stealing from people is wrong, young lady." Elena stroked the girl's long blonde hair at the same time she reprimanded her.

The con artist chiding the little thief. Ariana shook her head and wondered if her mother realized what a contradiction she presented. She bit down on the inside of her cheek and wondered what to do with the runaway teen.

While Sam stared at her hands, Elena walked over to Ariana and whispered in her ear. "Her technique must be good if you didn't notice your wallet was missing," Elena said in awe.

Oh, she'd noticed earlier this morning. She'd just assumed the planner had fallen out on the floor of the car, as often happened back home.

"But still, she's too young to be doing such a thing," Elena said softly.

Ariana agreed. She glanced at Sam. "You took my wallet but you came to return it. What gives?"

Sam shrugged. "I took it 'cause I liked you," she said, mumbling, her voice filled with embarrassment.

A headache had begun to develop and Ariana pressed her fingers against her temples. "You wanted a reason to see me?" she guessed.

Sam nodded and once again the lump of emotion inside Ariana grew. Though she had problems with her relatives, at least she had a family of her own. "I bet people are looking for you."

"They think I'm at school."

"And won't school call home when you don't show up?"

Sam kicked at the kitchen tile with her sneakered feet. "It doesn't matter."

"Unfortunately it does. I'm going to have to call Quinn." Ariana glanced at Sam. "Unless you want to call your foster parents yourself and let them know you're okay?"

Sam shook her head. "I don't want to talk to them. But Quinn's gonna kill me."

"Nothing that drastic, I'm sure." Ariana stood and reached for the portable phone. Leaving her mother alone with the runaway, Ariana dialed Damon's and asked to be connected with Quinn.

Half an hour later, the doorbell rang. "I'll get it." Ariana left Sam and her mother in the kitchen and opened the door for Quinn.

As if she hadn't even seen him last night, she devoured him with her gaze, surprised at how good it was to see him. He hadn't shaved yet today and a darkened shadow covered his cheeks. His eyes were glassy and he looked tired. Like her, he probably hadn't completely recovered from his late night. If this was how he looked in the morning, she definitely wouldn't mind waking up beside him. Her body tingled at the seductive, heady thought.

And when he spoke, his severe tone sent shivers of another kind through her. "Where is she?"

"In the kitchen. But before you see her, I think you need to take a deep breath first."

"Easy for you to say. Her foster parents called me two hours ago. I've been making phone calls and driving around looking for her. I'd finally given up and gone back to the hotel. Then you called."

She placed a hand on his arm to calm him. "I'm sorry. I called you as soon as I knew she was here. Unfortunately I don't know how long she was outside with my mother. They bonded," Ariana said wryly.

"At least she's safe." He glanced at Ariana, a flicker of warmth and appreciation in his gaze.

Ariana smiled. "Now that you've collected yourself, let's go talk to her and see why she pulled a disappearing act."

"I know why. She'd been led to believe if things worked out with Aaron and Felice, they'd consider adoption. The way things were going, there was no reason to think anything would mess with that. I mean, they couldn't have kids, and Felice wanted a girl. Despite the few times the little pickpocket tested them, Aaron and Felice understood. Hell, *I* thought they'd adopt her." He ran a hand through his hair, his frustration evident.

"And then Felice got pregnant," Ariana said. He'd told her as much yesterday.

"Yeah. It shouldn't make a difference to them. But it does. And I've seen it time and again. I should know better than to hope. Damn, I should have known better than to let Sam hope."

Ariana's heart twisted with emotion, for Sam and for

Quinn. The fact that he'd given her insight into his feelings was shocking. So too was the depth of his caring. For as much as Ariana didn't know about him, she liked everything she'd already learned. He had a good heart despite his secrets. "You're doing your best for Sam."

"Yeah, and I hate it that my best isn't enough. I was so sure that *this* perfect looking couple with their perfect little house would make room in their hearts and home for a beautiful young girl."

She was shocked by how much she wanted to help him, not just with Sam, but with his feelings and his pain.

Without warning, Quinn pulled away from her touch as if realizing how much he'd revealed. "I need to talk to Sam."

Ariana nodded. "Just remember she's hurting, too."

She led him toward the kitchen, and as they entered the room, Quinn bellowed, "Samantha!"

"So much for taking my advice," Ariana muttered.

Sam winced at his yell, and Spank the monkey, who'd been sitting at the table letting Sam paint her nails, dove underneath the table and covered her head with her hands.

"You scared her," Sam said accusingly to Quinn. She obviously wasn't intimidated by his bluster.

Then again the kid lived in foster homes and never knew where she'd be next. She wouldn't fear much, Ariana thought sadly.

"Spank doesn't like loud noises." Elena held a hand out to the monkey.

Spank let Elena pull her out from her hiding place. She turned to Quinn, gave him a raspberry with her tongue, then climbed into Sam's lap.

The young girl giggled and Quinn stopped himself from yelling and demanding an explanation for her behavior. He hadn't seen Sam laugh. Ever.

He was furious at the scare she'd given him, but he didn't know what made him angrier, that Sam had run away or that she'd come here instead of calling him when she was upset. But as he'd told Ari, at least she was safe.

"Let's leave Sam and Quinn alone, Mom," Ari said.

He stopped himself from asking her not to leave. He could have used her support about now, and that shocked the hell out of him. For a man who'd always lived life on his own to need a woman who wanted nothing more than to find her sister and disappear from this town, well, it wasn't a smart move.

Elena looked at her daughter and nodded. "You're right. Come, Spank."

Sam shook her head and wrapped her arms tighter around the damn monkey. "I want you all to stay."

"We've imposed on them enough, Sam," Quinn said.

"Nonsense," Elena said. "She's welcome here any—"

Ariana interrupted her mother by pulling her out of the room, dragging the monkey she took from Sam along. As Spank reached the doorway, she lifted her skirt. Damned if the monkey hadn't mooned him on purpose. But what marked this meeting for Quinn was

101

Ariana and her obvious insight and understanding of him and what he needed.

He still couldn't allow himself to get too close or too attached to the woman, but that didn't mean he wasn't developing feelings for her anyway. Damn him. He turned his attention to Sam instead.

"You gonna yell at me for stealing Ari's wallet?" Sam asked.

He blinked. "You *what?*"

"Oops." Sam blushed a furious red. "She didn't tell you?"

He shook his head. "Obviously she protected you. But at least now I know how you found Ari," he said, solving the mystery he hadn't been able to figure out. He already knew why Sam had taken off. "Running away isn't smart," he told her.

"Why the hell not?"

"Watch your mouth, Samantha," he said through clenched teeth.

"Well, tell me why not. It's not like Aaron and Felice give a sh— I mean, it's not like they care."

He pulled out a chair and, straddling the back, sat down beside her. Her defiance was a shield from her pain, her big, glassy eyes a better giveaway to her true feelings. Which led him to choose his words carefully now. "They care about their responsibilities," he said, slowly. "And they get to give a recommendation. I don't know about you, but I don't want you labeled as trouble for new placement."

Her eyes filled with tears. "Let me live with you? Please? I won't cause any trouble, I promise. I'll clean up after myself and I'll even disappear if you want to bring a lady friend home," she said, too wise for her years. "I swear you won't even know I'm there."

"That's the problem, kid." He knew exactly how she was feeling, had begged and said those same words to different people in his past. His throat nearly closed and he wished he could give her what she wanted. "*I'm* not even there. It's not a supervised home. I wish I could let you stay with me, but I can't."

"Won't." She folded her arms across her chest. "You're no different than Aaron and Felice or any one of the other homes I've been in."

Each word she uttered was another dagger in his heart. Just when had this kid come to mean so much to him? he wondered.

"You just play the do-good act better than most," she said, hurt and accusation in her tone and in her gaze.

He swallowed hard. "You don't believe that for a minute. I do care." He held out his hand and then, lowering his voice, he said, "Let's go. I'll take you back to Felice."

"For how long?" She sniffed and wiped her eyes on her arm, ignoring his outstretched palm.

"Until Social Services finds another home." Her running away had been the excuse Aaron and Felice needed to decide to call Social Services and tell them they were opting out as foster parents.

The knowledge caused a raw, painful feeling in his throat. But there was no point in telling Sam. The couple would have backed out anyway, she'd just made it easier for them to walk away. Though how anyone found it easy to give up a kid was beyond him.

To his surprise, Sam didn't argue. Refusing to take his hand, she stood up, slid her chair under the table, and came up by his side.

As he led her out, his gaze fell on the manicure stuff spread over the table. He wondered when anyone had cared enough to let Sam be a girl. Play. Just have fun. Even if it was with a monkey, she'd had an hour of normalcy in this crazy house. A house Sam ran to— and Ari ran from.

Ariana cleaned off a table with a damp rag, then placed her tray on the bar. She couldn't think about anything except Sam, who'd come to find her. Obviously the girl saw her as some sort of salvation and for a brief time thought she'd found it in Ariana's home. Which was ironic, since Ariana knew well that her eccentric family wasn't the best influence.

Then there was Quinn, who'd looked so distraught, she'd wanted to do nothing more than take him in her arms and make him forget. Her own thoughts had become so overwhelming, she wished she could do the same.

"I'm taking a break," she told Connor during a lull at the bar.

"Don't take too long. You never know when it's going to pick up again." He looked across the room, seeming to nod at someone.

Ariana turned, but didn't see anyone. She narrowed her gaze, wondering if she'd imagined it. "Don't worry. I just need a quick breather."

"Understandable," he said and winked at her before turning back to his duties behind the bar.

Ariana made her way to the employees' restroom because thankfully it lacked the hustle and bustle common in the larger restrooms inside the casino. Though she wasn't alone here, Ariana still relished the peace. She sat on the couch in the outer lounge, leaned against the backrest, and sighed aloud.

"It's hard working for a living."

Ariana glanced up as Maria walked into the restroom's lounge area. "It's not the same as my old job," Ariana replied, "but work is work."

The other woman strode over to the mirror and adjusted her skirt and top, then opened her purse to pull out a tube of lipstick. "What was your old job?" she asked, then began the meticulous job of applying a rose-colored lipstick while watching Ariana in the mirror at the same time.

"I'm a psych professor, but I've waitressed before. Back when I put myself through school." This was Maria's first attempt at civil conversation, and Ariana didn't want to blow it by coming off as too academic.

"Returning to your roots?" Maria's gaze narrowed while her tone indicated she still didn't like or trust Ariana.

Since she didn't have the time to play games, Ariana opted for the truth. "No, I'm looking for my sister."

For the first time, Maria's hardened expression changed and softened. "She was real," she said. "We all liked her."

Ariana swallowed over the lump of emotion knotted

at the back of her throat. "Did you see her that last time she worked here?"

Maria shook her head. "I was out that night."

"Then did you hear anything when you came back? Anything unusual happen around here that day?"

The other woman paused, obviously giving the question some thought. Finally she shook her head. "Not that I can remember. Except everyone was really quiet after the police came sniffing around."

"I guess that would be understandable." If someone was covering something up, they'd definitely remain silent, Ariana thought. And if the employees knew nothing, they'd have nothing more to say. "What about Connor?"

Maria stiffened and Ariana realized she'd made a tactical error and hit a nerve. "What about him?" Maria asked, her walls and suspicions back up and in place.

"He's the bartender," Ariana explained. "He's here every night. If anyone was going to see or hear anything, wouldn't it stand to reason it would be him?"

The other woman shrugged. "It might. Then again you might be using your sister's disappearance to get closer to him."

Frustration filled Ariana and she clenched her teeth as she spoke. "If I was, why would you care? Danielle said you won't give the man the time of day, so why give me the cold shoulder over him?" She deliberately used another waitress's information as a means of confronting Maria.

"I have my reasons." She bit down on her bottom

lip, the first real hint of vulnerability Ariana had seen. "They're just none of your business. Just because you're a psychology professor doesn't give you license to pry into my life."

Ariana shook her head. She didn't need this crap right now. "Believe me, I don't give a damn about anyone who doesn't care about me, and you've made your feelings perfectly clear since the moment we met. All I want to do is find my sister and go back to my life."

"Then we both want the same thing."

"Insecurity's not attractive," she told the other woman. The psychologist in Ariana came out despite her resolve to keep quiet. "Besides, I'm not after Connor and I'm no threat to your seniority here."

"You'd better not be, since I need this paycheck and any upcoming raise to support my kid." She clamped her lips shut tight.

"Then I suggest we both get back to work." Ariana headed for the door, frustrated that she had no more information now than before.

Maria stopped her with a touch of her hand on Ariana's arm. "Wait."

Ariana turned and waited.

"I liked your sister and . . . well, I have no real reason to dislike you. What's going on between me and Connor has nothing to do with you."

Since the woman appeared to be choking as she swallowed her pride, Ariana figured that was as close to an apology as she was likely to get. Grateful for even that much of a concession, Ariana smiled. "Then maybe things can get more pleasant around here?"

Maria nodded. "And since I've been such a bitch, the least I can do is give you one piece of information."

"I thought you didn't see or hear anything about Zoe that night."

"It's just that what I heard and what I trust are two different things. And since I saw you kissing Quinn, I didn't know if I *should* tell you."

Ariana's fingers clutched her purse tightly, her knuckles turning white and her nerves prickling with anticipation. "I want to know anything about Zoe. Even if it involves Quinn." *Especially* if it involved Quinn.

"You haven't been here long but I'm sure you realize Quinn's considered a prime catch."

Ariana raised an eyebrow. "I hadn't heard."

Maria rolled her eyes. "Come on. He's single, he's gorgeous, and he's Damon's right-hand man. Who wouldn't want a piece of that?"

"I don't know," Ariana murmured. She didn't want to think of other women ogling Quinn or his interest in them. Not when *her* interest in Quinn was growing with each passing day. "What does this have to do with my sister?"

"Well, he's also a prime topic for gossip and speculation, especially since unlike Damon, he keeps to himself instead of choosing from his pick of women."

Do tell, Ariana thought.

"Anyway, when Zoe disappeared and then the police came around, people here wondered if he had something to do with it." Maria shook her head. "But it never sat right with me, you know? Quinn can be cold and disinterested. It's the strong, silent quality that attracts women, but . . ." She shook her head.

"But what?" Ariana pushed harder. Maria had come so far in confiding in Ariana. She couldn't stop now.

"Look." Maria waved a hand through the air. "I've been in a bad relationship and I like to think I'd recognize a guy who'd do wrong by a woman. Quinn just isn't one of them." She pulled the door open. "I just thought you should know," she said before slamming the door behind her.

Ariana let out a long stream of air. She wanted to agree with Maria and in her heart she did. But if she was here to investigate, she had no choice but to pursue leads, no matter where they led.

And so far her only tip pointed to Quinn. A man Ariana had already decided to get to know better.

Connor wiped down the bar and poured himself a beer. They were closed for the night and all his waitresses were long gone. Except for Maria. Though she was normally the first one in and the first one out, tonight she stuck around even longer, helping him clean. He watched the sway of her hips and the determination she put into everything she did. Man, he had it bad.

Returning to business, he recalled the brief conversation he'd had with the "customer" who was actually working along with himself and Quinn. He'd signaled her to follow Ariana to the ladies' room and make sure she stayed out of trouble. The woman had been able to eavesdrop on Ariana's conversation with Maria. The two waitresses still hadn't hit it off, but Maria had come around and given Ari some vague information, the woman had told him.

Maria hadn't done anything more than supplied the realities and the rumors as she'd heard them. At least Ariana hadn't gone snooping around any of the offices, which was what he and Quinn were afraid of and was the reason he'd had her followed. The same way he'd had her tailed after her shift ended since Quinn hadn't shown up to take her home. Damn Damon anyway, Connor thought. The man was a pain in the ass. Both Connor and Quinn would be happy to see the last of him.

A low tune interrupted his thoughts and the happy humming settled inside him, warm and comforting. *Maria.* She was still cleaning, happy in her work despite the late hour and the grueling time on her feet.

He admired her. "You've cleaned enough. I can already see your reflection in the tables. Care to tell me why you're still hanging around?"

She seated herself on a barstool and met his gaze, propping her chin in her hand. "I've been asking myself that same question."

"Are you reconsidering my invitation?" He'd been asking her on a date nightly since they'd met. Of course only an idiot put up with so much rejection, but there was something about this woman that wouldn't let him shelve his desire and forget about her.

Perhaps it was because she gave him a glimpse of

himself. A solitary person needing a break from the daily grind. They'd have hot sex, that much he knew for sure, and the desire thrumming through him backed up his hunch. The fact that sometimes he wanted to know her secrets wasn't something he liked to contemplate. He was a man used to being alone. He didn't know how to open up and he didn't care to try.

Flirting, however, was another story. "Well, sweet-stuff?"

"I might be thinking about changing my mind." She studied him closely as she chewed on a piece of bubble gum. She blew a bubble that he tried in vain to pop before she sucked it back between those lips he was dying to kiss.

"Dare I ask why the sudden shift?"

She shrugged. "Sometimes the harder you try to avoid something, the more it crowds you." She stood and slid her hand into her apron pocket. "If you're serious, you can pick me up at noon on my next day off." She handed him a scrap of paper.

He glanced down and saw her handwritten address. He was completely taken off guard, and for a split second, his stomach churned with all the excitement and anticipation of an adolescent who'd just gotten a *yes* to his first date. "I'll be there."

She started to walk away, then turned, uncertainty in her eyes. "Remember what they say."

"What's that?"

"What you get may be much more than you bargained for."

He laughed, but once again his gut tightened. He

had the distinct impression this date could change his life forever.

CHAPTER SEVEN

Damn Quinn. If he was going to insist on being her chauffeur, the least he could do was show up to drive her home. At two A.M., Ariana had no desire to hunt around the casino looking for him. She started with the small bar where she'd seen him the first time, but he wasn't there. Now she headed for his office, her thoughts in turmoil.

Nothing she'd learned about Quinn or Zoe made any sense. She recounted the facts that worked against Quinn: She didn't know much about him and he'd been less than forthcoming about who he was and what his relationship had been to her sister. People at Damon's wondered if he'd had anything to do with Zoe's disappearance, and though he claimed to know for a fact her twin was alive, he refused to divulge more information. Until tonight he'd kept close tabs on Ariana during her time in the casino—because he was afraid she'd discover he was somehow involved? All the circumstantial evidence didn't place Quinn in the best light.

But she wasn't ready to count him out. Wasn't it possible that Maria, who'd been a bitch since day one, had intended to cause problems for her and Quinn? Ariana shook her head. *That* theory didn't work, because it served Maria's interest to have Ariana involved with any man other than Connor.

But ironically also working in Quinn's favor was the fact that he claimed her sister was alive. Added to that, her crazy family seemed to like and trust him. His deep caring for Sam proved he was a decent human being. And Ariana was falling hard for the man.

Her last relationship had been with a fellow professor who'd been as excited about Freud as he was about her. Sadly, that passion hadn't translated physically for either of them. They'd agreed to be friends, went to university events together, but there'd been no real romance in her life for way too long.

Quinn gave her excitement. He made her feel desired and sexy and completely feminine even when he was in one of his darker, not-speaking moods. While she was in town, she wanted to get to know him better. Her search for Zoe had suddenly become as much about clearing Quinn from guilt as finding her sister.

She obviously couldn't rely on fact or logic, and frustration shot through her. She'd just have to confront Quinn. She'd already checked his office, but the door had been locked. She checked the paper he'd given her with his phone number in case she had to reach him. Sure enough, he'd also included his room number.

Her gaze strayed from the house phones to the bank of elevators. The easy way or the hard way? Ariana wondered. Which would it be?

Apparently, since her return home, she'd acquired courage she hadn't known she possessed. Not five minutes later, Ariana was knocking on Quinn's door. Her fists clenched tight as she waited.

Finally he jerked open the door. His gaze fell on Ariana and his eyes opened wide in recognition. "Oh shit. I forgot all about you."

"Nice way to impress a lady," she said wryly. "You never showed up at the bar to take me home." That was unlike him, and for the first time she wondered if he'd gotten sick.

A look at his furrowed brows and she realized he was preoccupied, nothing more. If he'd let her drive to the casino and leave on her own, he wouldn't have to add her to his list of concerns, something she opened her mouth to mention.

"Come in and let me get dressed," he said, and all rational thoughts fled.

Her stare drifted from his troubled gaze to his muscled chest. His bare muscled chest, sprinkled with just the right amount of sandy-colored hair and tapering to a trim waist. Lower down, a thin scar traversed his lower right abdomen and led into the waistband of his unbuttoned jeans. Her hands twitched with the desire to feel his skin's texture, to dip her fingertips into the worn denim and explore further.

"Unless you'd rather wait in the hall?"

His voice startled her, and feeling as if she'd been caught, she quickly raised her gaze. Her body had already flushed hot at her thoughts, and now she was certain a blush covered her cheeks as well. "No. I'll come in. Thanks." Ariana stepped inside, tripping over the raised wooden saddle on the floor.

He righted her with a hand on her elbow and if he knew why she was suddenly flustered, at least he was gentleman enough not to say. Instead he gestured with a grand sweep of his arm around the suite. "Be it ever so humble."

"There's no place like home," she finished for him, and to distract herself from all that blatant testosterone pummeling her, she glanced around.

The place he called home wasn't anything like the private domain she'd imagined he occupied. Instead the room was a sterile suite with plenty of luxuries and amenities but lacking any warmth. From the cold, industrial-type carpet to the pictures and furniture common to all hotel rooms, there was nothing personal to indicate anyone *lived* here. Oh, Quinn stayed here, that much she could tell, since his watch lay on a dresser beside some spare change and his clothes had been haphazardly tossed around. But there was nothing of *him* inside this room.

"Sorry about the mess. I wasn't expecting company," he said, as if guessing her train of thought.

She shrugged. "Not a problem." She sat down on the couch and waited while he buttoned his jeans and then reached for a sweater he'd left on the arm of a chair.

In front of her was a mass of paperwork, and though she didn't plan to pry, Sam's name jumped out at her from the top page. And suddenly Ariana knew the reason he'd forgotten about her.

"Will you have trouble finding Sam a home?" she asked softly.

Surprising her, he took a seat by her side. He still held his shirt in his hands, and his body heat emanated off him in waves. "Unfortunately, yeah. Finding her a new place won't be easy."

"But she's such a great kid." Ariana couldn't imagine a couple not wanting her. "What happened to her real parents?"

He eyed her steadily. "Her father's a drug dealer doing a life sentence, and her mother's dead. Caught by a bullet meant for her father."

Ariana winced and her eyes filled with tears. Embarrassed, she wiped them with the back of her hand. "That's horrible."

"That's the kind of life she's been exposed to."

Ariana paused for a steady breath. "Is it the kind of life you've been exposed to?" She knew he'd also been in foster care, and wondered what had happened to his parents.

He shook his head. "No, my folks just didn't give a shit." He let out a bitter laugh. "At least Sam's mother made an effort at giving her kid a decent life before a bullet got in the way." He'd changed the subject back to Sam, and Ariana knew that's all she was likely to learn about him for now.

But that was okay, since she'd plumbed unexpected depths and gained a deeper understanding of what made him tick. She still couldn't put all the pieces together, but she'd made a start.

"Social Services will have no choice but to place her in a group home filled with mostly troubled teens. But she needs love and stability and she sure as hell won't find it there." He rubbed the heel of his hand over his eyes.

"Maybe another couple that can't have kids will want a teenager?" she asked hopefully.

He shook his head. "Not likely. Sam's got so many strikes against her I don't know where to begin."

"What else is there besides her age?"

He cocked his head to one side. "You met the kid, so you shouldn't have to ask. She's a wiseass for one thing, and you experienced her petty-theft tendencies firsthand."

"But underneath it all, she just wants to be loved. Surely somebody will see past the facade," Ariana said. She had seen past it the first time they'd met.

Quinn shook his head again, his eyes wide with obvious disbelief. "You don't really buy into that humanity crap, do you? Not everybody's got the rosy family you do."

She bit her cheek to keep herself from giving him a wise-guy comeback about her family, because he was right. At least she'd had a loving home to grow up in. "Okay, I get your point, but there's got to be a solution."

"I wouldn't leave my dog with half the applicants on this list, and besides, they're looking for younger kids. Anyone who'd consider a teen will be hard pressed to take her, given her history."

"But she's got reasons for the way she acts." Ariana knew she was grasping at straws, but like Quinn, she already cared about Sam.

His anguished gaze met hers. "The reason she acts

out doesn't matter. The facts in the reports do." With a wave of his hand, he trashed the papers, sending them sprawling to the floor. "I'm going to have to work on Felice and Aaron, because nobody decent wants a troubled teen."

In Quinn's gaze, in his expression and in his posture, Ariana could see traces of the little boy who had once been in the same position as Sam. He still remembered being the kid nobody wanted.

But he wasn't that teen anymore, he was a man. A man whose hurt she wanted to ease and who she desired more with each breath she took. Knowing it wasn't wise, she reached out anyway and placed a hand on his shoulder, a safe distance away from the hair-roughened chest that interested her so.

His heated stare locked with hers and she realized there was no safe place to touch or to run. There was no way to escape from her mounting desire for this complicated man.

He leaned closer, his lips hovering near hers. Every time she inhaled, she smelled his masculine scent and her nipples puckered tighter against her stretch tee. Desire pulsed inside her, and from the fire burning in his gaze, he needed her, too.

"This is crazy," she said softly.

He nodded in agreement. "Then walk away."

"I can't." Once again it was that simple.

She didn't know who kissed who first, but finally, blessedly, his lips were on hers, hot, devouring, demanding, and giving her exactly what she'd yearned for.

They were combustible and the fire between them flared out of control. Her hands started at his waist, slid upward, her fingers trailing over his skin and taking in every contour and sensation. His flesh was smooth to the touch, made coarser by the liberal sprinkling of hair. And everywhere she touched, his skin was aflame.

He held her head in place with one hand and all the while his tongue dipped and swirled inside her mouth, setting the pace. One she gladly matched. He was a man who obviously liked being in control, and if it made her feel this good, she didn't mind allowing him the liberty. Not as long as she could take a few of her own, and she did, as her hands came to rest over his chest, his hard nipples spearing her palms. He let out a slow groan of intense satisfaction and she took pleasure in knowing she could affect him as easily as he did her.

His lips slid over hers, then down her neck. "You drive me insane."

"You do the same to me."

With shaking hands, he pulled her top high around her midriff until he cupped her breasts in his hands. He'd anticipated her need, as he fed her hunger, his warm hands plumping and kneading her aching flesh. His hands worshiped her breasts and desire pulled a straight path to her center while a rush of liquid trickled between her legs.

A pulse beat harder in her throat as waves of temptation beckoned to her. He caressed and plucked her nipples with his fingertips, each movement creating a pull of exquisite desire throughout her body. She realized she was trembling, her hips gyrating in time to his unspoken commands.

He understood what she desired and pulled her onto his lap. Though it took some adjusting, she managed to straddle his legs, her thighs bracketing his. Her skirt inched up and only a thin scrap of cotton and his denim jeans provided a barrier between mutual, aching need. As his erection pressed warm and full between her legs, a delicious heat spread through her. She tipped her head back and let out a slow moan, allowing the pleasurable sensations to infuse her body, mind, and spirit.

"Let go," he whispered in her ear. "Let me make you come."

She had no doubt he could. Without him ever touching her *there,* he had the ability to make her lose control. But that was the thought that cut into her pleasure and forced her to think instead.

Her control was the very thing that had kept her sane. She had always held herself in check, deliberately forced composure because doing so distinguished her from her family. Her more dramatic, emotionally freer, bordering-on-crazy family. Control distinguished her from her twin.

Their moment had passed and Ariana scrambled off him, pulling down her skirt as she moved. "I can't do this."

She'd come here to question Quinn about Zoe. Instead she'd taken one look at his distraught face, seen his pain over Sam, and fallen into his arms with no questions asked.

He met her gaze, looking as shell-shocked as she felt. But he wasn't the one who'd made a mistake. She had. Because while she was sitting in Quinn's hotel room, shirt and skirt hiked up, breasts bared, her precious control nearly shot to hell, her sister was missing.

And Quinn, who was masterfully taking charge and encouraging her to let go, knew where her sister was. And he refused to say.

Just wonderful, Ariana, she thought to herself.

Quinn sat in silence as Ari adjusted her clothing, pulled down and retucked her shirt. He wished he could say he was sorry, but damn it, damn *him,* he wasn't. Because for the moment, he'd been able to forget.

He'd been able to put Damon, the case, Sam and her problems, and Quinn's whole sorry life, out of his mind. No woman ever had the power to make him lose focus and forget. And he'd needed to lose himself in Ari more than he'd needed to breathe. So he wasn't sorry.

Even if she obviously was. "What's going on?" Not the most tactful way to approach her, but she hadn't looked at him since pulling away.

She met his gaze through hooded eyes. The desire still lingered but a wealth of other emotions obviously flooded her, too. "Where's my sister?" The question was quickly becoming a chorus.

He ran a hand through his hair, frustration welling

inside him. "I can't tell you."

She strode closer and leaned down so she could whisper in his ear. "Is this place bugged?"

He heard the hope in her voice and knew she was wishing there was a reason for his silence that she could understand. There wasn't. His room had been swept clean, something he made certain of daily. He put up with Damon's meddling in the office, but his private domain remained sacred.

He shook his head in answer to her question. No bugs, he thought silently. "I just can't say."

"That's what's wrong." Disappointment laced her tone and kicked him in the stomach, sucking the life out of him.

She rose from her seat. Her clothing was still awry, her face red from his razor stubble, and still she appeared sexier than any woman he'd ever known. Even if her expression made it clear that she couldn't be more disappointed in him. He'd rather be hit by a barrel of someone's gun than face her disapproval. Which shocked him, since Quinn Donovan never gave a shit what anyone thought.

"Rumor has it you had something to do with Zoe's disappearance." She shivered and rubbed her arms with her hands.

He knew better than to offer comfort, just as he also understood her need to push for answers. "I didn't."

Ari narrowed her gaze. "Then tell me why and how you got to know Zoe. Because from what I can see, you don't have much to do with the dancers. Why did you have a relationship with my mother? Why with Zoe?

Why were they different?"

He admired her intellect. But that intelligence would also be his downfall, Quinn realized, since she was beginning to put together pieces of information.

How long before his cover was blown?

"Your mother was just plain friendly," he told her truthfully. "As for Zoe . . . You're going to have to trust me." He held his hands out toward her but she refused to come near.

"Just because I'm sexually attracted to you doesn't make me stupid," she said, her exasperation obvious. "For all I know, the rumors are true and you did have something to do with Zoe's disappearance."

"I didn't. Not in the way you mean, anyway."

"Oh, okay. That's clear as mud." Disgust etched her features, and those lips he'd kissed earlier turned downward in a frown.

The desire raging through him hadn't lessened, only now it was accompanied by frustration. At Ari for her persistence and at himself for his inability to give her the answers she needed.

"Give me one more week," he said, thinking back to Damon's insistence he'd go away next weekend. If he could stall Ari for another seven days, he'd have the proof he needed to put this case to rest.

She shook her head. "Not without a reason. Some kind of proof that I can trust you."

"Besides my word?" he asked, not missing the irony in that statement.

"Sorry but that's not enough." A hint of regret flickered in her eyes.

Maybe at least a part of her wanted to believe him. "I had nothing sinister to do with your sister's disappearance," he told her, once more for good measure.

Her wry laugh sliced through him. "Do me a favor, Quinn?"

"What?" he asked through clenched teeth.

"Take me home."

An awful stench greeted Ariana as she walked into the kitchen early the next morning. As she'd told Quinn, her mother didn't cook, she ordered in, and this odor was a testament to the reasons why. Her mother had pulled a barstool away from the counter so Spank the monkey could sit and watch while she cooked. A fact that struck Ariana as more normal than the sight of her mother in an apron, stirring something in a large pot.

"So, what are you cooking?" Ariana asked diplomatically.

"Not cooking. Creating." Her mother continued to stir the ingredients with a wooden spoon.

"I hope it's nothing like the drink you made the other day," Ariana said.

"It's another version," Aunt Dee said from her place at the table.

"This recipe is for facial cream. I'm waiting for it to thicken. The combination of ingredients has restorative qualities for the skin. It's an old family recipe. Don't you think our new spa should have a product unique to the Costas family?" she asked.

Ariana raised an eyebrow. She didn't know her

family claimed anything but cons to pass down from generation to generation, but she didn't want to insult her mother by asking whether she'd made up this story for the public relations benefit it would offer the spa.

Instead she tackled the more surprising revelation. "You said *Costas* family spa. Does that mean Dad's willing to move away from the Addams family?" she asked hopefully.

"He will eventually," Elena said with certainty. "He only holds on to it as security because the persona lets him forget he was sick during his treatment. It's been a long time. He just needs the right prodding to let go. He'll come around."

Elena sounded so sure of herself that Ariana knew her mother would have her way. She glanced into the pot only to have herself smacked away by her mother's hand.

"Leave it be," Elena scolded her.

"What's the main ingredient?"

"Other than fish oil?" Aunt Dee asked.

Ariana swallowed, attempting not to gag. "So that's what the odor is." She winced and decided once and for all not to try to look into the pot again. "I know I'm going to regret asking, but why?"

Elena glanced heavenward. "I'd think that was obvious. Have you ever seen a wrinkled fish?"

Ariana blinked. Only her mother would come up with such absurdity. "Only a scaly one," she muttered. "Assuming you can even get anyone near this stuff given the odor, I think you're going to have flaking problems." She wrinkled her nose in distaste.

"She hasn't added the scent yet," Aunt Dee assured her.

Ariana doubted anything would cover the fishy smell, but decided to shut up now. "I'm a little surprised Spank wants to be anywhere near this stench."

At the mention of her name, the monkey grinned.

"Well, there's also Greek valerian in here." Her mother placed a cover on the pot and lowered the dial to simmer. "Historically, it's a scent that has been known to attract cats," she said, as if that explained Spank's attraction to the vile odor.

Ariana shook her head. "Do you mean valerian root?" She named an herbal remedy she'd once heard of.

Her mother laughed. "I think *Greek* valerian sounds so much more apropos for us, don't you? Besides, that's the correct name for what I purchased."

"Whatever." Ariana was through asking questions. Even if she did wonder what legal steps her mother planned or didn't plan to take in order to market this new treatment. Once she eliminated the odor, that is. "Since the stove's overloaded, I think I'll go to Aunt Kassie's for something to eat."

But she'd be shocked if her sinus passages cleared and the odor in her nostrils disappeared enough for her to regain her appetite.

"Are you working tonight?" her mother asked.

When Ariana had told Elena the truth about her job at Damon's, her mother had merely grinned and said,

"Quinn will protect you." Ariana had gritted her teeth and smiled.

Though Elena thought a man was the answer to life, Ariana had learned the hard way to rely on herself. Her first few months in Vermont had been lonely, and more than once she'd had to suppress the urge to run home to her family despite the chaos and insanity. But she'd been determined to carve out her own life and she had.

Her neighbor, Jill, had become a close friend, as had the younger professors at the college, while one of the older deans had practically adopted Ariana and they shared tea once a week. It was the staid, predictable, comfortable life she'd sought, but coming home showed her all she'd been missing, both good and bad.

And she was about to embark onto the bad, snooping around the casino in the hopes of finding her twin. As long as her mother was calm about her resolve to remain at Damon's, Ariana didn't care if trust in Quinn was the reason. Even if she didn't trust him herself.

Though he'd never promised her anything, she was furious at him for disappointing her and even madder at herself for caring. *Because she'd been starting to care about him.* Because she still did. But the fact remained he didn't trust her enough to confide the truth and so he'd put the wall between them.

She glanced around the pot-filled, cluttered kitchen and inhaled the awful smell. All were a reminder of the childhood embarrassments she'd been running from. Yet despite her resolve to keep her distance as well as her sanity, she couldn't deny she loved her family as much as they loved her.

So she forced a smile for her mother's sake. "Actually, I'm off tonight. I haven't had time to visit with Aunt Kassie and the cousins since I've been back." The more grounded side of the family, Ariana thought. Which, considering the Costas clan, wasn't saying much.

CHAPTER EIGHT

Quinn dribbled the basketball around the old gym at the rec center and took a shot at the basket. The ball hit the rim and bounced off. Damn, his concentration was off, Quinn thought, and it didn't take a genius to figure out why.

Only hours had passed since he'd had Ari in his hotel room—warm, willing, and all over him. She'd been so close to coming apart. Yet he hadn't even had a chance to indulge in his deeper fantasies of sinking his fingers inside her warm, moist body and feeling her clench around him. He'd never been so affected by a woman in his goddamn life. She was all he could think about.

But she obviously had her mind elsewhere. She'd ignored him unless she was coolly making conversation that was forced on her by proximity. Worse, she'd done everything she could to undermine his attempt to keep her safe at Damon's. She'd left ahead of him, driving herself to work. This was something he'd discovered after the fact, when he'd gone to pick her up. While he was being mooned by the monkey *again,* Ariana was one step ahead of him. He'd then caught her trying to pick the lock on his office door with a bobby pin, and she'd remained stubbornly silent about what she was looking for. In general, she'd been causing him trouble.

He grabbed the ball off the floor and tossed it toward the basket, but missed again.

"You still suck," Connor called out to him.

Forcing his mind to clear, Quinn dribbled some more and took a free throw from the middle of the court, sinking the ball clean. "I'd like to see you hang one like that."

Connor dribbled to the far end and made his shot with ease, then let the ball bounce its way off.

"Lucky," Quinn muttered. "What are you doing hanging out around here?"

"I needed to work off some energy." Connor retrieved the ball and began a steady dribbling while they talked.

"Lady problems?" Quinn chuckled.

"Hey, at least Maria's talking to me."

Connor's jibe hit home and Quinn winced.

Connor paused in his bouncing and hiked the ball under one arm. "I'm taking her out tomorrow."

Quinn let out a slow whistle. So Connor had finally made progress. "Good luck, buddy." Considering his friend's track record with relationships, he'd need it.

"Right back at you," Connor told Quinn. "Who'd have thought the professor had the guts to give you such a good runaround." Connor shook his head in amazement.

Ari definitely had turned out to be a worthy adversary, and though Quinn respected her guts and moxie, he was frustrated just the same. "She thinks I'm pond scum. She knows I'm involved in Zoe's disappearance but she can't figure out how. And every stunt she pulls brings her closer to blowing my cover sky high trying to figure it all out."

"She's already questioned Maria."

Quinn shrugged. "Doesn't matter. Maria only knows what we wanted everyone to know. It was bound to get back to Ari eventually. She's questioned everyone, including the janitor," he muttered.

Connor lowered himself onto one of the bleachers. "No matter what she thinks she knows, she won't blow your cover. No one knows enough, except me and I'm not talking."

Though his friend and partner had a point, Quinn wasn't sure how much longer he could live with the guilt of letting Ari agonize over where her sister was.

"Just don't go do anything stupid," Connor said into the silence.

He didn't need to spell out what he meant. Quinn knew. He shook his head and groaned. "She deserves better."

"We've got two years invested in this operation and it's nearly over. Remember your career, because it'll be the one thing that's there for you when this is over."

Quinn nodded. They'd perfected that line during their time at the police academy when things got tough. They had each other's backs. No one else in life could be counted on to stick around for the long haul.

"Don't worry. I'm thinking with my head," he told Connor, as much to convince himself as the other man.

"Just make sure it's the right head, because from where I'm sitting, the only reason you'd tell her the truth would be to get into her pants." Connor nodded, obviously certain he'd come to the right conclusion.

He hadn't. Quinn's truth was far worse. When it came to Ari, sex wasn't the only thing driving him. She hit an emotional chord inside him, one he didn't ever remember feeling before and one that gave light into the deepest recesses of his soul. He just wasn't about to admit it aloud.

"I wouldn't jeopardize a case just to get laid," he said in disgust.

"Excuse me if I don't want my only friend to end up on a slab at the morgue."

"Maybe you need to make some more friends. Just in case," Quinn said, laughing.

Connor shook his head and laid a brotherly hand on Quinn's shoulder. "Remember one thing. When all this is over, she's still going back to her cozy little home in Vermont."

"Hell yeah, I know." And Quinn told himself he wanted it that way.

Yet after whipping Connor's ass at a game of hoops, he'd showered and headed to Ari's parents', hoping to find her home on her night off. Plain old desire to see her was driving him and he knew he was in deep.

Although she wasn't at the house, it had taken a long while to make his escape from her family. He sniffed his sleeve but wasn't sure whether he smelled of fish or if the stench was permanently embedded in his nostrils.

An hour later, he finally walked into Paradeisos, the diner owned by Nicholas's sister Kassie. Quinn had never been to the diner before, but judging by the warm decor, he figured he'd be back again. Glancing around, he noticed Ari sitting at the counter in the back.

"Can I help you?" a dark-haired woman asked, menus in hand.

"Actually, I'm looking for someone. I'll just go on back to the counter, if you don't mind?"

"Of course not." She smiled, her gaze raking him over from head to toe before she gestured toward the rear of the restaurant.

He strode back, all the while feeling the presence of the hostess following close on his trail as she *click-clack*ed in her high heels. He reached Ari and chose a stool beside her, glancing over. Her hair had been pulled back into a ponytail and little makeup adorned her face. He liked her fresh, natural look better than the made-up-doll look she chose for her nights working at the casino.

"Hi there," he said, laying one hand on the stool behind her.

She turned. Only the slightest widening of her eyes told him she was surprised to see him. "Following me even when I'm off duty?" she asked, the chill in her

132

voice obvious. "Pretty silly of you, since there's not much I can find out from my own family."

"Oh, you'd be surprised," he said, thinking of all Zoe knew. The usual gut-twisting guilt followed. To distract himself, he took in the basic diner look—linoleum floors, vinyl seats, tables in the center and booths by the windows, with individual coin-operated jukeboxes for each.

But considering this was a Costas restaurant, there was a unique flair. Every table had its own centerpiece of what looked like a Greek god. A naked Greek god with some portion of the anatomy left to hold flowers.

"So this is your Aunt Kassie's place?"

"Mmm." Ari focused her gaze on the milk shake in front of her, stirring the thick liquid.

Obviously she was going to make him work for conversation. "Is that dinner or dessert?" He pointed to her drink.

"It's comfort food," the hostess said.

He'd forgotten she was even there.

"Ari always drinks a milk shake when she's got a lot on her mind. At least she used to when she lived at home. She's been gone so long, none of us really knows what she likes anymore—"

"Go away, Daphne," Ari said in a singsong voice. "She likes to lay the guilt on me. It makes her feel better, since she gets so much of it from her mother," Ari explained to Quinn before tipping her head back to Daphne. "Get a life, cousin," she said good-naturedly.

Aah, Quinn thought. So these two women were

related. He'd never experienced ribbing from a family member, and he envied Ariana even this luxury.

"Here's your Burger Deluxe." A man dressed in black pants and a white shirt placed a plate in front of Ari.

The delicious aroma wafted under Quinn's nose and his mouth watered.

"What can I get for your friend?" the waiter asked Ari.

"What makes you think he's my friend?"

Ari's voice held a trace of boredom Quinn didn't buy for a second. Her hand was gripping her fork so tightly she'd have nail marks in her palm when she finally let go.

"His hand's on your stool and you no tell him to get lost," said the man whose name tag read *Gus*. "On second thought maybe I just call him your *boyfriend?*" The man chuckled.

Quinn raised an eyebrow and watched as Ariana gritted her teeth. He stifled a laugh, saying nothing. In this case discretion was smarter, especially since Ari still held the fork in her hand.

"He's not my anything."

"Then you won't mind if I ask for his phone number." Cousin Daphne leaned close, her big breasts brushing against his arm.

Ari glanced at the sight and scowled. "Argh! I should have stayed home. At least the damn monkey respects my privacy."

Once again Quinn was tempted to chime in, this time to remind her of Spank's Peeping Tom tendencies. But being smart, he shot Ari an I'm-so-innocent look instead.

"I get you a burger, too," Gus said without asking if Quinn even wanted one. The other man strode off, pulling a laughing Daphne along with him.

"This side of the family is just as interesting," Quinn said once he and Ari were alone.

She poured ketchup onto her plate then poked at the red puddle with a thick french fry. "They've all sent more than a few men running for the hills."

Quinn hadn't been a cop this long without learning how to read people, and Ari's sarcasm was a definite cover for her share of pain. Though he enjoyed her eccentric relatives, she didn't. She had no idea how fortunate she was to have family in her life, he thought. But apparently she'd been given good reason to distrust people's reaction to the Costas clan.

He snagged a french fry and dipped it in the ketchup, eating it before addressing her comment. "Those men you mentioned? I'm sure they were pansies."

She tipped her head to one side. "Lesser men than you, you mean?" she asked wryly.

"Can I help it if the men in your life don't measure up?" He shot her his best boyish grin and she rolled her eyes.

"Coke for you," Gus said, placing a glass in front of Quinn.

"He's got a point, you know, Ari," said Daphne, who'd returned, popping up along with Gus.

"Don't you have work to do?" Ari asked her cousin.

"Ari's last boyfriend—well, her last boyfriend we know of, since she's so silent while going to live on her own in Vermont—well, that guy was a real piece of work. A stuffed prig with no sense of humor." Daphne gave an exaggerated shudder.

Quinn leaned an elbow over the back of his chair. "Do tell."

"Oh, don't encourage her," Ari said on a sigh.

"If she doesn't tell, I will," Gus said.

"Gus," Ari said in warning, "if you snitch, I'll tell Uncle Constantin you've been giving the pretty girls free drinks."

"And it'd be worth his roar." Ignoring other customers around the room, Gus sat down in the chair next to Quinn. "Did you know Cousin Ari is famous?"

"More like infamous," she muttered. "Do we really have to revisit my youth?"

A beautiful woman, with teased dark hair and a bone structure similar to Nicholas's, leaned over from the other side of the counter. "Oh, are you going to tell my favorite story?" she asked.

"I'd prefer he didn't," Ari said, and before Quinn could ask, she introduced the woman as her Aunt Kassie.

Quinn shook Kassie's hand, then glanced at Daphne and Gus. "I want to hear everything."

Ari's face turned a delicious shade of pink, and without thinking, Quinn placed a reassuring hand on her knee. Beneath her jeans, her leg twitched, her surprise obvious, but she didn't say a word. And he didn't give a damn if the reason was that she didn't want to call attention to the familiarity in front of her relatives. He was happy to be touching her, feeling the simmering heat beneath the denim and even enjoying his own body's response.

As for her family, other men might have run off in the face of their odd behavior and eccentricity, but not Quinn. He intended to soak up as much of Ari and her relatives as he could get.

"Well," Daphne began, "the story goes that Ariana's mother wanted to tan the twins for an Indian princess act she would perform on the boardwalk."

"The girls were little," Gus chimed in, his accent making his *i*'s sound like *e*'s. "Such cute twins." He lowered his hand to indicate about toddler height. He paused and added, his voice cracking, "May Zoe return to us soon."

"Amen," Daphne and Kassie said, and Quinn's stomach churned with extra guilt.

"Anyway, Aunt Elena used instant tanning lotion. Which turned the twins orange," Daphne explained.

"And John, he called the paper. What is the name?" Gus snapped his fingers, trying to remember.

"The *National Enquirer*," Ari said, resigned.

"And *this* was the result." Aunt Kassie pointed proudly to a photograph of the twins hanging on the wall, with the heading "Alien Twins Invade New Jersey" above it.

Ariana had known she couldn't stop them from telling the story, but being prepared didn't stop the humiliation from rising inside her. It was, as the photograph's enlarged presence on the wall both here and at home proclaimed, her family's proudest moment.

If Quinn hadn't run by now, this story surely would do the trick. It had been the start of Jeffrey's departure. Her father's fake lie-detector test, purchased at a garage sale, had acted as the final kick out the front door. He'd used the gadget on every one of his daughter's boyfriends. She could still recall Nicholas's serious face as he asked her first high school boyfriend—"You sure you like girls and not boys?" The poor boy's voice had squeaked as he answered.

Then there was Jeffrey, who'd been subjected to the question that had sent him running. Gathering her courage, Ari glanced at Quinn.

He was laughing and he didn't look taken aback by her family's stories. The same stories had always been fodder for gossip and teasing by friends and had sent more than one boyfriend ducking for cover. She was amazed at Quinn's fortitude. Then again, he had nothing invested in Ariana. And the Costas family was always good for a laugh.

She glanced at her aunt and her cousins. "Go away," she yelled at them, and to her surprise, her family scattered.

She and Quinn shared a burger in silence. She didn't know why he'd sought her out, and until he was ready to talk she wasn't about to ask.

When they finished, he reached into his pocket and pulled out his wallet.

"You can't pay. You'll insult the family," she told him. Another thing that bothered macho, I-want-to-pay-my-own-way kind of men.

He inclined his head. "Okay, then let me thank your aunt and we can be on our way."

"We?"

He nodded. "I need you to come with me."

She raised an eyebrow, unwilling to accept anything at face value. "Where?"

"I can't say."

She exhaled a frustrated breath. "Why am I not surprised? Tell me something, Quinn. What *can* you tell me?" She was so tired of asking for answers and receiving nothing.

He extended his hand. A peace offering? She didn't know but reluctantly she placed her palm in his. Her skin tingled and warmth reached all the way through her body. Damn the electricity between them anyway. It was what had gotten her into trouble the other night in his hotel room and was destined to be her downfall with him now.

He curled his fingers around hers. "You shared some of your history with me."

"Not willingly," she muttered.

He laughed. "I'm just going to return the favor."

She had no idea what he meant, but her rapidly beating heart prompted her to go with him. They said goodbye to her family and Aunt Kassie made him promise he'd come back soon. Then Ariana followed him to the parking lot and his familiar black truck.

Dusk had fallen and darkness had begun to settle around them. She glanced back at the rental she'd parked close to the building. "What about my car?" she asked.

"You can pick it up later."

"I don't want Uncle Constantin reporting I've been kidnapped." Then she'd have the entire family in an uproar, and that was definitely something they didn't need.

A smile pulled at his lips and Ariana felt ridiculously validated at the sight. "The cops would have a field day with that, since I'm one of them," Quinn said, taking her completely by surprise.

"You're a cop?" she asked, glancing his way.

He stopped short and drew a deep breath. "I meant I'm feeling more and more like one with all this damn watching over you," he said, correcting himself.

"Aah. Now that makes more sense." Even if his true explanation caused her stomach to roll over in disappointment. He hadn't sought her out for the pure pleasure of her company as she'd begun to believe. "So you're just here tonight to make sure I don't go over to the casino and ask questions." Ariana folded her arms over her chest defensively.

"It would make my life easier if that was the reason." He shook his head and placed his hand beneath her chin.

Warmth spread from his touch throughout her body. Delicious, tingling warmth, and she didn't want to lose the feeling.

"Let's just forget about the casino and everything about that place for tonight, okay?"

Ariana found herself wanting to give in.

After all her worrying about her sister, uprooting her life and trying to help out, was it so bad to give in to her wants and needs for a little while?

She swallowed hard and met Quinn's deep gaze. "Okay."

Quinn drove to the rec center in silence. He had no business bringing this woman deeper into his life, but he couldn't help feeling the desire to do so. He'd seen her reaction to her family, the mortification and embarrassment. Maybe if she saw the kids at the center, those with no family—embarrassing or otherwise—she'd feel better about her own.

And maybe if he spent some time with her away from the casino, he'd get over his growing feelings. *Yeah, right.*

He pulled into the parking lot and shut off the motor.

"Would you believe I pass this place all the time but I've never been inside?" Ari asked.

He nodded. "No reason for you to come here. But there are people I want you to meet." A scratching sound distracted him and he turned. "Did you hear something?" he asked Ari.

"No. I—"

"Okay, okay, I confess," a small, familiar voice said from behind him. From much lower behind him.

"Shit." He reached over and grabbed, coming up with a fistful of clothing, and pulled.

"Ouch!" Sam yelled from her crouched position behind the seat. "I can get up myself."

"Then do it. Now."

"Sam?" Ari asked in shock. "How long have you been there?"

"Too long." Sam sat on the back seat and stretched out her legs, groaning as she moved. "God, Quinn. How long does it take you to eat a stinkin' meal, anyway? You were in that diner place forever!" she complained.

He glanced at Ari, who was obviously biting the inside of her cheek to keep from laughing.

He was pissed at Sam for running away again and even more annoyed at himself for being so distracted by thoughts of Ari, he hadn't even noticed the kid who'd snuck into the back of the car while he was at the rec center with Connor.

"Sam, you can't pull stunts like this," Ari said in her soft voice. "What if someone had stolen the truck with you in it?"

"Nobody wants this hunk of crap."

"Samantha," Quinn warned before turning to Ari. "If someone had taken the truck, they'd have returned her and her smart mouth in no time. Get out of the car, miss," he said to Sam, pulling out his cell phone as he spoke.

"Do your foster parents know you're here?" Ari asked.

"I'm just about to find out." He started to dial at the same time Sam burst into tears.

CHAPTER NINE

Midnight. Unable to sleep, Ariana paced the floor in her sister's room. She'd tiptoed in and now glanced around, memories of the past, both happy and sad, overwhelming her. Ariana often wondered why Zoe hadn't moved out of her parents' home. Why, beyond college, she hadn't taken that step toward becoming an independent adult. But any time Ariana asked, an argument had ensued. Zoe would berate Ariana for her feelings toward the family and her need to stay away, and Ariana would tell Zoe she could do so much better than a life as a showgirl/con artist.

One of the reasons Ariana had taken off for Vermont instead of teaching at a local college was so she could escape not just the lifestyle but the constant disagreements. Now Ariana would give anything to have Zoe standing in front of her so they could have a good old-fashioned sisterly fight.

Ariana was already feeling raw and the earlier scene with Sam hadn't helped. Quinn had returned Ariana to the diner for her car, then taken Sam back to her foster parents, but not before Sam had indulged in a full-blown scene. She'd cried and begged him to let her stay with him, while blaming him for choosing Felice and Aaron in the first place. Ariana's heart had twisted with pain for them both.

The end result was that Ariana felt twice as guilty over the rift with Zoe, because at least she had family, while Sam had none. And she agonized because she couldn't find a way to fix things for an innocent child, the victim of other people's decisions, not her own.

A knock sounded on the door and Ariana turned, startled. Her mother strode inside, tying her black silk robe around her waist as she walked. "I heard noises and thought I'd find you in here."

Ariana swallowed hard. "I'm sorry if I woke you."

"It wasn't you. Your father's snoring did that hours ago."

Ariana laughed. Nicholas always fell asleep, mouth open, the most obnoxious noises coming from deep in his chest. When they were kids, she and Zoe would toss popcorn at his open mouth in an effort to see who had the best aim.

She glanced at her mother and grinned. "I don't know how you stand it." Her mother had been complaining about her father's irritating habit for years.

Elena shrugged. "When you love someone, little things like snoring don't bother you." Elena placed a hand on Ariana's shoulder. "And one day, you'll have feelings so strong, you'll understand what I mean."

Without warning, Ariana thought of Quinn. She wondered if he snored—and if she'd ever find out.

"Now tell me. How's Quinn?" her mother asked as if reading her mind.

"He's fine, as you well know, since you sent him over to Aunt Kassie's place earlier."

"And how was your dinner?" she asked, casual as she pleased.

"What would you expect with Daphne hovering and

Gus telling him our sordid stories?"

Elena smiled. "At least Quinn knows what he's getting himself into. And this one's got strong character. He won't run just because your family's got their own special quirks." Her mother brushed a strand of hair out of Ariana's eyes. "I always told you that Jeffrey had a stick up his behind."

"Mom, please. Let's not relive history, okay?"

"Of course not. I just want you happy and I think Quinn's a good man."

"Good enough to make me come back home, you mean?" Ariana figured it was time to deal with all that was unsaid between mother and daughter.

"It isn't normal for a daughter to move out and not return for five years. You needed your own life? Fine." Her mother spread her hands out in front of her. "But to stay away so long? Are we so bad a family?"

Ariana twisted her fingers together and tried to find the words to explain why she'd made the decisions she had. "I was right to leave, because I needed space and I needed to find out who Ariana Costas really was." But since coming home again, Ariana was forced to acknowledge the scary truth to herself—she still didn't know.

But there was another truth. And this one she could admit to aloud. "I was wrong not to come home. That was the coward's way." She realized that now.

"I still don't understand why you stayed away."

Ariana met her mother's gaze, reaching out for her hand at the same time. "I think that's the problem. I don't understand all of you any more than you understand me. But I promise to try harder, okay?" She made a vow to do just that. She couldn't look at Sam, who had no family, and turn her back on her own.

"Will you stay then?" her mother asked.

Ariana couldn't go that far. She shook her head. "I need to live my own life. But I'll come to visit this time," she promised.

"If you have such a good life, how come you never discuss it?" Elena asked. "How come I don't know anything about friends? Men? Your job?"

Ariana winced because her mother had hit a nerve. The life she didn't talk about was dull compared to life here. Compared to Quinn and the excitement he brought into her days and nights, her life in Vermont was routine. Nothing out of the ordinary ever occurred. Her friends were carbon copies of herself, professors in conservative suits who met for coffee a few nights a week, and turned in early to work the next day. Nothing like her bright and cheery twin, whom she missed badly.

It was exactly the life Ariana had been seeking when she'd left her family behind. She didn't expect them to understand it and so she kept details to herself, especially now when that life seemed pale in comparison.

She met her mother's inquiring gaze and had no idea how to explain, so she merely shrugged. "I'll try to be more open," she promised her mother.

Elena nodded, a slight smile lifting her lips. "Okay then. How about you start with Quinn?" she asked, not being subtle at all.

Ariana laughed and hugged her mother tight. "I

146

really did miss you," she told her.

"Then prove it by talking."

She grinned. "I hate to admit it, but I really like the man." She drew the line at discussing exactly how much she liked him with her mother. "Unfortunately he's got his share of secrets. He's a hard man to get to know."

"Aah," her mother said, a knowing sound that gave Ariana the chills. "It's not like you're an easy nut to crack yourself," she reminded Ariana. "Which means you two will have no trouble maintaining the element of the unknown that helps keep things interesting early on in a relationship. As for sexual attraction, well, I've witnessed the undercurrents between you. That's not a problem either."

While Ariana blushed at her mother's frank talk, Elena nodded, pleased with what she obviously considered a good match. "Just remember, if you're going to make it for the long haul, secrets have to give way to trust."

"There is no long haul. He's a loner and I'm only visiting," she felt compelled to remind her mother.

Elena shrugged. "Then just sleep with the man. You wouldn't want to miss out on a good time. Just make sure you use protection."

"Mom!" Ariana said, appalled at such a suggestion from her mother.

"I'm not the one who dismissed the more serious possibilities." Elena sent her a pointed look.

Ariana didn't like being cornered by her own words.

As if sensing her daughter's feelings, Elena changed

the subject. "So, why can't you sleep and why are you in your sister's room?" She sat on the bed and patted the mattress, motioning for Ariana to join her.

Ariana curled her legs beneath her. She was happy to end the subject of her love life and welcomed the chance to talk to her mother about something more important. "Sam ran away again tonight."

"Oh no."

Ariana nodded. "Apparently her foster parents bought furniture for the baby's room, which is the room Sam is staying in. It was delivered today."

"Of all the thoughtless, inconsiderate . . ." A low growl escaped Elena's throat.

"I agree. But there's nowhere Family Services can place Sam right now. They're waiting for a space in a group home to open. As long as she doesn't cause trouble, her foster family has agreed to let her stay on until then," Ariana said, explaining to her mother what Quinn had told her earlier.

"How understanding," Elena said, not bothering to hide her sarcasm.

Ariana ran a hand over her eyes, which burned from lack of sleep and the tears she'd already shed.

Her mother rose from the bed and paced the floor. "Those people don't deserve to have that child in their home."

"Again, I agree. But there's no denying that Sam's better off there than in a group home." Ariana shuddered at the mere thought. "But trouble is Sam's middle name. She's just not helping her cause." Ariana wished she could do more for both Sam and

Quinn, who felt somehow responsible for the young girl's predicament.

"If Sam thinks she's not wanted, she's only going to act out more. I ought to know how teenage girls think, considering I raised two of them—" Elena snapped her fingers in the air, as if she had just thought of something important. "That's it."

"What's it?"

"Me. Raising teenage girls."

Ariana raised her eyebrows. "Sam? Are you talking about bringing Sam *here* to live?" she asked in shock.

Her mother nodded. "I have to go talk to your father. Of course, I need to soften him up first." She shrugged her silk robe off her shoulders in a provocative gesture. "Now, you keep this between us until I'm ready to broach the subject with him at the right time."

"But . . ." Before Ariana could discuss the subject further, her mother glided out of the room, a determined woman on a mission.

Her mother wanted to bring Sam here. That idea brought up a load of memories and questions Ariana wasn't sure she was ready to deal with. She and her sister had been raised in this house with two very different results. But given the alternatives, Sam could certainly do much worse. At least she'd be safe and cared for here.

In the meantime, it hadn't escaped Ariana's notice that she and her mother had discussed every touchy and painful subject between them—except Zoe.

The notion that something might really have happened to her sister was a pain too great to contemplate.

If Quinn held the secret to Zoe's disappearance, Ariana just had to trust he'd confide in her soon.

She glanced around her sister's room, not knowing what she was looking for, just that she desperately needed a connection to the twin she loved but didn't understand. And then, unexpectedly, she found the link she needed. Reaching across the bed, she pulled a small crocheted pillow into her hand and ran her fingers over the nubby stitching. *Sisters and Best Friends 4 Ever.* Ariana had made the pillow as a birthday gift for Zoe when they were young. She couldn't remember exactly how old they'd been, just that she'd given it to her twin.

She had no idea Zoe had kept the gift, but she had. Through the arguments and the rift, Zoe had held on to a link between them. At this moment, their last argument stood out in stark contrast to the past. The night Ariana had left for Vermont, she and Zoe had agreed that they'd never understand one another. Never agree. That distance was best for them both.

Distance, Ariana thought. Not a permanent gap. She wondered now how she'd stayed away for so long. And she hoped it wasn't too late to make amends.

The persistent sound of banging woke Ariana from a fitful sleep. She rolled over and realized she'd dozed on top of her sister's bed. She was still wearing her robe, which had twisted uncomfortably around her waist, and the pillow she'd found was clutched tightly in her arms.

As she made her way downstairs, the noise, which

she realized now was hammering, became louder. "What's going on?" she called to her father, who stood looking out over a window with a backyard view.

"We're starting construction on the addition for the spa," he replied, just as loudly, speaking over the noise.

"Why didn't you say anything?"

He shrugged. "We told you we'd be doing remodeling on the house."

"You just didn't say when. I work nights and need to sleep days," she reminded him.

"You're young. You need less sleep."

A loud crash reverberated throughout the house. Ariana jumped at the same time a bizarre shriek sounded in her ear and the monkey dove into Ariana's arms.

"She hates the noise." Her father spread his hands wide, indicating he was at a loss as to what to do.

"I take it you're not any happier than I am?" she asked Spank.

The banging grew louder and the monkey buried her face between Ariana's neck and shoulders. "How long is this going to go on?" she asked her father.

"As long as it takes," her father said.

"I was afraid of that. Where's Mom?"

Nicholas glanced over his shoulder. "She went to the library. She said she had research to do. I think she needs to figure out how to thicken the facial cream she's been working on. But she was in an exceptionally good mood," he said and winked at Ariana.

She rolled her eyes. When her mother played her

father, she was so obvious, Ariana didn't know how her father didn't see it. Everyone else certainly did. Then again maybe he just accepted her the same way Elena accepted his snoring, because he loved her. Ariana wondered how he'd feel once her "research" led to another child in this house. Because the one thing Ariana had learned was that whatever Elena wanted, Elena made certain she got.

With a shake of her head, Ariana left the kitchen, the monkey wrapped tightly around her. In the meantime, Ariana needed to find a place to stay where she could actually get some sleep while the construction continued.

Quinn was pouring himself a cup of strong, black coffee when the phone in his hotel room rang. "Donovan."

"Hey, buddy."

Since Connor didn't normally call from his post at the bar, Quinn was surprised. "I was just on my way downstairs. What's going on?"

"Our mutual friend looks exhausted. Ariana has broken more than a few glasses, and I'm thinking she needs to get out of here early, if you get my drift." Connor's low chuckle sounded through the phone line.

"Thanks. I'll check it out." Quinn wondered what was going on with Ari and headed to the bar to find out.

He took one look at the woman in the skimpy cocktail waitress outfit, noting the lack of makeup and the dark circles under her eyes, and he'd seen enough. He grabbed her elbow. "Come with me."

She met his gaze, startled. "I can't leave with you. I have work to do."

"And there's plenty of people here who can cover for you." Quinn leaned closer. So close he could smell the shampoo in her hair and the scent that kept him awake at night. His groin tightened and the desire to make love to her overwhelmed him. "Let's go."

"Okay," she said, surprising him. "Just let me get my purse." She tilted her head, meeting his gaze.

The same need that beat like a drum inside him shimmered in her glassy eyes. When it came to attraction and desire, they were definitely on the same page. His libido kicked into high gear. Only her complete and obvious exhaustion had him breathing deeply and reminding himself she had more important things going on than thinking about sex.

Once they'd reached the lobby of the casino, where the throngs of people and the glittering lights and mirrors made them just one of the crowd instead of the object of the other employees' curiosity, he pulled her into an empty corner. "You look like hell."

She laughed but even that sounded strained. "Way to flatter a lady."

He flattened his palm on the mirrored wall behind her. "What's going on?" he asked in a low voice.

"I'm just tired," she said with a sigh. "My parents started construction on the house this morning, which works well for people on a normal schedule, but with my night shifts, I couldn't get any sleep today."

He slanted her a disbelieving glance. "Somehow I don't think that's all that's bothering you." He raised her chin with his hand, looking into her weary eyes. "You can talk to me." He wanted to hear what was really going on with Ari—and he wanted to help. Not in the I'm-a-cop-and-it's-my-job kind of way, either.

Ariana looked into his sincere gaze and she believed his words. She needed to take him up on his offer and confide in him. Maybe it would let him trust her in return, but if not, she still wanted to let him wrap his arms around her and make her feel better, if just for a little while.

"I really am exhausted, but it's not just physical. It's emotional, too. It started with Zoe disappearing," she explained. "Then it was the stress of coming home. You must realize I have family issues." She felt ridiculous complaining about family when he had none, but when he squeezed her shoulder, urging her to continue, she instinctively knew he understood. "Then last night everything hit me all at once," she went on.

She drew a trembling breath and he waited patiently. "Watching Sam fall apart like that got to me. I mean, she's so young and vulnerable and she has no one. While I have a sister whom I haven't spoken to in years for stupid reasons and now she's missing." Her voice cracked and her eyes watered. Embarrassed, she sniffed, wiping her eyes with the back of her hand. "On top of that, I couldn't fall asleep last night and then the construction woke me today . . . God, I feel like a basket case." Her voice quavered and she shook badly.

"You'll have a chance to fix things one day," he promised her, determination and something so compelling in his voice, once again, she couldn't help but believe him.

"Add a little sleep and you'll feel much better." He brushed a stray tear beneath her eye with his thumb, and she shuddered at his comforting yet oh-so-seductive touch. "Come. You can crash upstairs for tonight and tomorrow. I think I have the perfect solution to your construction problem."

Going up to his room could only lead to one thing, and despite her exhaustion, her palms grew damp at the heady thought.

He let out a frustrated groan. "Look, you need sleep, so will you change your mind if I promise not to touch you?" he asked, obviously misreading her silence.

"If you make that promise, I'll definitely change my mind." In other words, if he didn't touch her, why bother going upstairs? she thought wryly, and bit the inside of her cheek to keep from laughing.

But there was nothing funny about her desire or her feelings for this man. "I don't want you to keep your distance and I definitely don't want you to keep your hands to yourself." She forced herself to be the bold and brazen woman she imagined her sister to be, then held her breath and waited, hoping Quinn would react the way she wanted him to.

His eyes darkened and he lowered his head until his lips hovered over hers, just enough to tempt her with his coffee-scented breath. Her heart pounded in her chest and an overwhelming rush of arousal trickled through her, slow, steady, and increasingly warm and exciting.

"You're a tease," she told him, then let her tongue dart out and caress the outline of his mouth.

A low groan rumbled from deep in his throat and he pulled her against him. Having gone this far, Ariana wasn't about to back down now. Hoping to take Quinn off guard, she slipped her tongue between his barely parted lips. Kissing him felt like coming home, a sensation and experience both foreign and welcome at the same time. She entwined her arms around his neck and pressed her breasts against his chest to ease the aching need building there. All the while his tongue tangled with hers, letting her know he wanted her every bit as much as she wanted him.

The kiss went on, long and leisurely one minute, more hot and demanding the next. Her stomach swirled with the exquisite sensations he created and her body craved his.

"Sweetheart, I think we're making a scene," he said, barely breaking the kiss.

"So?" Her blood flowed like warm liquid and she wanted more of the boneless feeling he provided. She wanted more of him.

"So we need to go upstairs."

The next thing she knew, he had lifted her into his arms. Ignoring the shocked stares of the strangers around them, he carried her into the private elevator reserved for Damon's closest associates. Soon she found herself in Quinn's hotel room, and he lowered her to the bed.

"You need to relax and I'm going to make sure you do." His voice held a determined edge as he maneuvered their positions so that she lay on her back, her head between his crossed legs. "Shut your eyes."

This was one order she didn't mind obeying, and she let her lashes fall. His fingers moved from her jawline to her forehead, and he began a steady massage of her temples. His touch was electric and she responded, her breasts tightening with need, while lower down, a pulsing of a different kind began between her legs.

"Breathe in," he said in that deep voice that had mesmerized her from day one. "And out."

Despite the desire flowing through her body, her mind responded to his request. For the first time since receiving a phone call about her missing twin, she let herself relax. She calmed down, feeling herself sinking deeper into the mattress as her tension eased. His caring caress nurtured the emptiness she'd been experiencing from being alone and being the only one *doing* something to find Zoe.

She wasn't alone anymore. She had Quinn. And although he wasn't revealing answers, he wasn't leaving her to fall apart either. He nurtured her emotions as well as he fed her hunger. And she had a hunch *that* would be the next need to be filled.

CHAPTER TEN

Quinn watched Ariana sleep in the king-size bed in his hotel room. She'd taken him off guard with that heated kiss in the lobby, even more so by making him promise he'd remain hands on, not off. But no sooner had he begun to massage her temples in an attempt to relax her, than she'd fallen into a deep sleep, leaving her head in his lap and him completely aroused.

He'd moved her head to the pillows and covered her with the blanket, then stripped to his boxers and climbed in on the other side. He lay far from where she was curled into the pillow and far from temptation, because despite her seductive words, she needed sleep. Still, keeping his hands to himself wasn't easy.

Neither was falling asleep, and as he turned on his side, he couldn't help but stare. Although technically this wasn't *his* bed, something about having Ari here with him felt too damn right. Her black eyelashes covered her paler skin and she slept peacefully. More so than he'd been able to manage since she'd unloaded her feelings on him earlier that night. He'd asked for it but that didn't make the guilt and sense of responsibility he felt easier to bear.

The distinctive ring of a cell phone broke both his thoughts and the quiet around him. A glance at the nightstand told him his phone lay silent, and he realized the muffled sound came from inside Ari's large purse. The phone rang again and she stirred. Not wanting her to awaken, he swung his legs over the side of the mattress and looked through her bag for the phone.

By the time he found it, the ringing had stopped and the display showed only MISSED MESSAGE with her mother's phone number. He wasn't sure whether or not to wake her, and glanced down at the items he'd removed from her purse. He couldn't help but notice a crocheted pillow staring up at him with stitching that read *Sisters and Best Friends 4 Ever.*

Shit.

"Quinn? What are you doing up?" Ari's voice called to him. "Come back to bed."

A smile quirked his lips. "Now, that's an invitation I can't refuse."

"I don't expect you to." She laughed, a sultry, sensual *Come here* he couldn't possibly mistake.

"Your phone was ringing," he forced himself to tell her.

"Did you check the number?"

"Your mother. Do you want to call back?" He palmed the cool metal in his hand.

"Come here, Quinn. And leave the phone."

He placed the cell in her bag. "What's going on?"

"I want to see your eyes," she said softly.

Curious, he walked to the edge of the bed and met her gaze.

"The only reason I'd call my mother back now was if it was an emergency." Her compelling, serious gaze stared into his.

"It's the middle of the night. Doesn't it stand to reason any call would be important?" he asked.

She shook her head and rolled her eyes. "You know my mother by now. She'd call at this hour just to ask me to say good night to the monkey," Ari said wryly. "So I'm asking *you,* is it important?"

In other words, were her parents calling about Zoe? Quinn could all but read her mind. All the while her steady gaze never left his. She obviously trusted his word that much. Trusted him.

He swallowed hard. "It's not an emergency."

She smiled, patting the mattress beside her. "Then come back to bed."

Though her question should have overloaded his sense of responsibility, instead her blind faith freed him to be with her right now. He strode around to his side of the large bed with every intention of making it feel a lot smaller. After all, Ari knew he had secrets that affected her and she accepted him anyway. Maybe a better man would deny himself this opportunity, but hell, when had Quinn ever considered himself a candidate for sainthood?

He lifted the covers and climbed back in beside her only to discover she'd already slipped out of her skirt. Wearing a tight "Damon's" top and skimpy panties, she curved one finger his way, silently asking him to close the gap between them.

He moved from his now cold side of the bed to her much warmer one. His entire body was on fire, burning with his wanting her for so long. "Be sure," he warned. "Because once I touch you, there's no turning back."

Her green-eyed gaze met his. "How's this for sure?"

Taking him by surprise, she grabbed the hem of her shirt and pulled it over her head, revealing a black lace bra and creamy mounds of flesh.

He exhaled a sharp breath, taking in her softly rounded cleavage and erect nipples waiting for his hands, his fingertips, his mouth. "You do realize that your quiet-professor image doesn't suit you?" Maybe because he saw the woman inside. One who was willing to take risks for her twin and slowly grow more emboldened by her actions. He couldn't put Ariana into the conservative mold in which she painted herself.

"I think it depends on your perspective," she murmured.

Her answer took him off guard. It damn well figured that when he finally had her just where he wanted her, half dressed in his bed, they were getting to some serious conversation he couldn't let slide.

He tipped his head to one side. "Are you saying I see a side of you others don't?"

"Right now you do." A naughty smile tilted her lips.

Unwilling to end their talk but unable to not touch her, he drew a finger down one side of her face. "I've come to know you pretty well."

"You think so?"

He nodded. "Yeah. And I'd say the professor's clothes and her uptight demeanor are a cover."

"I thought *I* was the psych major," she reminded him in a teasing tone.

But he didn't miss the fact that her voice quivered beneath the lighthearted banter. Yet another signal he'd struck home and she was afraid. Afraid of him getting too close. "You might be the smarty-pants psych professor, but I'm the—"

Quinn bit the inside of his cheek, catching himself in time. "I'm the people-watcher around here. I can recognize a con and a cover in no time." He'd been about to say that he was the cop, good at reading people with something to hide. He couldn't allow himself to slip again.

It looked like they both had good reason to fear each other. Being with Ari allowed him to let his guard down in a way he never had before. This was dangerous stuff and they were both walking a fine line here. He sensed the precipice they were on, their abilities to reach inside each other—and that was something he couldn't allow. Not while he was still undercover.

Instead of trying to figure her out, he ought to just take what she offered and be satisfied. Since when wasn't a woman's offer of her body enough for him?

Since the woman was Ari.

"Don't you think we've done enough analyzing for one night?" she asked.

"Not nearly," he said, easing her shoulders down onto the pillow. "I could spend the entire night researching *you*." The time for talk had ended.

He reached for the front hook of her bra and he released the clasp and slowly lowered the straps down past her shoulders to her forearms, then peeled the cups away and revealed her bare breasts. Against the cooler air, her nipples puckered into rigid peaks, and against his boxers, his groin grew thick and hard with wanting her.

He leaned forward and brushed a lingering kiss over her lips, letting his tongue dart inside her moist mouth and taste all of her, before trailing equally wet kisses down her neck and throat, her chest and cleavage. He ended exactly where he wanted to be, inhaling the fragrant scent of her skin, his mouth on one breast. With his tongue, he traced the slope of one mound of her flesh, encircling her nipple in teasing strokes.

She sucked in a deep breath, then let out an electric moan of satisfaction when he pulled her into his mouth and began an insistent suckling that had her writhing with obvious burning need. She threaded her fingers through his hair, urging him closer, silently begging him to continue. And he did, grazing on first one breast, and then, when the sensation obviously became too great for her, he switched to the other, laving and giving it equal attention. It seemed he'd been waiting forever to have her come apart for him. Feeling her quiver with need and shake with desire beneath his hands gave him more pleasure than he'd ever imagined.

So much that when she reached for him, obviously intent on reciprocating, he shook his head. "I'm not finished with you yet."

She forced heavy eyelids open and a sassy smile curved her lips. "But you can't deny me equal time after."

His body tensed at the mere thought. "Honey, I

wouldn't dream of it." But first he had other objectives to complete.

With her arms safely at her sides—because he wouldn't last a second if she touched him—he eased one finger into each side of her panties and, with her help, brought them down over her legs. He tossed them onto the floor, glanced at Ari lying naked but for a flimsy bra securing her arms, and thought he'd died and gone to heaven. But heaven couldn't possibly look this good or offer so much, Quinn thought as he came over her, easing her legs apart.

She looked at him, wide-eyed and shockingly trusting. It was the trust that wreaked havoc with his heart, and that same trust he tucked away to think about later.

"You're playing so unfairly," she said while her body quivered with expectation and anticipation.

"I don't think you're really all that upset." He chuckled, then rested his hands on her thighs and dipped his head, his intent clear.

She let out an exaggerated sigh. "I suppose not," she said, too languidly for his liking, so he dipped his head and tasted her for the first time.

At the first touch of his silken tongue, Ariana's back arched off the bed and tremors shot through her body. "Oooh, *definitely* not," she said, a low ragged moan rumbling from her throat. She swallowed hard, barely able to think at all.

His warm breath combined with his slick tongue and just the right pressure of his teeth on her most sensitive spot had her trembling, on the verge of climax.

164

She closed her eyes and he reached for one hand, wrapping his fingers through hers. That small act was so intimate, a surge of emotion enveloped her, bringing her higher still.

His tongue dipped inside her and another wave of tremors began. As if sensing the moment, he pressed against her with the palm of his hand, coaxing her closer still. Without warning, the feelings converged. The slide of his tongue, the delicious rolling of his palm over her mound and the delicate rasping of his teeth, all exploded into one long spiraling climax that seemed to go on and on. Just as he went on and on, wringing every last drop of sensation out of her.

The tremors continued even after Quinn released her hand and began to ease himself upward. She realized he'd managed to pull off his boxers, because his lean, hard, naked body touched every inch of hers as he moved. All muscle and defined male, he came over her. He bracketed her head with his hands and aligned their bodies so they came into intimate contact, his straining erection nestled in the vee of her legs.

That easily she came alive again. The desire she thought he'd sated returned, letting her know the previous orgasm, though incredible, had been but a prelude. Her body pulsed with need as an aching emptiness begged to be filled.

Needing to touch him, she pulled her arms free of the restricting bra straps and wrapped her arms around his waist so she cupped his behind in both hands.

Quinn let out a low groan. "What you do to me . . ." He shook his head. "It defies description."

His groin pulsed low and hard against her feminine mound and she couldn't help but smile. "That's good to know, because I'm pretty swept away myself."

He rolled to one side, opening the night table drawer and pulling out a sealed box of condoms. Ariana couldn't believe how ridiculously happy she was to see that he hadn't used them before. With no discussion, he opened them and sheathed himself, then he returned to pick up where they'd left off.

But Ariana wasn't content to let him have his way this time. She hooked her leg around his and maneuvered him onto his back.

"Looking to be in charge?" he asked wryly.

"You don't seem like you're complaining, either." She lowered herself over him, slowly, deliberately taking him inside. As she felt him full, hard, and completely in her body, the mix of emotions was almost too much for her to handle and she closed her eyes.

"Ari. Look at me."

She did as he asked and Quinn used that precise moment to thrust upward, impaling himself deep inside her. Their gazes connected as tightly as their bodies, forcing her to acknowledge her own feelings, even if she didn't voice them aloud.

No matter his intent, looking into his darkened gaze made her come face-to-face with the wealth of emotion he pulled from her. And then he shifted beneath her and she couldn't think at all. Her body began another rapid climb toward fulfillment, this time more satisfying with Quinn joining her for the ride.

Her hands grasped his and she gyrated her hips in a

circular motion until her most sensitive spot ground tight against him. Clenching her internal muscles, she gripped him in warm, wet heat and again her body reached higher until together they found a matching rhythm all their own.

His hips pumped upward, hers downward, faster and faster, the intensity spiraling beyond reason. Unable to maintain any semblance of control, she stretched herself over him and ground her hips into his, her climax beginning and peaking almost at the exact same time.

Waves and waves of rapture washed over her and she rode the crest, rode him, prolonging the exquisite sensations and feelings until she was wrung dry.

Ariana woke up to the most pleasurable feeling of being wrapped in complete warmth and safety. She couldn't ever remember such utter bliss and she inhaled deep. Musky scents assailed her, scents of passion and Quinn. Unwilling to let herself think and possibly spoil the moment, she eased back into him. He was spooned around her, holding her tight.

"You're up?" he asked in a low, morning-roughened voice.

"Mmm-hmm."

He nuzzled her neck in reply. "You smell delicious in the morning."

"That's ridiculous," she said and laughed, but she'd thought the same thing about him. "You don't snore." The words popped out without thought.

"Did you expect me to?"

"No. It was just an observation." She wasn't about

to explain her mother's views on men, love, and snoring, since they couldn't possibly mean anything to herself and Quinn. Not at all, she reassured herself. But her heart was pounding hard in her chest while her panicked brain reminded her *this* was temporary and her life was hours away in a small college town in Vermont.

A knock sounded from the other room, louder with each successive rapping noise. "Did you hear that?" she asked.

"Unfortunately, yeah." Quinn got out of bed, but not before rolling her onto her back and treating her to a morning-after kiss that rocked her world and aroused her all over again. "Wait here."

As if she had anywhere else to go, at least for the moment. "I'll just call my parents back while you get the door," she said.

He had risen naked, then pulled on a pair of jeans he'd tossed over a chair, zipped them but ignored the button. The result was disheveled and sexy, and would convey a message to whoever was at the door that they'd interrupted and were unwelcome.

She bit the inside of her cheek as he walked out of the room, pulling the door shut behind him. Left alone in his bed, she had to admit she liked being the bad girl who'd spent the night in Quinn's bed, then had to sneak her way home in the morning wearing last night's wrinkled clothes. Maybe she was making up for lost time, because Lord knew she'd never been a bad girl before. That had been Zoe's job.

Zoe. She'd trusted Quinn's word that Zoe was safe

and her parents' phone call had nothing to do with her missing twin. Trusted him in favor of a night of blissful lovemaking in his bed. *Blissful sex,* she corrected herself, but her rapid pulse and full heart didn't back up her claim.

She scooted to the bottom of the bed and reached to the floor for her bag. She dialed home but nobody answered, meaning they were either ignoring call-waiting or Spank had pulled the answering machine cords out of the wall. Then again, it could be the workmen. Either way, if her mother had needed her that badly, all she'd have to do was call the hotel and ask for Quinn's room. Certain everything at home was fine, she rose and found a large T-shirt of Quinn's that she pulled over her head, and then started for the bathroom.

She passed the door to the outer suite on the way, and since Quinn hadn't shut the door completely, she clearly heard the sound of raised voices traveling toward her. And though she told herself she shouldn't eavesdrop, she couldn't help but listen anyway. Especially once she realized the man in the other room was Damon and Quinn was obviously not happy with the man's interruption.

Quinn didn't appreciate being woken in the morning any more than he liked Damon's obvious attempt to find out who he'd brought up to his room. Quinn leaned against the wall beside the bedroom door and contemptuously eyed the man who'd barged in.

Where Damon was concerned, the stronger Quinn

came on, the more the boss respected him and the more responsibility he gave. "I work for you but my private life is my own," Quinn said.

"Have a cup of coffee and chill." Damon held a hand up in front of him. "I just heard rumblings downstairs that you were hot and heavy with some broad in the lobby, and I came upstairs to give you my congratulations. You've been like a goddamn monk since coming to work here, and I figured it's about time you got some action."

Quinn rolled his shoulders to relieve the building tension. "Let's say this has been long overdue." In ways this man couldn't begin to understand. Being with Ari had been destined from the moment he'd saved her ass on the beach, only now he was in deeper than ever before.

"It's *her,* isn't it?" Damon stepped closer, lowering his voice.

Quinn wanted Damon gone, and playing along was the only way to accomplish his goal. He nodded. "You said to keep an eye on her, didn't you?"

"And you're ever the loyal employee." Damon belted out a laugh and slapped Quinn on his forearm. "Just make sure she doesn't find out you offed her twin or you'll be back to being a monk in no time."

Still laughing, Damon strode toward the door, turning before he walked out. "My trip's still on, so make sure you're not distracted over the weekend," he said with a nod toward the bedroom.

"Don't worry. I'll be one hundred percent business," Quinn said. If for no other reason than he was dying to wrap up this case and return to his real life.

No sooner had Damon shut the door and it locked behind him, than Ari stepped into the suite, wearing his shirt and an extremely wary expression on her face. She'd obviously heard what Damon said, leaving Quinn to wonder where the hell he stood with her now.

Ariana tried to swallow but since hearing Damon so callously discussing how Quinn had supposedly "offed" her twin, she felt like she had paste in her mouth and a huge lump in the back of her throat.

"I don't suppose you'd care to explain?" she asked Quinn. But since he'd been less than forthcoming until now, she really didn't expect any answers.

But she refused to stick around on the basis of pure trust. Not anymore. She'd given him her faith and her body. It was time he offered something in return. But since being on the receiving end of Jeffrey's ultimatum, Ariana didn't believe in giving her own. Folding her arms over her chest, she stared at Quinn. And waited.

"You can't believe everything you hear."

She laughed, but the sound was as bitter as she felt. "Try another one."

He spread his hands open wide. "Things aren't always as they seem?"

A reluctant smile pulled at her mouth. "Better." But not enough.

She turned and headed back into the bedroom to get dressed. Back into the room where they'd made love. And because they'd been so close, so intimate, because she'd seen him with Sam, in her heart Ariana knew Quinn hadn't had her sister *offed*. No way in hell.

But she needed to hear the truth from him or she was through. He still wasn't talking. She began the embarrassing morning-after process of retrieving her clothes that were scattered around the room. She bent down for her T-shirt when Quinn laid a hand on her shoulder. Her heart beat triple-time in her chest and her skin tingled, memories of last night overwhelming in their intensity.

He knelt down beside her, his breath warm against her neck, and whispered softly in her ear. "I'm an undercover cop and your sister's safe. There's nothing else I can tell you."

She sucked in a startled breath. "You're a—"

He placed a hand over her mouth. "Do not repeat that word out loud. Especially not here. Understand?"

She nodded and he released her.

Her cheeks tingled from his touch as surprise and something so much deeper coursed through her veins. His last slip of the tongue had been real. Quinn was a cop, not one of Damon's goons. Unless he'd turned, but she knew that wasn't even a remote possibility. She'd always known he was a good man. She wouldn't have slept with him otherwise. And she'd sensed his nobleness even when he refused to give her the answers she needed. Which was why her feelings and emotions regarding this enigmatic man were bizarre, conflicting, and now that she'd slept with him, even more complicated.

He turned her toward him. "I've swept this place for bugs but I'm not about to risk a lengthy discussion here." He still spoke at barely a whisper.

Ariana remained silent, the enormity of what he'd revealed just now settling over her. Not his occupation, which was enough of a shock, but the fact that he'd trusted her with the information. She understood what that must have cost him.

The most she could do in return was accept his request to remain silent. Reaching out, she cupped his cheek in her hand. "You didn't sleep with me because Damon said you should stick close to me."

"Did it *feel* like that's why I slept with you?"

She sealed her lips over his in reply.

CHAPTER ELEVEN

Connor pulled up to a small house in a town about thirty minutes from Damon's casino. The outside was well maintained, unlike the dilapidated older houses surrounding it. He double-checked the number against the paper Maria had given him, before climbing out of his car and walking toward the front door.

He'd been waiting for this moment for so long, his palms sweat like he was on his first date. In Connor's life, not much affected him anymore. Until he'd met the dark-haired sexy woman with a smart mouth and an obvious reluctance to get closer—which was just fine with him since he didn't want anything long-term or serious either. He just couldn't get her out of his head and he hoped like hell this date would be a good start.

He was heading up the driveway when a young kid, probably a neighbor, followed a basketball that rolled across the grass and came to a halt by Connor's feet. He appeared about six or seven years of age. His dark hair stood straight up as if he'd slept wrong, had a cowlick that wouldn't tame, and had been avoiding a hairbrush for days.

"Hey, mister."

Connor knelt down on one knee. "Hey, yourself."

"Whatever you're selling, we don't need." The boy puffed out his chest as if he were the man in charge and stared Connor down.

Connor could well relate to the kid's bravado, having been a similar tough guy in his day, and he stifled a laugh. "Don't worry. I'm no salesman. But who are you anyway, the neighborhood welcoming committee?" he asked wryly.

The kid shook his head. "I just take care of what's mine."

"Then go on home and do that," Connor said, chuckling. Gone were the days when a kid should play alone in the streets, and Connor glanced around, wondering if someone was looking out for him.

"I am home." He pointed his thumb back toward the gray house and wrinkled his nose, looking at Connor as if he were a complete moron.

An uneasy feeling crawled up Connor's spine at the same time he heard a familiar voice call out. "Joseph Anthony, get yourself into the house now!"

Connor stood, looking toward the house to see Maria standing beside the open screen door. Ignoring him, she waved toward the kid, motioning for him to come inside.

"Aw geez, Mom." Joseph stomped up the driveway and into the house, ducking under his mother's arm.

His mother. Holy crap, Connor thought.

Maria said something low to the kid, something Connor couldn't hear, before she stepped back out onto the front porch and shut the door behind her. She folded her arms across her chest in the defensive posture Connor had come to recognize. "I see you found the place okay."

"I have a good sense of direction," he said, finishing the short walk up the stone path to the house.

She nodded. "You can leave now if you want to."

He narrowed his gaze. "Tell me why you think I'd want to." Stupid statement since he now understood her reasons for keeping him at a distance and putting off any overtures he'd made.

"Because you wouldn't be the first, for one thing." She studied him warily.

Hell, he thought, running a hand through his hair. He should have just accepted her signals and backed off. He was a guy who only knew how to take care of himself and chose his women accordingly. He'd made a promise at a young age—he'd never be a bastard like his father and run off on a woman and a kid. Someone who wasn't an adult and wasn't responsible for the choices of those around them. The easiest way to accomplish that had been to pick women who liked their affairs free and easy.

His nerves jumped as he walked up the two steps and joined Maria on the small stoop. He found himself at an unusual loss for words.

In full defensive mode, Maria stared him in the face, daring him to glance away or back down. "I'm sure your interest in me didn't include a kid. Joey and I are a package, so now that you know, why don't you save us both a lot of grief and take off." Tension and distrust emanated from her in waves.

She was obviously testing him. Forcing him to make a decision before anyone got hurt. Smart woman, he thought. Once again he wished he'd heeded her signals, yet at the same time, he was still drawn to her, even more so now that he knew there was more to her than just the cocktail waitress he thought would be good in bed. Oh hell, he'd sensed that all along. Wasn't that why he'd pursued her relentlessly?

"Maybe you underestimate me," he said. Just as he'd obviously underestimated her.

She shrugged. "That remains to be seen."

He glanced at her and felt his reserve softening. He'd only seen her at work, in a tight "Damon's" T-shirt and black miniskirt. Now he viewed her in a different light. Dressed for their date, she wore a pair of black pants and a light blue sweater with a nice, deep V that accentuated her lush curves. Gone were the sneakers; in their place, black shoes with a slight heel. And when he looked into her wary eyes, he noticed she'd put on a minimal amount of makeup, enough to entice but no heavy artifice to cover the real Maria.

She hadn't hidden a damn thing from him now. "You look nice."

"Thanks," she said, ducking her head.

He'd obviously taken her off guard and was about to do so again. "Where's his father?"

She shrugged. "Couldn't tell you. There's fifty states. Since he's not paying child support and my attorney can't find him, I'd assume he's somewhere in the other forty-nine."

Connor nodded. So that explained her wariness. Abandoned himself, he understood. "And you expect me to run scared like he did."

"Like I said, you wouldn't be the first." Her voice quivered despite the outward show of bravado, reminiscent of her son.

Connor turned and glanced at his car parked on the street. Freedom lay a few feet away. He rolled his shoulders, the pain lodged in his back intense. He should just walk down the steps, climb into the car, and take off, putting miles and distance between himself and Maria and her son. He wanted to run before he replicated the mistakes his father had made. Before he hurt a kid the way he'd been hurt. And if he spent any time with Maria and got to know her kid, that *could* be the end result.

But a distinct memory stopped him from taking off. The one of his mother, dressed for a date just as Maria was now, dropping Connor off at a neighbor's who watched him when she had to work. He doubted he could call it babysitting, since no money was exchanged. They were two single parents doing each other favors in order to make ends meet. His father had already been long gone. And his mother had never come back. The neighbor, as nice as she was, couldn't afford to keep Connor in addition to her two other kids, and his trip through foster care had begun.

Connor had always blamed his father for the kind of childhood he'd had, while making excuses for his mother's decisions. Looking at Maria now, Connor was forced to acknowledge that he'd been wrong. His mother's choices were as selfish as his father's had been.

Maria waited, saying nothing while Connor sifted through his memories and his own choices. Here stood a woman who cared enough about her child to put his needs before her own, and he admired her for it.

And here he stood, a man who could follow his heart and get to know this woman or let fear rule his life and make him walk away. Connor swallowed hard. "Who watches him while you're out?"

She tipped her head toward the run-down house next door. "A neighbor."

Connor winced at the similarity. For years he'd worked with the kids at the center, and their stories didn't affect him on a gut level. This woman and her child did.

Just go, a voice in his head yelled to him. *Before it's too late to get out.* But then he'd never know what he was missing in life.

So instead he heard himself saying, "Why don't you get him and we can all go out for a burger."

Maria's eyes opened wide, then a cautious smile tilted her lips and he relaxed a little more. He owed it to himself to take this chance and prove to himself he wasn't like his old man. He hoped like hell he could handle it.

Quinn drove to Ari's house while she followed in her own car. It was hard for him to believe they'd made love a few hours ago and he'd compromised his case and his integrity as a result. He trusted her, dangerous as that notion was.

He heard the sound of hammering from inside the truck as he pulled to a stop in front of Ari's parents' home. He exited the vehicle and met her on the front lawn near where she'd parked on the street behind him.

"Do you hear that?" She shook her head. "I can't stay here."

Without thinking, he grabbed for her hand. "You don't have to." He had the perfect solution for her problem. "Do you like dogs?"

"More than monkeys, though I have to admit she's growing on me." Ari gestured to the window Spank had appropriated as her own.

He chuckled.

"Why?"

"You can stay at my place while your parents are constructing. My *real* place," he amended. Quinn hadn't realized what a huge burden he'd been carrying until he'd unloaded the truth on Ari. With her knowing he was a cop, he didn't have to tiptoe around her and could bring her deeper into his life. Something he hoped he didn't come to regret later.

She stopped and turned toward him. "You'd let me stay there?"

"As long as you watch my dog." The companion he trusted to be there without conditions.

Her eyes opened wide. "Isn't that like the equivalent of giving me a drawer in your apartment or us sharing a toothbrush?"

He was scared to death that it meant more than a mere dating convention, but what the hell. By admitting he was a cop, he'd entrusted her with his life. How much more serious could this possibly be?

To forestall any further conversation on the subject, he plucked her key out of her hand and led her into the house. "Did your mother say what she wanted?"

Ariana had finally called Elena back and she'd instructed Ari to bring Quinn home for a "chat."

"Just something important that affects us all," she said, her words vague. "Mom? Dad? Anybody home?" she called out over the workers and the noise.

"Let's try the kitchen," he suggested.

"Nothing good ever happens in there," she muttered.

Laughing, he took the lead and walked into the room. The sight in front of him proved Ari right.

Spank sat in a baby's high chair with various jars of creams set out on the tray. And Sam straddled a chair in front of her, brush in hand, painting a white mask over the monkey's face. "It smells delicious, Elena," Sam yelled without looking over her shoulder.

"Just rank them in order of what you like best,"

Elena called from another room.

"Aren't there laws against animal cruelty?" Ari asked jokingly.

"In addition to truancy laws." Quinn strode toward Sam, tired of the kid's games.

She turned to face him and rolled her eyes. "You always think the worst of me."

"Because lately you've been proving me right." He leaned a hand against the counter, meeting her gaze.

"Well, not this time. It's a half day. Parent-teacher conference, not that I have any parents."

"Ouch," Ari whispered in his ear. Then to Sam, she said, "So what are you two doing?" In an obvious attempt to lighten the mood and break up the argument, Ari pulled a chair up beside Sam.

"Elena wants me to see how these smell." Sam waved a hand over the jars. "But Spank decided to try them on herself, so I figured why not help her?" She giggled and Quinn took three steps back.

This was the second time since meeting Sam that he'd heard her laugh from pure joy. Both times had been in this house. "So you're playing dress-up?" he asked.

Ari shot him a look at the same time Sam said, "You're so dense. We're testing scents, but don't worry, they're all natural. Nothing's gonna hurt Spank."

"I am *so* relieved," he said.

Ari kicked him in the shin. "I take it Mom gave up on the fish oil?"

"Fish oil?" Sam wrinkled her nose.

"Don't ask." Ari ruffled Sam's hair. "As long as she's moved on, we're all in good shape. Hey, it's quiet in here." She glanced around, suddenly realizing the noise had stopped.

Quinn had just noticed the same thing.

"I think the crew took off early today. Igor said they had to finish up another job." Sam rose and pulled some paper towels off the roll, wet them, and sat down with the monkey again.

"Who's Igor?" Ari asked.

Sam cleaned off Spank's face, then released her from the high chair. "He's the foreman in charge of this job," Sam said with the authority of someone who lived here.

Quinn narrowed his gaze. "Where did you say Elena was?"

"I didn't." Sam shoved her hands into her jeans pockets. "She's in the other room but I know she wants to talk to you guys." She fidgeted in her chair. "Elena, Quinn's here to talk to you," she yelled at the top of her lungs. "Hurry up and come here."

Elena laughed as she strode into the room. "There's no rush, Sam. I'm not going anywhere."

Sam glanced up at Ari's mother with wide-eyed adoration. "Okay, okay. Can I stay when you tell him? Please, please, please?"

Ari put a hand on Sam's shoulder. "Why don't you and I go into the other room and let them talk. You can tell me what's going on with you."

Quinn rolled his shoulders. If Ari didn't want to remain and hear what Elena wanted to discuss, she probably already knew what it was. "Why do I get the feeling that everyone in here knows what Elena wants to discuss except me?" he asked, looking at Ari.

She shot him a guilty look. "I don't know for sure, but I have a hunch. Let's go," she said, holding a hand out to Sam, who left the room grumbling.

"What's going on?" he asked Elena.

She placed a folder on the counter. "I've been doing some research. I contacted the Division of Youth and Family Services about becoming a foster parent for Sam."

Shock rippled through him. Whatever he'd been expecting, it wasn't this. "That's a huge responsibility."

Elena nodded. "I raised two girls. Of course I know that."

He lowered himself into one of the kitchen chairs. "And how does your husband feel about this?" Quinn asked, all the while sorting through the idea in his mind.

There was no doubt Sam needed a home and every possibility Elena and Nicholas could provide one. A good one. One that would make Sam happy. Quinn had thought he was out of options, a group home being the only solution. Now Ari's family was offering him hope and he had to admit he was optimistic. Cautiously optimistic.

Elena joined him at the table. "Nicholas is fine with the idea. He's a good man, and when he heard about Sam's situation, of course he agreed she should come live with us."

He pinched the bridge of his nose. "It's noble, Elena, but you can't . . ." How could he say this delicately? he wondered. "You can't adopt Sam just to help fill the void left by Zoe's absence."

Elena whacked him on the shoulder. "Bite your tongue at such a suggestion. First off, Zoe's coming back. And secondly, both my girls are adults. They live their own lives, and Sam coming here would have nothing to do with that," she assured Quinn.

"What did Family Services say?" he asked next.

"They went into a lengthy explanation about the requirements, the classes, home inspections, and time it takes to approve a family." Elena waved a hand, dismissing the process as unimportant. "But Sam doesn't have that kind of time. She can't go on living in an environment where she knows she isn't wanted. It's not healthy and it's bad for her self-esteem. Besides, she can stay here."

"Can I, Quinn, please?" Sam came bouncing back into the room.

"I tried to restrain her." Ari followed after her, a concerned expression on her face. "But Sam insisted on being here when Mom told you her idea," Ari said to Quinn, neither expressing support for her mother's decision to take Sam in, nor protesting it.

And given her family history and problems with her relatives, Quinn couldn't figure out which side she came down on. Right now he only wanted to smooth the worry lines and promise her everything would be okay. How could he when he wasn't sure what was bothering her?

He only knew what upset him and he turned to Elena. "So Sam knows about your plan?" Quinn asked.

Elena's nod confirmed his fear. Nothing about the foster care system was easy or guaranteed, and he hated to have the kid's hopes raised once more only to endure disappointment later. It was one thing for *his* heart to beat faster in his chest and for him to feel the potential excitement of a solution he once thought impossible. It wasn't okay for Sam to be led on a journey of false hope.

"Isn't it cool?" Sam asked. "And Elena's willing to look into adoption," she said, awe in her voice. "Somebody wants me!"

Oh shit. This thing had gone too far in a short time. "I have some connections," he said, trying to take back some control. "Let me see if I can speed up the reference and home check." His being a cop who vouched for the Costas family would go a long way toward helping with references.

Neither Zoe nor Ariana had mentioned anyone in the family having a criminal record, but the department ran thorough checks, including fingerprinting, and that was just the beginning of potential problems and snags.

"Hey, Quinn." Sam poked him in the shoulder. "Me and Ari and Zoe can be sisters! Did you see pictures of Zoe? She looks just like Ari. How awesome is that?"

It was frigging fantastic, Quinn thought. *If* he could make it happen. Until then, everyone had to keep their wits about them.

"When she comes home, my Zoe will love you," Elena assured the young girl.

He glanced at Ari. She leaned against the counter and remained silent, looking as torn as he was. But the one thing that stood out as if he could read her mind was her guilt over her knowledge about her sister. Now that she knew Quinn was a cop and she could believe his claim that her twin was alive, keeping the truth from her mother was eating away at her. Quinn understood.

Like Ari, he hated the deceit, but Elena was too unpredictable to trust. She'd just proven she would act on emotion, not common sense. And he was certain Ari agreed or she would have begged him to fill her mother and father in on the situation regarding Zoe, too.

He shook his head, pushing thoughts of the Damon sting out of his mind. He had to deal with Sam first and he walked over to her side. "There are no guarantees this will work," he reminded her. "Elena and the whole family need to go through the approval process."

"They'll pass," Sam said with certainty. "And then even Spank can be my sister."

She laughed again, but her words sobered Quinn. There was also a home evaluation they'd need to pass. "I'm not sure the monkey's going to help this situation," he said, imagining one of the uptight social workers walking into the house, with construction and various relatives all around them and a monkey diving into their lap. He shook his head. Why couldn't life ever be easy?

"What are you saying?" Elena asked.

"Is having a monkey living with you even legal in this state?" Quinn wondered aloud.

"Quinn!" Sam wailed, while Elena glanced away.

Apparently she hadn't checked out the legalities, and he wasn't one bit surprised. As a cop he had to know many things, but this wasn't something he'd encountered before.

He ran a hand through his hair. "Okay, one step at a time. Since teenagers are so much harder to place, the department's been known to put things through faster if something special comes up. Let me make some phone calls and let's see if we can get the process going. Elena, you and Nicholas are going to have to take eight weekly training sessions."

Elena swiped her hand through the air, a gesture she seemed to favor. "I raised two children. What can they possibly teach me that I don't know?"

He rolled his eyes. "Nobody gets out of those classes, so get yourself signed up and start them *immediately.* They're three hours each," he added for good measure.

"Do not tell that to Nicky," she ordered everyone in the kitchen. "He has no patience for classes, but once he's there, he'll do it for Sam."

The girl beamed and for the first time Quinn realized she wasn't wearing her hat. Her hair was hanging long down her back, and she was truly happy. He'd just have to make sure this worked out for her or die trying.

"What about Spank?" Sam asked, holding the monkey's hand. "If my caseworker sees her and it's not allowed, they won't let me come here and that can't happen."

A long, drawn-out sigh came from the other side of the room. Quinn glanced over at Ari. "I suppose if I can handle a dog, I can handle a monkey," she said, obviously resigned to doing her part in this scheme. "Since I can't stay here and get any sleep during the day and since Spank hates the noise, I'll take her with me," she explained to her mother.

"Where?" Elena asked, hands perched on her hips.

"I'll be staying at a friend's," she said vaguely. "We'll work out the details later, okay?"

Elena kissed her daughter on the cheek. "You're a good girl, Ariana. But let's see if Aunt Dee and Uncle John can take her first. They're used to her from spending their days here, and that would keep her close for Sam."

Ari smiled, but there was no eager light in her eyes.

Quinn wasn't sure exactly what was bothering her, but she'd offered her help along with his house. Because that's what Sam wanted.

His gut told him the Costas house could very well be the right place for this child. Sam felt it. Hell, he enjoyed their warmth and giving spirit. Even their eccentricity appealed to him, making him feel at home in a way he'd never experienced before. He felt himself sinking deeper into the quicksand of this family and damn but he didn't mind at all.

Yet when he looked at the woman who had spent

the night in his bed, the woman who was his most intrinsic link to the Costas clan, he realized despite Ari's offer, she'd begun to withdraw from her family.

And he had a hunch if he didn't get her out of here, then Ariana pulling away from him would come next.

CHAPTER TWELVE

Ariana couldn't get out of her parents' house fast enough. Although the rational part of her knew her family could give Sam a good home, the irrational part of her—the one that hadn't parted with the adolescent in her who was embarrassed by her odd family—worried about Sam. Thirteen was an impressionable time and, more than most, Sam needed a support system that included friends. Not people who'd laugh behind her back and set her up as the butt of cruel jokes.

To his credit, Quinn remained silent on the ride to his house. They were headed toward the beach. More than once, he looked into the rearview mirror longer than usual, and took what seemed to be an out-of-the-way route to the ocean.

Although she had a lot on her mind, she sensed he was preoccupied, too. He glanced in the mirror again and she couldn't take it anymore. Her head pounded as she broke the quiet in the truck. "What's wrong?"

"What makes you think something's up?" He squeezed her hand in reassurance.

"You're antsy. You keep checking the mirrors. And though I don't know where your house is, I'm certain we've circled around a few times."

"You're quick, Ari." He grinned, shaking his head. "I'm just being careful, that's all."

"About Damon?" Chills walked all over her skin.

He nodded. "He knows I have this house, so it's not going to be a problem if he is having me watched, but I'd rather know about it going in." He rolled his shoulders in a definite release of tension.

"Understandable." She rubbed her hands up and down her arms. "I don't know how you live like this."

He turned his head to the side, glancing at her. "It's getting harder," he admitted. "But it's almost over. Now, what's going on in your beautiful head? You've been completely overwhelmed since the whole foster-care talk back at your parents'."

Ariana couldn't believe how perceptive the man was. "It's my family. Or rather Sam and my family. My parents have to give up being pickpockets and cons," she said, stating what had been preying on her mind.

Quinn sighed, his understanding clear. "I'll talk to them."

"The new business, the spa. It has to be legit." She was revealing more than he knew about her relatives.

He nodded. "I know. I'll make sure I oversee it. Nicholas likes me," he said, and when she turned her head his way, he shot her his most endearing grin.

This time she squeezed his hand tighter. "I like you, too, Quinn."

"Then tell me what's really bothering you. It's not just concern for Sam. I can tell."

She shut her eyes tight as he pulled into a short driveway leading to a two-car indoor garage. "How about you give me the ten-cent tour first," she suggested, stalling.

"You got it, but then there's no more hiding from the truth."

"You'd know all about that, wouldn't you?"

"Low blow, Ari. And being angry at me won't change the fact that you obviously have a hell of a lot to come to terms with. You might as well start somewhere." He turned the key in the ignition, shut down the motor, and climbed out of the truck.

She joined him at the foot of three wooden steps leading into the house.

"You can park in here." He gestured to the empty space beside his truck. "I have an extra garage remote in the kitchen drawer, if I can find the damn thing." He unlocked the door and unset the alarm. "The code is 1213," he told her.

"Random choice?"

He let out a harsh laugh. "My birthday. I remember my mother telling me she knew I'd be bad luck from the minute she went into labor on Friday the thirteenth."

Ariana winced and as they walked into the kitchen, she turned toward him. "Are you trying to convince me of what a spoiled brat I am because I have problems with my family?"

He shook his head. "It's not my place to judge. The

only measure anyone can use to judge life by is their own experience. Having a family doesn't necessarily mean you found growing up to be easy."

Grabbing her hand, he led her to a cozy room with a cabin-like feel, and they sat on the couch.

"So tell me, *are* you feeling like a spoiled brat?" he asked.

"I'm feeling like childhood memories are over-whelming me." She rubbed her eyes and leaned back, sighing. "What if Sam has the same problems I did living with my family?"

"I'm not sure. You've never told me what those problems were." He met her gaze, hoping that by now she knew she could confide in him. When she remained silent, he added, "I don't have to come from the same background as you to understand."

She leaned forward. "Let me ask you something. Do you find my family a little . . . weird? Unusual? Strange?"

He laughed. "Well, yes, but that's what makes them special."

"Try growing up with that specialness. I'd bring friends home and never know what my mother would be wearing, what language she'd be attempting to learn, or what con my father would be concocting."

"Like the Indian princess act?" he said, trying not to laugh.

"Or the Martian one."

He raised an eyebrow, dying of curiosity.

Ari sighed. "When we were thirteen, Zoe and I fell asleep on the beach. Unfortunately we'd covered ourselves with baby oil and fried to a crisp. We were beet red for days. Mom couldn't help but take advantage of the situation."

"How?" he asked, hoping to coax more information out of her.

She rolled her eyes. "She dyed our hair green and snapped pictures of the Martian Invasion. Except by then the *National Enquirer* had caught on to her schemes. Add to that kind of insanity the fact that my mother was a showgirl, which for other kids was tantamount to a stripper. I was the laughingstock of the school." She ran a hand through her hair. "And the guys? Oh, they just loved the lie detector," she said. "Even they tended to steer clear, too."

Knowing it wasn't the time to laugh, Quinn tried keeping things serious. "What about Zoe? Did she have problems with that kind of behavior?"

She shook her head. "Zoe was different. Her sense of humor was as wicked as my mother's, and she loved the limelight just like Mom did." Her eyes glazed over as she remembered. "Maybe Zoe wasn't different, maybe it was me. Zoe wanted to be just like Mom. She dressed in tight clothes and flouted any convention. It didn't matter to her what the other kids thought, because she obviously had a stronger independent streak." She clenched and unclenched her fists as she spoke. "And don't think I don't realize how ungrateful and awful this sounds, but—"

He placed a finger over her moving lips, trying like hell to ignore the erotic sensations that just touching her inspired. "I'm a cop. I was also a kid once. I know how cruel other kids can be, and you don't need to make excuses about your feelings. They're yours and you are entitled to them. But I don't think you need to worry about Sam. She'd be happy to play along and tell the other kids where to go if they dared to make fun of her."

"That's probably true. In psych lingo, I'm probably just transferring my fears and insecurities onto Sam. In my family, normal didn't fit in. *I* didn't fit in." She shrugged. "But Sam already has been through the hell of being different. If someone makes fun of her, she can handle herself a lot better than I ever did."

He laid one hand across the back of the couch and turned, slanting his head toward her. "Now that's the truth. I really wouldn't worry. Sam wants to be there and she already knows exactly what your family's like. They adore her and she already loves them. If it works out, it's a perfect solution."

Leaving me as the misfit once again, Ariana thought.

"Now tell me about the stuffed-shirt boyfriend your family mentioned."

She laughed, grateful he'd changed the subject to something that wasn't quite as painful. Not anymore. She didn't like her cousins giving her a hard time over Jeffrey, but she was fine with sharing that part of her past with Quinn. "Like the family said, he was a pompous ass. But he was everything they weren't."

"Conservative and normal?" he guessed.

"Yeah. And I needed that at the time." She stared out at the water, the turbulence there somehow familiar.

"He was a break from the insanity at home, and I thought if he got to know me first, they wouldn't seem so different, or at least he wouldn't care."

He reached out and massaged her shoulder. "What happened?"

"My father asked him one of his infamous questions. He used to hit up any guy who walked into the house with one."

"What did he ask poor Jeffrey?" Quinn, not the least bit fazed, was laughing already.

"He asked him if he had enough goods to satisfy his girl," she said, shaking her head at the memory. "Jeffrey turned five shades of red and changed the subject, and my father told him he'd take that as a no."

Quinn burst out laughing. "I assume that didn't go over well?"

She sighed. "Jeffrey gave me an ultimatum. He told me to choose between my family and him because there was no way he'd have a life that had anything to do with *those wackos.*"

Quinn visibly cringed.

"In other words, if we got married and had kids, my parents wouldn't be acknowledged as their grandparents. He was headed into corporate America, where his family was already established, and he said they'd all see my relatives as a liability." She shrugged, but the memories were far from casual. Reliving them truly hurt more than she'd thought they would.

Quinn's eyebrows drew together, his expression one of outrage. "He's a jackass," he muttered.

A smile pulled at her lips. "Yeah. He actually

thought I should consider myself fortunate he was willing to continue to see me at all, considering my bloodlines."

Quinn rolled his eyes. "I take it you told him to go to hell?" Because as far as he was concerned, the man wasn't fit to step into the Costas home, let alone have a worthy place in Ari's life.

And you are? a voice in Quinn's head asked. He hadn't struggled with that internal self-doubt in years, and fought against allowing his damn insecurities to resurface now. He wasn't that unwanted kid in foster care anymore, and damned if he'd act like it.

"Oh yes, I did," Ari said, her eyes finally lighting up with the memory. "And then I packed my bags and left for Vermont. I transferred, finished up school there while working my way through, and then I got a job teaching at a local college."

"Never to darken your parents' door again until now," he finished for her with the ending Zoe had already told him. "Why?"

She swallowed hard. "You don't ask easy questions, do you? It must be your cop training."

He raised one eyebrow and waited.

She rose and paced the hardwood floor in front of the sliding glass doors. "I was running away, is that what you wanted to hear?"

"I want to hear the truth," he told her. "Besides, sometimes running isn't so bad as long as you face what you were running from eventually."

"Well, I had no allies at home. At least I didn't feel like I did. Not even my twin. Zoe was just like my parents. She was always up for a good con, and I thought she was wasting her life. She thought I was an uptight prig and should loosen up, and I thought she ought to grow up and do something worthwhile."

She inhaled deeply and Quinn could feel her pain. But he had a hunch she'd never discussed this aloud, and the only way for her to deal was to face things. She'd need to come to terms with her past before she discovered how wrong she'd been about her sister. "So you two argued?" he asked.

"Oh yes. And then I left. I just shouldn't have stayed away."

Gratitude for her honesty overwhelmed him and he was glad he'd opened up to her first.

"I'm sick of talking about myself," she said.

He grinned. "Then come here." He held out a hand toward her. "And we can do something besides talk."

She started her walk across the room, determined and sultry in her steps, but not before turning to the glass doors once more.

He stared at the beach, seeing his backyard from Ari's perspective. Sliding glass doors overlooked the sand, and he realized how fortunate he was to have been able to purchase this place at auction. He also recognized how much he missed living here.

"So this is your home," Ari said, interrupting his thoughts. "I knew the hotel room didn't reflect the real you."

"The real me?" Quinn asked. "Just who is that?" He wanted to know how she viewed him, what she saw when she looked at him, especially now that she knew he was a cop.

She came up to him and settled close by his side, curling one leg beneath her. Finally a relaxed smile twitched at her lips. "You're a bundle of contradictions, Quinn."

"Men like to be as mysterious as women," he joked.

"Well, you did a good job. And I kept asking myself, which is the real Quinn? Is it the guy who tackled me on the beach? Damon's goon? Or Sam's guardian angel?" Reaching out, she caressed his cheek, cupping his face in her hand. "And that sterile hotel room didn't provide any answers. Now I know it's because your so-called room wasn't really yours."

He studied this woman who seemed to want to understand him as much as he wanted to get inside her head. "Nothing at the casino is real. It's all part of the job, which reminds me." Though he hated to break the bonding moment between them, work called to him. "We need to talk about how things are going to be once you go back to the casino."

"In what way?" she asked curiously.

"We don't want Damon suspicious of me, so you're going to need to play your part. Continue to look for information on your sister, ask the right people the right questions, but do not get into serious trouble."

"Trouble? Me?" She shot him her most innocent look.

He rolled his eyes, laughing. "You know exactly what I'm talking about. But if you need an example, no lock picking and no snooping around Damon's office," he ordered her.

"I can handle that." Despite their banter, her intent gaze indicated she understood how serious he was.

And he wasn't finished. "And when it comes to *us,* as far as the employees and Damon are concerned, you still need to cozy up to me, pretend to use me to find out what happened to Zoe."

She licked her lips and he knew something big was coming. "What did happen to my sister?" she asked, her voice tight with emotion.

Finally. She had finally asked the question Quinn knew had to be brewing inside her.

"I mean if you're a cop, then what was Zoe doing being involved with you?" she asked. "I know my mother said she borrowed money and Zoe was working to help pay back the loan, but why would Damon want her . . . killed?" Ari swallowed hard, the words obviously difficult for her to say.

He inhaled deep before answering. "She was snooping around where she shouldn't have been. Just like you started doing. But you had a sister you were looking for. Zoe just got herself into trouble," he said, still being deliberately vague. "Damon's putting up with your amateur sleuthing because he knows if you turn up missing, too, it'll look bad for him. Plus this time he's got me watching out for you whenever possible. He knows I won't let you find anything."

Ari narrowed her gaze. "What was Zoe looking for? Come to think of it, what are *you* looking for?"

He sighed, wishing he could give her so much more than he was about to offer. "I think your sister's involvement in all this is something she needs to explain to you herself. As for me, it'll all become clear in time. The less you know, the less trouble you can potentially get into."

He'd revealed enough about their operation already. As for her sister, Zoe's true occupation and why she'd kept it secret was her story to tell.

Ari frowned. "And when will that time finally come?" she asked, her frustration evident.

"With any luck, at the end of this weekend."

"Aah." She nodded slowly as understanding dawned. "The seven days you asked for."

"That's right. And until then, for Damon's sake we continue the charade of being lovers."

"Quinn?" she asked, meeting his gaze. "It's not a charade."

Relief was sweet and he grinned. "I hoped you'd say that." He wasn't about to press her on exactly what they were to each other. He'd never been one to label a relationship anyway. For now he'd take whatever she offered.

He noticed she had begun to undo her blouse. One button at a time, she slipped open her shirt, a provocative smile on her face. Watching her, he broke into an appreciative sweat. "You do know how to prove a point."

"It's one of the benefits of being with a teacher," she said on a sultry chuckle.

He laughed. "Not one the school board would advertise, I'm sure."

"Maybe not." She dropped her blouse onto the sofa

cushion beside her. "But I don't see you complaining."

"That's because I'm a smart man." He reached out and with one finger, drew a line from the base of her throat, down her neck and chest, until his fingertip nestled in the warm vee of her cleavage.

He sucked in a shallow breath, enjoying their banter and foreplay. "So tell me a little about this brazen side of you," he urged her. He'd already told her that he thought the conservative teacher was a cover for the real Ari.

When he'd met her, she was wearing an uptight suit, then he watched her discomfort in the miniskirts and tight tops slowly disappear, proving to him that so much passion and depth lurked beneath the priggish professor persona. Now he wanted to know why the cover was necessary. Why she couldn't be that delightful mixture of Ariana and Ari that he knew her to be.

"Aren't there things you'd rather do than talk?" she asked in a husky voice, since his finger had begun to make its way across her left breast.

He inclined his head. "Yes, and we'll get to that. As soon as you tell me why you keep this side of you so well hidden from everyone you know." Beneath her lacy bra, he drew lazy circles around her nipple, careful to avoid touching her there and eliciting the wanton woman he knew she could be.

She exhaled and a low, trembling moan came out instead. "You expect me to talk right now?"

He nodded. "If you want satisfaction later, I do."

She arched her back, which had the effect of pushing her breasts taut against her silky bra. "That's blackmail," she complained.

"And you're stalling." He shot her a bad-boy grin and started to withdraw his finger.

"Professor Ariana Costas is safe," she admitted at last.

As a reward, he cupped her entire breast in his hand and began kneading her soft flesh.

Her eyelids fluttered closed, a happy sigh on her lips. "Safe how?" he asked.

She swallowed and her throat worked convulsively. "*Ari* is what the family calls me."

It's what he called her, too, but he wasn't about to mention it just yet.

"And *Ari* hits too close to home."

"How so?" he asked, curious.

Ari sighed. "Well, Ari is the little girl in the tanning cream who turned orange and liked it. She's the one who played lookout and laughed while her sister stole the principal's spare keys to the boys' locker room." Her lips twitched as she recounted the memory. "Zoe wanted to douse the football team captain's shorts with itching powder after he started spreading rumors about her."

Quinn stifled a laugh. It was important that he continue to focus on Ari more than on Zoe's pranks. "And Ari's the one who walked into Damon's casino dressed like that twin?" he guessed. "The one who slept with me? Who just undressed in front of me now? And who liked it?"

"You know me too well." She looked at him through heavy eyelids.

Through caring eyes, he hoped. Still his life had always been about watching people leave and never getting too close as a result. She was guaranteed to do just that once her sister returned, and he couldn't invest too much in her.

"I'm not sure what to think about us," Ari said.

Quinn nodded, accepting her honesty. He wasn't sure what to make of them either. He only knew when she was around, the world seemed brighter and he liked everything more. He'd gotten more revelations than he'd counted on, and he didn't want to risk driving her away too soon.

"Then how about you don't think and just feel?" he asked, and shifted his palm so that he could turn teasing into torment by rolling her nipple between his thumb and forefinger at the same time he leaned over and sealed his lips over hers.

He slipped his tongue between her lips, molding his body to hers. The need to make love to her, bury his body deep inside and lose himself in her, was overwhelming. But without warning, the doorbell rang, interrupting them.

"This can't be happening." She echoed his thoughts exactly.

He rose to his feet, pulling her to a sitting position. "Unfortunately, it is. I forgot I told Wolf to bring Dozer over when he got a lull at the center."

Ari scrambled to dress, pulling her shirt over her head.

"The bedroom's back that way and the bathroom's inside," he said. "Go on and I'll handle Wolf."

"Thanks, Quinn." She treated him to a smile that made him harder than he'd been before they were interrupted and, worse, caused a distinct warm feeling in his heart. So much for not investing too much in Ari.

Ari buttoned the blouse she'd changed into at home, then glanced in the mirror over the sink and vanity in Quinn's bathroom. With the meager contents of her purse, she quickly fixed her makeup and, after a moment's hesitation, picked up a comb lying on the counter and brushed through her hair. She'd pulled herself together on the outside, but inside she was still trembling and aroused.

And one thing had nothing to do with the other. Arousal seemed obvious and understandable. The trembling came more from their conversation than from unslaked sexual desire. Thanks to Quinn, she was an emotional mess, feeling more vulnerable than usual and susceptible to a whole host of insecurities. All combined to prove just one thing.

She didn't know who she really was. She couldn't say she missed Ariana Costas, the uptight and boring teacher with an equally boring life.

On the other hand, she still thought that the insanity surrounding her family was too great. Her views on that hadn't changed in the time she'd been gone. But she liked the woman she was around Quinn—the more open and less repressed, and even less judgmental, Ari.

In coming home, she was starting to view her family from an adult perspective and appreciate their idiosyncracies a bit more than she'd like to admit. So much so that she no longer minded thinking of herself the way her family did: as Ari, the child who'd willingly participated in their pranks and games.

So it wasn't a coincidence that she could no longer think of herself as Ariana. Being caught between two personalities and two worlds raised a scary question—just where did that leave her now?

CHAPTER THIRTEEN

Quinn stood in his office watching the rows of television monitors. His anger was contained and he merely rocked on his heels and waited for Damon. By the time his boss strode into the room, it was close to midnight.

"The tables are hopping and the bar's packed." Damon slipped his hands into his slacks, obviously pleased with himself. "All in all, it's a damn fine night."

The man's arrogance knew no bounds and was getting on Quinn's frigging nerves. "I guess that depends on your perspective. I don't appreciate being tailed to my own goddamn house." Though he'd told Ari he was just being cautious, he'd lied. He just hadn't wanted her to panic.

"A smart man trusts no one, Quinn."

He clenched his jaw tight. "And what did you find

on this fishing expedition of yours?"

"That you're having a good time on the job, not that I blame you. It's smart to keep Ariana close by. This way she can't be asking questions around here. I'm impressed with you," Damon said, nodding.

"Then call off the tail or I'm out of here." And though he had no intention of walking away, Quinn's boiling frustration was evident in his threat.

Damon waved a hand, dismissing him. "Go downstairs, have a drink and relax. You're too damn uptight."

"I wonder why." Quinn let out a harsh laugh and, ignoring Damon, headed out the door. To keep himself sane, he needed fresh air.

And he needed to see Ari.

Not five minutes later, he'd settled himself on a barstool where Connor was busy mixing drinks and sending pathetic mooning looks Maria's way. Not that he was one to talk, he silently acknowledged, watching Ari's hips sway as she maneuvered among tables.

"I'm not sure how we came to this," Connor said, leaning on the bar during a lull between patrons. "Hung up on two babes."

"We always liked women," Quinn said, laughing.

"Yeah, but they never presented such big challenges before."

"Is that what you see in Maria?" Quinn asked his friend. "Is it just the challenge?"

Connor wiped down the bar with a damp rag. "Hell, if that's all it was, do you think I'd be taking her and her kid to Great Adventure?"

"She has a kid?" Quinn let out a slow whistle. "That must have been some first date."

"Instead of having hot sex, we shared hamburgers, fries, and milk shakes, then watched Joey play with his friends at the school playground." Connor stared at Maria for a while, long enough for her to turn and acknowledge his searing gaze. "And I'm still not going anywhere, which shocks the hell out of me."

"Scares you, too, I'll bet."

Connor barely acknowledged the comment with an imperceptible nod. "Be right back." He turned to pour a round of beers from the tap for one of his waitresses, then returned to hang out with Quinn.

"When's the trip to the amusement park?" Quinn asked.

"Next weekend."

After they'd closed down this operation, Quinn thought. Maria would still be around. In all likelihood, Ari would not be.

Connor pulled out a Corona, opened the top, and handed Quinn the bottle.

Quinn shot him a questioning look and Connor shrugged.

"You looked like you could use one. My guess is Ari's got you tied up in the same knots. Anything you want to admit to?" Connor asked, laughing.

"Hell no." Which both men understood meant *Not here*. But there were some things about the situation he could discuss. "She's not like Zoe."

"That much I had figured out."

"She's more intense. More . . ."

"Repressed?"

Shutting his eyes, Quinn recalled how easily she had slipped out of her blouse, how close they'd come to making love on his couch with the ocean as a backdrop. He shook his head. "Not the word I'd use, buddy." He met his friend's amused gaze. "But she's so scared of being like her crazy family, she's lost sight of how to have fun."

"So remind her," Connor said as if it were simple.

And maybe it was. He and Ari had spent all their time in an intense situation. What they needed was relaxation and fun. *She* needed relaxation and fun. She'd spent too much time hiding behind the conservative facade she thought distinguished her from her family, and not enough time giving in to her true nature.

Quinn intended to bring out her "Ari" side. Not only did he want her to have fun but he wanted her to see she could embrace her natural instincts and emotions without fear of turning into a sideshow freak. She'd come to understand how special the real Ari was. The upside to his plan was that they'd be putting on a show for Damon at the same time.

He reached across the bar and slapped Connor on the back. "Every once in a while your intelligence shows through." He chuckled but knew Connor understood he was damn grateful for the insight. "Now get back to work."

Quinn slid off his chair and walked to where Ari stood at the other end of the bar, where she was calculating a bill. "Hey there, beautiful," he whispered in her ear.

A light blush stole across her cheeks. "Stop that, I'm working." But a pleased smile told him she was happy to see him.

"You know what they say about all work and no play. Which brings me to my proposal."

She turned and he captured her against the bar. Her heart beat more quickly in her chest and her breathing grew more rapid. "You're excited," he said softly.

"Yeah, well, I think we've established that you do that to me." Her eyes flashed bright and eager.

He grinned. "Well, what would you say to upping the excitement quotient? Let's plan a night of hot gambling." He leaned closer so he could whisper in her ear. "And even hotter sex."

Her body trembled against his. "You're bad," she said, nestling her cheek against his in an intimate gesture that did so much more than just turn him on physically. He had an emotional tie to this woman that had the potential to hurt him in the end.

But he couldn't walk away without giving it his all. Without giving *her* his all, including showing her how to have fun, let go, and not be afraid of being more like her outgoing family.

It was a gift he wanted to give her, just as more time was a gift he needed to give himself. "I'm officially giving you tomorrow night off. We're having dinner on the rooftop restaurant and we're going gambling at the tables. I'll send a car for you at eight. Dress is elegant."

"Now, how can I argue with that?" she asked, the pleasure obvious in her voice.

"That's the point. You can't." He'd deliberately phrased things as a done deal.

"Excuse me," Connor said, clearing his throat as he cut in. "I hate to interrupt, but there are tables that need your attention."

Quinn shot his friend an annoyed glare, but to Ari, Connor was her immediate boss and she jumped to attention.

"I'm going," she said as she ducked under Quinn's arm.

Which was fine with Quinn, since tomorrow night she was all his.

Ari had no dressy clothes to wear for the night Quinn had planned. Her conservative suits would send him running in the other direction, and she didn't want to wear her sister's hand-me-downs. Instead she'd gone to the hotel boutique and purchased the sexiest dress and shoes she could find. But all the while, she wished she'd had her sister to rely on for advice on what outfit to choose, how to act, and any other questions she had. It had been so long since she had felt any close emotional bond with Zoe, and, with her twin in hiding somewhere and Ari staying alone at Quinn's house, she missed her sister more than ever.

She walked through Quinn's house, his dog Dozer trailing everywhere she went. Though he was a mixed breed, outwardly he was all chow. His golden fur resembled a lion's mane but he acted more like a baby in need of attention. Considering she was feeling fairly lonely herself, Ari was grateful for his company.

Kneeling down, she ran her fingers through his fur and he stretched, rolling over. "You're so affectionate. Quinn's lucky to have you," Ari murmured.

She accommodated his shameless request for a belly rub, laughing. "And I'm lucky Aunt Dee took the monkey to her house, or else you might not have been a happy dog. I wouldn't want to deal with some sort of perverse sibling rivalry," she muttered.

Besides, when Zoe returned, she'd have her own sibling strife to deal with, and theirs would make the monkey and the dog's potential problems seem like an absurd cartoon. She stood and, with excitement swirling in her stomach, headed into the bedroom to get ready for the night ahead.

An hour later, a black limousine that looked absurdly out of place in the small neighborhood pulled up to Quinn's beach house. Adrenaline fueled her walk to the car, more so when the driver opened the door and she found Quinn waiting inside.

Quinn held Ari's hand and helped her into the back of the limo. A long black coat protected her from the cold and blocked him from seeing the outfit she'd chosen. Her bare ankles and strappy high-heeled shoes told him she was wearing a dress, while her sexy, musky new scent revealed she'd indulged in a sensual change he enjoyed.

She'd pulled her hair up, leaving soft strands to fall around her fully made-up face and caress her cheeks. He shook his head, letting out an appreciative whistle. "You look fantastic."

"Thank you." A pleased smile turned up her lips. "You look pretty hot yourself," she said, treating him to a sultry, you-ain't-seen-nothing-yet look.

She'd obviously taken his request to loosen up and have fun to heart. She settled in on the seat beside him as the car got under way. "I didn't expect you to come pick me up."

He grinned. "Life's full of surprises. I told you I'd make sure you had a good time. I'm a man of my word."

"I know that."

And those words obviously meant a lot to her, since she then snuggled closer to him.

"I've never been in a limo before and the ride wouldn't be nearly as much fun if you hadn't surprised me."

"Didn't you go to your prom?" Even in foster care, he remembered working at a gas station and saving money to pool with some guys at school and take a girl whose name he couldn't remember to the prom in a limousine.

"I was so happy I had a date, I didn't want to subject him to my father's question of the moment," she said, a glazed look in her eyes as she remembered. "I met him on the street corner and we drove with some friends." She tilted her head upwards, her gaze locking with his. "So this is a first for me. Thank you."

She brushed a quick kiss over his lips before sitting back in the seat.

But brief contact wasn't enough. Quinn was already hot with wanting her. Desire fueled him as he leaned over and finished what she'd started. She immediately parted her lips and he found her mouth warm and moist. Her tongue locked with his. She was so giving, so ready for him, he almost told the driver to turn around and head back to his house.

Making love to a woman there would be *his* first, but he reminded himself that tonight was about Ari and giving her the freedom to let go and explore her inner self. And so he sat back against the seat, breathing heavily, giving the intense need a chance to subside.

He glanced over while she reapplied her red lipstick. He started to wipe his lips with the back of his hand, laughing when he saw the swipes of dark color on his skin.

"Let me." With a tissue, she cleaned the remnants of lipstick off Quinn's mouth with shaking hands.

If she continued to touch him, with her scent so powerful and her cleavage too close to his lips, his restraint would vanish along with his good intentions. Thank God the car pulled up to the front of the hotel and reality intruded in the form of glittering neon lights and an attendant who opened the car door.

After that, the evening went just as he'd planned. Dinner was an intimate meal with a rooftop view of the ocean and a close-up view of his date. She'd chosen a strapless dress in a deep blue with a plunging neckline that had him drooling.

She glowed with confidence. It was obvious she knew how her sex appeal affected him, and she teased him mercilessly. But more than once, she paused in thought, as if shocked by her open actions. Feeding him a shrimp from her shrimp cocktail, her eyes opened wide as if to ask, *Who is this uninhibited woman?* All he'd had to do to bring her back was to continue the playful moment—nip her fingertip with his teeth, soothe with his tongue—and she was back in what he thought of as her Ari mood and persona. Seeing how happy she was with him, he wondered how she'd lived so long hiding behind the suits and uptight facade.

She flirted and teased, her fingers walking up his thigh beneath the table as she whispered in his ear. They danced to a slow song the band played and he held her tight, unwilling to let her overthink and pull away because Ariana would act more appropriately in public. They shared coffee and a fruit tart for dessert, and not even Damon, sitting a table away viewing them with undisguised interest, seemed to dim her enjoyment or enthusiasm.

Quinn found equal pleasure in just watching her, and though he could have stayed in their private booth forever, he had more planned for her this evening. "Ready to hit the tables?"

She nodded.

Quinn placed his napkin down and rose to his feet.

"I'm not much of a gambler," she admitted. "But I guess I could learn."

The hesitancy was back, something Quinn wouldn't allow. "Maybe Professor Costas isn't a gambler, but the sexy lady in front of me certainly is." He winked and extended his hand.

Without hesitation, she placed her palm in his and followed him to the elevators that took them back down to the casino. He exchanged money for chips, refusing to accept any cash she offered. "The night's on me, remember?"

"I suppose you'll expect payback later on?" she asked in a deliberately sultry, teasing voice.

"I'm certain I won't say no." He laughed but the sound was strained, his body was so overheated and hard. "So what will it be? Craps, baccarat, blackjack . . ."

"Slots?" she whispered, obviously embarrassed by her moderate choice.

If she expected him to tease her, she was in for disappointment. He merely turned back to the change windows and collected rolls of quarters instead.

He opened them into a bucket and handed her the large tub. "Let's go pick a slot machine."

He pulled two stools up to her chosen machine, then settled in to watch her in action. Popping one quarter at a time, Ari won some and she lost some, and gained confidence as time wore on. She yelled, cheered, and groaned, and an hour later, she was still almost even. She was a determined gambler, the adrenaline from hoping for that next big hit keeping her parked at the machine, refusing to move.

"Ready to switch to the tables?" Quinn asked. No matter how much he enjoyed watching her, he was

215

ready for a different kind of action.

She bit down on her lower lip as the question took on enormous proportions. Finally she shook her head. "Nope. Can't do it. Can you imagine if I walk away and somebody else sits down and this thing spits out millions?"

He shot her an amused gaze. "I'd hate to see how competitive you'd be if you actually rolled the dice at the craps tables."

She shuddered at the thought. "Oh no. I can see those cigar-smoking men eating me alive."

"Honey, they'd *love* you." Hell, he was afraid he already did.

Love her. Stunned by the impact of the thought, he reeled back, leaning against the heavy metal machine. Loving Ari wasn't part of the equation. Not if he wanted to walk out of this assignment whole.

"Quinn?"

It wasn't the concern in Ari's voice but the reminder that he was still on assignment that jolted him back to reality. Quinn latched onto the idea of work. Hell, it was as convenient an excuse as any to not deal with his emotions, and he pushed thoughts of his feelings for Ari aside, to be dissected later when he was alone.

"I got distracted. Let me prove to you that you can handle the tables." He tugged on her elbow, urging her to make the move, and to help him shift his attention, too.

She glanced down. Four quarters remained in the machine's tray. "Just let me have one more try here first."

She inserted all four pieces into the machine at once—the first such daring move she'd made all night—then pulled the handle. Without glancing back, she rose and started to walk away from the machine, obviously certain she'd tossed away a dollar.

The bells, lights, and whistles caught Quinn off guard and he turned. Her machine was glowing with flashing lights and a loud siren as accompaniment.

He blinked, stunned. "You won!"

"Who won?" she asked.

She pivoted toward him and he grabbed her around the waist, spinning her around in midair. "You did!"

She let out a shriek. "How much did I win?" she asked, oblivious to the fact that she was starting to draw a crowd.

"I'd say about five thousand dollars. You're a lucky lady."

Damon's voice killed Quinn's pleasure and he turned to face the other man. "It's nothing in comparison to the night's take," Quinn said, wanting the boss to leave.

"Actually it means nothing without the right person to share it with." Ari came up beside him and placed her hand around his waist, squeezing tight. "Quinn's been showing me a good time," she explained to Damon, gazing up at Quinn with adoring eyes.

But tension radiated from her in waves and he sensed the fact that she was acting. For his benefit, she was following directions and being cozy and nice around Damon even if she wanted to throttle the man.

"He's a loyal employee," Damon said. "I hope you enjoy your winnings."

"I wish my sister was here to share them," she added pointedly.

Quinn winced. "I was thinking of taking this celebration up to my room," Quinn said to Ari, opting for a subject change before she could get any deeper into conversation with the man who'd ordered her sister killed.

"I'll have a bottle of our finest champagne sent right up," Damon said. "On the house."

"You really are as kind as my mother said." Ari fluttered her lashes for effect. "Thank you. But I was thinking of going home after this." She squeezed Quinn's waist.

"Sounds like a good plan." He wasn't about to argue with her, even if he didn't know what she had in mind.

Damon nodded. "Then I'll make sure a chilled bottle is ready to go with you . . . as well as your winnings. You can pick everything up at the window."

Around them, security guards gathered to escort her to the cashier's window.

Damon turned to Quinn. "Remember we're meeting before I leave to go over the weekend plans?"

Quinn nodded and Damon took off without looking back.

Quinn let out a slow exhale. Every day was another day closer to getting this nightmare over with and being able to go home.

Only one unanswered question remained, Quinn thought, pulling Ari close. What the hell would remain of his life once the end came?

"Why don't you want to go upstairs?" he asked, forcing himself to push reality aside in favor of Ari, his ultimate fantasy.

"You gave me a special night and I don't just mean winning," she said, gesturing to the slot machine behind them. Genuine appreciation glowed in her cheeks and sparkled in her eyes. "I want to do the same thing for you, and I want to do it away from here."

She leaned so close her cheek nestled perfectly against his. He inhaled, taking in her perfume and her heat. "I can understand you wanting to get away from reminders of Damon."

"It's not for me." Her hands stole around his waist and she pulled him close. "It's for you. I want you to have a night away from this place and its tensions. I want you to have a night where you can completely be yourself." She hugged him tight, her cheek still resting against his.

And with that innocent gesture, his heart slammed hard against his chest. She understood him in a way no one ever had. She knew, even without his explanation, that the man he was here wasn't always the man he could be away from the job. Appreciation for her insight and gratitude for her caring overwhelmed him, and a desire that far outweighed the need for sex grew inside him.

"What do you say?" she asked softly, as if afraid she'd stepped over the line.

He separated them long enough to gaze into her eyes

and stroke her cheek. "I say we go home."

Nobody had ever told Ari that buying a sexy garment was one heck of a lot different than waltzing out of the bathroom wearing one. Especially when the guy she wanted to impress waited on the other side. And he was probably naked. Magnificently so, and not the least bit insecure about showing off his . . . assets. Which meant she shouldn't be either.

Ariana might worry about what Quinn would think, but *Ari* wouldn't. Not any more than Quinn would be disappointed. Squaring her shoulders, she pushed aside any insecurities and reminded herself he cared for *Ari*. A lot.

With that thought in mind, she marched out of the bathroom and into Quinn's bedroom. He waited in bed, but to her surprise, he'd turned off the overhead lights, leaving one small lamp on, more for mood than vision, while music played softly in the background.

"Only a confident man would play the *Lion King* soundtrack at a time like this."

"And only a confident woman would model an outfit like that." He eased himself up against the pillows. The white sheet fell to his waist, revealing his muscled chest and the dark sprinkling of hair that tapered down low on his abdomen, sexy and inviting.

"It's not as easy as you might think." She forced a laugh as she crossed the carpeted room. His words registered and she forgot all about feeling self-conscious. "What do you mean, *modeling* the outfit?"

He patted the mattress and she lowered herself

beside him, close enough to see his eyes dilate with a now familiar need. "Do you really think you're going to have this thing on long enough to consider it any more than a quick modeling opportunity?" He slid one fingertip beneath a single, thin strap. Teasing her, he edged it down her shoulder until it dangled there, evidence of just how easily he could divest her of this expensive but flimsy outfit.

As he maneuvered closer, his thick erection brushed against her thigh and her insides curled in delicious anticipation. "I don't know. Why don't you tell me how long I'm going to be wearing it?" she asked in an attempt to push him to the edge.

"You're playing with fire," he warned her, his voice low and barely controlled.

"I'll take my chances." Because she wanted to see him lose control.

His unabashed desire dispelled her worries and allowed her to experiment with the ultimate power her femininity provided. Quinn did that for her. He allowed her to revel in her abilities to affect him and toss any cover or facade out the window. He saw the real woman.

He'd taught her to begin to see Ari again and to embrace her. From his smile and pleased expression, he obviously knew it, but he didn't know what else she had in store for him.

She let her fingertips trail along his skin, taking a direct path to the sheet hovering so temptingly over his stomach. She watched in fascination as the sheet moved, his response to her teasing touch obvious.

"Should I put you out of your misery?" she murmured.

He let out a strained laugh. "Either take me out back and shoot me or have your wicked way with me." He lifted his arms above his head, sank backward into the pillows, and gave her complete, unfettered access to his body.

Talk about trust, she thought, and sucked in a shallow breath, concentrating on Quinn and nothing else. She pulled the covers off him, revealing his naked body for viewing.

He was pure hard, erect male, yet when she wrapped her hand around his straining shaft, embracing his length and learning every rigid inch of him, she was mesmerized by the silken softness beneath her fingertips. And when her thumb came in contact with moisture, blocking out emotion and feeling was no longer possible. Not when faced with the very essence of Quinn.

He'd given her so much, she wanted to give back. That decision came easily and she lowered her head, taking him into her mouth. She ran her tongue down his shaft and he let out a groan that reverberated through her. A swell of desire took hold as she worked him, both with her lips and her hands.

His hips bucked, his body trembled, and suddenly he pulled her upward, flipping her onto her back and coming over her in one deft movement.

Her breath left her body in a hard whoosh of air. "Pretty slick move," she managed to say.

A slight grin tipped up his lips. "I've been trained to

respond in any situation. And I wanted this to last a lot longer than it would have if you'd continued—" He cut his words off as he sealed his mouth over hers.

He thrust in his tongue hard, mimicking the action with his hips, his erection tempting against her mound. Moisture slickened between her legs and a distinct heaviness pounded there, too, while above her, Quinn's body rubbed insistently between her thighs and a low groan rumbled from deep in his throat.

She shut her eyes, reveling in the knowledge that she'd sent him over the edge, pushing him to take control. And he did. With one easy yank of his hand, he snapped the flimsy strap of her teddy and pushed it down over her breasts, hips, and thighs until she kicked the garment aside. Cool air rushed over her and her nipples puckered harder. She lay naked beneath him, her skin becoming even more sensitized as awareness and anticipation took hold.

His gaze never leaving hers, he hooked one foot around her ankle and spread her legs wide so she opened before him, vulnerable and ready. Yet there was no one she trusted more than Quinn, with both her body and her mind. And it was her heart, which beat hard in her chest, that she refused to take into the equation.

"You feel it, don't you?" Quinn asked, taking her off guard.

"Feel what?" She was afraid he'd been able to read her mind. Afraid he would ask her things she wasn't ready to face just yet.

He brushed her hair off her forehead with a too gentle touch and a lump rose in her throat. Instead of answering, he lowered his head for a soul-searching kiss that culminated with him entering her in a long, deep motion. He filled her in so many ways and she wanted more.

Bending her legs, she took him deeper, as far as he could reach inside her body. And when he moved, he took his time, sliding in and out, starting slow so she felt every hard, solid inch as her body molded and joined with his. Then just as she began to build toward climax, he started to pump inside her faster, accommodating her need and taking her upward on a high, spiraling ride.

One she never wanted to end.

CHAPTER FOURTEEN

Quinn realized he hadn't used protection at the same time he accepted that he loved Ari. He was still buried deep inside her body, his breath coming in shallow gulps and his weight pinning her to the mattress. Rolling off her was the last thing he wanted to do, but he forced himself to move. No matter how happy his body was, his mind screamed he needed distance.

He was in love? He nearly snorted aloud. He had finally opened his heart, and who did he choose but a woman who picked up and left the people she cared about too damn easily. Just like the other people in his past.

"I'll be right back." Quinn pushed himself to the edge of the bed.

"Don't be long," she murmured, her fingers trailing over his back.

"Oh hell." He could search for some walls to erect to protect himself from her later. Right now he wanted to be with Ari again, he thought, and rolled back into her arms.

An hour later, they were sharing Ben & Jerry's ice cream in bed. Dozer lay on the edge of the mattress snoring and Ari was trying to decide what to do with her winnings.

She licked the spoon, her tongue lapping over the cool steel just as she'd taken him into her mouth earlier. He nearly groaned aloud at the memory.

"I could put the money in savings," she said, bringing him back to reality. "Or I could see if my parents need help with the spa."

As much as he loved her generous spirit, he wished she'd put herself first for a change. "Would it kill you to splurge a little? Treat yourself to something and put the rest away for a rainy day."

She nodded. "Maybe that's not a bad idea."

He persevered. "What would you spend it on? If you could buy anything you wanted, what would you pick?"

She laughed but he heard an almost desperate longing in the sound. "I couldn't afford my fantasies. Not even with my winnings."

"Let's hear it." He pushed himself up against the pillows and rested on one side. "Come on, spill your vices." He reached over and twirled her hair around his finger.

He wanted to know what secrets lurked in her heart. What yearnings she refused to admit aloud.

"It's nothing I can buy. It's just a sense of something that I'm looking for." She closed her eyes and curled into his arms. "I love this house. It's so cozy and warm."

"Same feelings I had the first time I saw it. I bought it at auction and did the renovations myself," he said, unable to disguise the pride in his voice. "This house was the one thing I splurged on." Ironic that when he asked Ari what she'd do with her money, her wishes were much the same as his.

Obviously she needed a place to belong as much as he had.

Just as obviously they needed each other.

"You made a good choice. It's on the beach and you can hear the surf," she said softly. "I feel good here."

Quinn buried his face in her hair. "You do feel good here." She also felt right here, in his house, among his things, and in his arms.

He knew better than to trust it would last. She was drowsy and her defenses were down. No doubt she'd feel differently very soon. When she learned the truth about her sister, when he'd finished wrapping up Sam's foster-care situation and the teenager was settled and Ari no longer worried about where Sam would end up. Then she'd have to decide who she was—Professor Ariana Costas or *his* Ari.

Quinn shuddered to imagine which one she'd

choose. And he could think of only one thing that might help her decide. "Ari? Are you up to taking a ride?"

She rolled her head to the side and met his gaze, suddenly more awake—and more wary than before. "A ride? Now? To where?"

"To see your sister."

Still trembling inside at the thought of seeing her twin, Ari walked into the garage. She waited as Quinn held open the door to his truck. Once she was settled, he slammed it closed behind her before getting in on the driver's side.

He glanced her way, questions in his eyes. "Are you okay?" He placed a hand on her thigh.

His touch was reassuring, but she fidgeted in her seat anyway. "I'm not sure what to say."

"I understand, and I'm sure you're going to be even more speechless as the night goes on. But Ari . . ."

She shivered at the sound of her name on his lips. She liked the familiarity and the intimacy it evoked, especially after the time they'd just shared. And especially now when she needed his support. "Yes?" she asked, swallowing hard.

"I'm breaking every rule I've ever lived by tonight." He cut off his own words with the sound of the engine turning over as he started the truck.

Her heart beat harder in her chest. Why *was* he breaking those all-important rules? Why do it for her? And why now? But she was too afraid to ask, more afraid of the answers.

Before putting the gearshift in drive, he reached back into a bag he'd already tossed inside. "I need you to put this on." He held out a dark scarf in front of her. "Blindfold yourself," he instructed, his voice leaving no room for argument.

She accepted the black garment with shaking hands. "It's already dark out."

"You need to trust me. I can't let you see where we're going. It's for your safety as well as your sister's."

Swallowing hard, she nodded, then folded the scarf and tied it around her eyes, sealing out what little light there'd been. "Where is she? In general?"

"A safe house," he said, just as the sensation of sudden movement took her off guard.

They were on their way. Knowing not to question him further, she remained silent as excitement and anticipation took hold. As if he understood, Quinn's hand returned to rest on her thigh, the sensitive spot just above her knee. Through her jeans, his touch branded her skin, and his palm remained there for the rest of the long, quiet ride to see her sister.

"Man, are you gonna get your ass kicked for bringing her here." Marco, the head of security at the safe house, gestured toward Ari, then took great pleasure in informing Quinn of his conclusion.

"Only if you open your big mouth," Quinn muttered.

Undaunted, Marco turned his wry wit on Ari. "Anyone tell you that you look just like the pain in the . . . I mean the *lady* inside?"

"A time or two." She smiled for the first time since Quinn suggested they make this trip.

He squeezed her hand tight. "Where's Zoe?"

Marco gestured over his shoulder down a long hall. "Probably in the bedroom. Any place she doesn't have to deal with me suits her fine," he said, then tossed his head in a pretty damn good imitation of Ari's twin. "Yo, Your Highness!" Marco yelled out.

The bedroom door flung open wide, hitting the wall with a loud noise. "How many times do I have to tell you, knock on the door if you expect me to answer you?" Zoe's distinctive voice sounded in the hall.

"Notice she answered me anyway," Marco said, chuckling.

"Who are you talking to?" Zoe walked down the hall, stopping short when she saw her sister. "Ari?" she asked, her tone incredulous, her voice cracking.

And for the first time, Quinn actually saw inside the federal agent to the softer, vulnerable woman. One who resembled her twin and who seemed frozen in place.

Quinn glanced at Ari. Her eyes were wide as she took a step forward, then stopped, insecurity halting her in her tracks.

He thought it wasn't pride that was keeping them apart, but rather shock and uncertainty. Quinn held his breath, wondering which sister would give in first.

Maybe it was the twin thing, but they ran forward at the same time, each engulfing the other in a hug so big, the emotions surrounding them excluded everyone else in the room. Quinn included.

He prodded Marco toward the kitchen in the back of the house, leaving the sisters alone.

He'd brought them together now instead of after the sting because he was pinning his hopes on Ari's reaction to her sister's true identity. Ari had always believed her twin had followed in her mother's footsteps, yet Zoe had actually managed to carve out a life for herself, separate and apart from what Ari called "the insanity."

Quinn was banking on that revelation to help Ari come to terms with her family and realize she could love them and still lead an independent life *here*. Just like Zoe.

Quinn hoped like hell his plan worked, or he was shit out of luck and on his own when she was gone.

Ari stepped back to study her sister. Zoe's hair fell to her back and she was as beautiful as ever. "You don't look like you've been suffering too much," Ari said, not sure where she was or what her sister was enduring here.

Wherever "here" was.

Zoe rolled her eyes toward the ceiling. "Looks are deceiving. You try spending twenty-four/seven with Marco. Insanity's about to set in. Speaking of Marco, I'm going to strangle him for letting you in the door."

Ari bit down on her lower lip. "That would be Quinn you'd have to strangle for bringing me here in the first place."

Zoe raised an eyebrow. "Mr. By-the-Book Donovan? *He's* responsible? I saw him here but didn't put two and two together."

Ari nodded.

Zoe strode up to her and looked her in the eyes. "Why? Why would Quinn bring you to me here? Now? When he knew how dangerous it was for you?" she asked, sounding more like an interrogator than a sister.

Her tone and her air of authority set Ari off. "Oh no. You're not the one who's going to ask questions, I am." Long-suppressed anger took hold at last and her voice shook as she turned on her sister. "Do you realize we thought you were *dead?* Mom and Dad are holding on to hope and going on with business as usual, but they're in pain. Do you have any idea how selfish that is? Just *who* the hell are you? What are you doing here? And where is *here,* for that matter, since I drove blindfolded just to see you?" She drew a deep breath. "You're my twin, but I feel like I don't know you at all."

A flash of guilt and more than a hint of hurt crossed Zoe's face. "I may have a lot to answer for, but you're not exactly blameless when it comes to not knowing who I am." Zoe marched over to a couch and settled cross-legged on a cushion. "It's not like you ever wanted to know. Or ever cared. You formulated all these high and mighty assumptions and they stuck." She lifted her chin in the air. "You were the professor, the academic, the smart one, and so much better than Mom, Dad, or me because of the choices you made."

Ari winced, knowing her sister was right. She'd held herself above her family and they'd all paid the price. But that didn't change the agony Zoe had been putting the family through.

But dealing with their relationship could come after both sisters understood the situation as it stood now. "I know Mom set you up to work at Damon's to get closer to him, thinking he was a good catch. But Mom also said she paid Damon back, so why were you still working there?" She ran a hand through her hair, frustrated at all she didn't know. "Because I've met Damon and I know you couldn't have fallen for him the way Mom had hoped."

To Ari's surprise, Zoe chuckled. "Mom's got these rose-colored glasses on, doesn't she? To think I could fall for that low-life sleaze." She shook her head, obviously as amazed as Ari had been.

"He definitely is slime," Ari agreed. "So . . ." She prodded Zoe back to her story.

"You should sit down, Ari." Zoe patted the seat beside her.

Ari sat, then she waited.

Zoe sighed. "I worked at the casino one night and figured out Mom had set me up. That Damon was no threat to her and the money she owed didn't amount to anything much. It doesn't take a genius or a federal agent—which by the way I am—to sniff out a setup."

Ari blinked, feeling as if she'd been hit by a two-by-four. "Say that again. Slowly."

"I . . . was . . . set . . . up. By our mother."

Ari shook her head. "No, the other part."

A wry smile took hold as Zoe reached for her twin's hand. The connection felt good after so long.

"I'm a federal agent, Ari." Zoe met her gaze, nodding slowly. "I work for a local division of the Secret Service, guarding diplomats and other high-level officials."

"Since when?" Ari asked, the truth much stranger and harder to believe than anything even her parents could have conjured up.

"I applied and started training right out of college."

"But I thought . . ." Ari sputtered, not sure what to say. "I mean you always acted like life was one big game. There was that jaunt cross-country where nobody heard from you for almost four months."

Zoe shrugged. "Training at Quantico."

"You worked as a showgirl when you needed money."

Zoe shook her head, her long hair swishing over one shoulder. "I enjoy dancing and it's good exercise, but I never worked as a showgirl. I left the house saying I was going to work. It's not like you ever saw me dance. And for the last five years, it's not like you were even home."

Ari was still unable to process what she was hearing. Or what her sister's words meant to her entire outlook on life. "Our family operates on the P. T. Barnum assumption that there's a sucker born every minute. How the hell can *you* be a special agent?"

Zoe laughed. "The same way you can be a psych professor. You have to admit with the family's eccentricities, nobody would suspect me of being with law enforcement. So?" She spread her hands wide. "Any more questions or do you finally believe I'm not wasting my life, just taking up space on this earth by operating one con after another?" she asked, repeating words Ari remembered using during one of their arguments.

Pain sliced through her at the memory. "Why didn't you tell me?"

Zoe's green eyes bored into hers. "Why bother changing a perception you found so comforting?"

"That's ridiculous."

"Is it? Come on." Zoe rolled her eyes. "You needed to believe the worst about us all or else you couldn't justify your fear and need to run."

Ari reared back, shocked by her twin's brutal yet dead-on assessment.

"You're not the only one who took psychology in school," Zoe informed her. "And if just once you'd looked at me like you cared about who I was inside, not who I appeared to be, I might have shared my life with you. I love you, Ari. And I never wanted to change any part of you. Except the part that wasn't accepting."

Ari wrapped her arms around herself and rocked back and forth on the couch. She took a deep breath and tried to push aside the hurt and anger overwhelming her.

Anger at herself, not Zoe. "I love you, too. And you're right, okay? I was judgmental. But only because I couldn't understand your life. A simple explanation and this rift between us would never have happened."

"You're wrong." Zoe hopped up from her seat and paced the floor. "It wasn't my place to explain. Or Mom's or Dad's."

"They *know?*"

"What I do for a living? Yeah. But like me, they figured you were comfortable with your assumptions, and we didn't want to shake your world." Her voice softened. "We knew how you felt about the way you thought I lived. I wasn't about to dispel the myth for you. And they agreed it was my story to tell. But I wasn't talking. Not until you accepted me for who I am inside." She stopped at a window, which not surprisingly overlooked a densely wooded forest.

A cover for this house, just like Zoe's entire life had been a cover. The same way Ari's had been a cover for everything she wasn't willing to face. And she had no words now for the sister she'd misunderstood and in many ways betrayed.

"Do they know you're alive and well . . . and here?"

Zoe shook her head, her eyes misting. "To tell them would have been to put them in danger."

Ari released the breath she hadn't been aware of holding. At least they hadn't withheld that. Although Ari hadn't told her parents she'd known Zoe was alive, her reasons were valid. She hadn't had proof. But double standard aside, she wasn't sure she could justify it to herself if they'd known and not told her that her twin was safe.

Zoe turned back to her. "Now are you ready to hear how I ended up in this godforsaken place with only Marco for company?"

Ari nodded. "Might as well give it to me all at once." She pressed her hand to her temples, feeling the beginning of a headache coming on.

"Once Mom set me up hoping I'd fall for Damon, I went to work there and immediately realized that something wasn't right with him. I couldn't say what, but my gut told me he wasn't as squeaky clean as he wanted the world to believe. I picked up little clues, meetings he lied about, dealings with shady characters, and I realized he had connections with known drug dealers. Money laundering seemed like the obvious answer. I just wanted a look at the books and then I planned on going to the authorities. But before I could even find out where the books were, Quinn caught me snooping. Damon walked in on us and ordered Quinn to take me out."

Zoe shook her head. "So Quinn dragged me out of the casino through the back entrance. Next thing I know, I'm learning that he's an undercover cop and I have to be stashed at a safe house until the operation is over."

"Well." Now that Ari understood everything about her twin, she almost wished she didn't. "I'm not sure what to say. 'I'm sorry' is a start, but it doesn't really erase the past, now does it?"

"I don't hold grudges. I'm not perfect myself." Zoe glanced down. "I mean, I could have been honest, but I was too stubborn. I wanted you to see *me* on your own."

A smile tugged at Ari's lips. "I guess we do come from the same egg. I was pretty stubborn in my beliefs, too."

"I'm so sorry I had to let you believe I was missing or dead." Tears filled Zoe's eyes. "I never wanted to hurt you that way. I just didn't want anyone going to the casino and risking their lives. I was so sure you'd hear about me and grieve, but you'd do it long distance." She wiped her damp eyes with the back of her hand. "Guess neither of us really knows the other, do we?"

"But we can change that, right?" Ari asked hopefully.

"Right." Zoe pulled her into her arms and Ari hugged her sister tight. "Now tell me all about Quinn."

Half an hour later, the sisters had caught up. To Ari's surprise though, she hadn't confided in Zoe at all about her intimate relationship with Quinn. Not because she didn't want to share with her sister, but because there wasn't anything to tell. There couldn't be anything beyond the here and now.

In discovering the truth about Zoe, her occupation, and the fact that she lived a life with direction and zeal, Ari had learned even more about herself. She was more judgmental than she'd believed and because of that she'd lost her sister's faith and trust. Ari couldn't say she liked the woman she discovered herself to be.

She'd come here with Quinn expecting a reunion with her twin. She'd gotten a life lesson instead. One that left her more confused about herself and her future than ever before.

• • •

Quinn's plan had backfired. He'd sensed Ari's with-drawal and emotional distance even before they'd left her sister behind. For her safety, Quinn still had to blindfold Ari for their return home, and she'd sat in silence for the better part of the ride.

Until finally she spoke. "Pull over."

"What?"

"It feels like we're on a highway, so find a rest stop or someplace safe and pull over. Please."

Quinn shot her a surprised glance.

Her jaw was clenched, a determined expression on her face. He'd sat in the kitchen earlier. The house was small, the walls purposefully paper thin. He and Marco couldn't help but overhear much of the sisters' conversation, and it had been far from the warm, fuzzy reunion he'd hoped for. Then again, what did Quinn know about family dynamics? Still, Ari was obviously upset and he figured it was best not to argue with her now.

He drove into an empty truck-weighing station. No markers showed where they were, so he removed the blindfold from Ari's eyes.

"Thanks." She blinked into the darkness, obviously trying to focus.

He inclined his head. "No problem." He placed his hand over the back of her seat. She was distant and preoccupied, and though he should heed her signals, his gut told him to act as if nothing had changed. Until she told him otherwise, he'd assume nothing had.

He let his fingers trail over her shoulders in an attempt to offer comfort. She subtly but noticeably eased back, away from his touch.

His stomach cramped. "What's up?" he asked. After all, stopping at a truck station wasn't an everyday occurrence. No more than reuniting estranged twins at an FBI safe house, he thought wryly.

"I wanted to talk." She glanced down at her intertwined hands. "You knew Zoe was a federal agent."

He shook his head. "Not at first. When she started working as a dancer, I had no idea. When I found her with confidential files in her hands after she'd broken into Damon's office, I thought she was just incredibly stupid. Then Damon showed up and ordered me to get rid of her." He gripped the steering wheel hard, the memories of his dealings with Zoe coming back to him. "The next day, your parents reported her missing."

"A disappearance you and Zoe staged."

Quinn nodded. "It would have gone down smoothly if—"

"I'd stayed in Vermont the way Zoe thought I would."

"That pretty much sums it up."

She sighed and Quinn felt her pain.

He'd dreaded this day from the moment they'd met, but he'd mistakenly believed he could orchestrate the twins' meeting and benefit everyone in the process. He shook his head. He certainly couldn't claim a relation to Dr. Phil. If anything, he'd screwed up Ari even more.

"What happened back there, anyway?" he asked, hoping she'd confide in him.

She shrugged. "Zoe pretty much let me know that it was my attitude and assumptions that kept me distant from her and the family." Ari rubbed her eyes with the silk scarf he'd used as a blindfold. "And she was right."

Indignation rose inside him on her behalf. "I've dealt with your sister and, believe me, she's no picnic. She does things her way. She could have confided in you and spared you both a lot of pain."

She shook her head. "She wanted me to accept her for who she was. Isn't that what I wanted from Jeffrey? From my family? Yet I couldn't do the same for them. I was arrogant, stubborn, and completely self-absorbed in my opinion of who Zoe was. God, I even dictated what kind of life she ought to live, when all along, she was working for the government!" Self-disgust rang in her voice.

"Look, I don't know much about family relationships, but I do know you two love each other. That counts for something. So you misjudged her. You'll make it up to her. In the meantime, look on the bright side. Look at the good in what you just learned."

Instead of her falling into his arms and telling him how smart he was, she stared at him as if he'd lost his mind. "And what positive thing did I just learn?" she asked, sarcasm in her tone. "Please do fill me in, because frankly I'm blank." She spread her hands in front of her.

Quinn drew a deep breath, then laid his final card on

the line. "Ari, you just found out Zoe's a federal agent, not a con artist with no direction. You must realize now that she's lived with your crazy family—*your* words, not mine—and she's still managed to take a positive direction despite it all."

Ari still stared at him blankly and frustration filled him. Obviously she wasn't ready to hear anything he had to say, let alone relate it to herself, her life, and ultimately to them. She needed time to process tonight, and he could understand.

"I need to know one more thing," she said.

He shrugged. "Just ask."

She laid a hand on his arm, then as if realizing she'd reached out for an emotional connection to him, she withdrew her touch. "Why did you bring me to Zoe now?" she asked. "Why didn't you wait until the case was over and the risk wasn't as great?"

He felt himself being led toward even greater disaster and refused to participate. "You aren't ready to hear the answer," he informed her. "Put the blindfold back on now." He placed his hand back on the gearshift, hoping she'd listen before he spilled his guts and drove her further away.

"I asked you a question and I'd appreciate an answer."

Damn stubborn woman. He exhaled a groan. "No, you wouldn't. It's like your sister all over again. You only think you want to know. Once you do, you'll run for the hills."

"I'm a lot tougher than you think. Especially after tonight. So tell me, Quinn. Why did you bring me to

Zoe? Why did you take the risk to this assignment? To your career?"

He grabbed her by both shoulders and pulled her to him. "Because I had to." By being vague, he was at once refusing to answer, yet goading her to press him for more.

A perverse part of him wanted her to keep pushing him until he bared his soul. And then what? he wondered, his head pounding with the knowledge that he was about to find out.

"Why?" she asked again. "In a few days I'll be gone from your life. You'll remember me as a woman you screwed with no strings attached. Most men would be thrilled with the situation, but you put yourself on the line. For me. And I want to know why."

She was so full of shit. She was using words to push him away, and he wasn't going to indulge her by letting an argument about semantics sidetrack him. "Because I hoped that if you talked to Zoe, you'd see that you could be a Costas, live among your family, and still have a normal existence. You could accept them and still be yourself."

She narrowed her gaze and he hoped like hell she was either thinking about his words or storing them to examine later.

"That's nice but why the hell do you care?"

"I think you already know, but for some reason you need it spelled out. Probably so you can have another excuse to run away," he muttered. "And I'm just stupid enough to give it to you. I needed you to reunite with your sister because I care. And again I'm just stupid enough to hope that you have the guts to admit you feel the same way about me."

Tears fell from her eyes but she remained silent. Which was okay, he told himself. He'd just added to her burdens by giving her more emotional crap to deal with. He trusted she'd come around.

She swallowed hard and stroked his cheek with her hand. "You're a great guy, Quinn. But you deserve a hell of a lot better than me."

And without meeting his gaze, she lifted the blindfold and tied it tightly around her eyes, closing him out.

Completely.

CHAPTER FIFTEEN

Ari rode with Quinn back to his house, but when he'd started to get out of the truck, she reminded him that he had to meet with Damon early in the morning. A not-so-subtle hint that she needed to be alone. But now her thoughts were muddled and sleep didn't come easily.

Quinn cared about her. Well, she cared about him, too, but that didn't mean she could admit it out loud. The fact that he'd brought her to Zoe, risking an entire case, his career, and heaven knew what else spoke to a depth of feeling that scared her. She had a life in Vermont. As staid as it was, as boring as she realized it had become, she had friends, a tenured job, and stability.

What did she have here? A family that she didn't

understand, parents and a twin who didn't trust her with the most basic information because she'd held herself above them. A monkey who was probably an illegal member of the clan, and a foster child she adored but who'd flip out if the monkey had to go. And a man who was caring and more understanding than she deserved.

Tired of tossing and turning, she rose at dawn and made her way to the small room Quinn used as an office, determined to focus on the one thing she could control. She turned on his computer and started to do some research on New Jersey laws and the fate of poor Spank.

Fresh from his meeting with Damon, Quinn was in a foul mood. Damon's trip had been delayed a few hours and Quinn was preoccupied, unable to let go of the colossal mistake he'd made by bringing Ari to her twin. Instead of reassuring her about her place in her family, the reunion had left her feeling more like an outsider than ever. As a result, she was pushing him away, too. He felt certain that in Ari's mind, by distancing herself, she was making her departure not only inevitable but easier.

He shook his head and decided to check out the action. He strode into the bar and saw Connor and Maria huddled in the corner, whispering and looking awfully cozy for two people who'd made sparring an art form. Obviously Connor was making progress with Maria, her kid proving not to be as much of a barrier as he would have thought. Watching them only served to remind Quinn again of his screwup with Ari and reinforce all that was lacking in his life.

He needed to get away and hang out with someone he understood. An hour later, he found himself at Elena and Nicholas's house. In hand, he had a copy of the letter of recommendation he'd filed with the Division of Youth and Family Services supporting their foster-care application as well as the request to apply for the fost-adopt program. But his real motive was the desire to hang out with Sam and remember what his life was like.

The construction had finished for the day and so the house was quiet, but when Uncle John let Quinn into the house, Quinn narrowed his gaze, unable to believe what he saw.

Spank sat in a cage. She was undressed, which was normal on any other monkey but strange for Spank, who typically favored frilly dresses and fancy bibs. One hairy arm hung limp at her side and her head was tilted at an odd angle. One word to describe the monkey was "pathetic."

Quinn stepped into the family room so he could get a better view of the sign in front of the cage:

We Don't Feed The Animal. *Unless they're all natural ingredients, which are the same ingredients we use in our products. Unless you want to end up deformed like the poor monkey we rescued from a cosmetics testing lab, pamper your face and body at the Costas Spa.*
Sincerely, The Management

Quinn rolled his eyes. This was the Costas family. He could definitely believe what he saw. He just had to keep his promise to Ari and put an end to the cons before Sam's placement was jeopardized.

He glanced around, but everyone had disappeared, including Uncle John. Quinn headed for the cage, but Sam's bubbly voice stopped him.

"Wait!" Sam said. "Don't you want to see her newest trick first?" She pointed to a change can he hadn't noticed before, which sat on a table beside the cage. A small sign said, HELP ELIMINATE ANIMAL TESTING. DONATIONS APPRECIATED.

Quinn raised an eyebrow at the sight. "This is ridiculous."

"No, it's really cool! Watch." Sam dropped a few quarters into the box.

As the coins fell, making consecutive clanking sounds, Spank smiled her infamous big grin.

Then Sam pulled a dollar bill from her jeans pocket and waved it in front of the monkey. Next Sam folded the bill and placed it into the can's donation slot.

Spank blew her a huge raspberry kiss.

"Ready for the best part?" Sam asked. She placed a single penny into the money holder. One solitary clink echoed in the room.

In return for the paltry sound, Spank turned around and mooned her, banging on her own backside like a juvenile delinquent looking for a laugh.

"Elena!" Quinn yelled at the top of his lungs. "Nicholas! You get out here now!" he bellowed.

"Geez, Quinn, what's your problem?" Sam asked.

"Is this normal to you?" He pointed to the monkey, who grinned, then waved with her good arm.

Sam giggled.

Quinn didn't find the situation funny.

Elena finally swept into the room wearing a kimono. "Do you like my outfit?" she asked, twirling around to give him a complete view.

"That depends. Are you opening a geisha house or a day spa?"

"Very funny," she said as she pinched his cheek. "Now, what did you need to see me about?"

"That." He jerked one thumb over his shoulder, refusing to look back at Spank and her antics.

"Oh, isn't she cute? Except for the pickpocket incident, she trains well." Her voice was infused with pride.

"Adorable." Quinn didn't want to ask who would be the recipient of the monkey's daily take.

"I fully expect she'll collect a fair share of donations as well as help sell our products. Did I tell you I finally gave in and hired someone to produce for us?"

He shook his head, ready to congratulate her on her good sense, then reminded himself not to get distracted. He had to make them see reason when it came to scams and to Spank.

"A family meeting is in order," Quinn told Elena. He fully intended to read the family the riot act. Much as he'd like to do it now, he knew it would be more effective coming from Quinn the cop. That meant a slight delay.

"No need," Elena said, waving her hand and dismissing his idea. "We're following the rules for Sam. Nicholas and I have been to one class and have another tonight. We filled out the forms and that cute little minivan came to visit."

"The DYFS Recruitment Mobile?" he asked of the vehicle that served as a mobile office for the Division of Youth and Family Services.

Elena nodded.

"And where was the monkey at the time?" he asked through clenched teeth, afraid he'd see Sam's last chance at adoption disappear.

"Across the street with my sister like I promised. It's just that we needed to *borrow* her for some work today. And Sam missed her."

The young girl, Quinn noticed, sat playing with Spank through her cage doors.

He shook his head. Why hadn't he realized how strong-willed and difficult these people were? And why did he like them so much despite it all? "Okay, this is how things are going to be," he said, intending to lay down the law and reinforce it when his undercover work was over.

Elena blinked but remained silent.

Quinn took that as a good sign. "The monkey goes back to your sister's and stays there." At least until he had time to figure out the laws and what to do with her. "And the cons and scams have to stop. Now. You will operate this spa legitimately. Understood?"

"What fun is that?" Nicholas asked, joining them in the living room.

"He's kidding," Sam told Quinn, trying to reassure him.

It didn't work. "And how would you know that?" Quinn asked her.

Sam clasped her hands behind her back and lowered her eyes, averting her gaze from Quinn's, always a sign she'd been in trouble.

A sinking feeling settled low in his stomach. "What'd she do now?" Quinn asked, looking from Sam to Elena and then to Nicholas.

All three remained stubbornly silent.

"Apparently Sam stole someone's lunch money," Ari said, her voice taking Quinn by surprise.

Quinn hadn't heard her come in, but he couldn't deny the leap of joy his heart took on seeing her.

"Hey, I gave it back!" Sam said, calling his attention back to the situation at hand.

"That isn't the point and you know it," Elena said, shaking her finger at the teen.

Nicholas stepped up to face Quinn. "You do not need to worry. I gave her a lecture on honesty and values," he said, putting an arm around Sam's shoulders. "And you can be sure that the next incident will result in punishment."

Ari cleared her throat while Quinn rolled his eyes. Did nobody but the two of them see the obvious? Quinn said, "Then I suggest you all start with setting the right example. How the hell do you expect Sam to straighten out if you don't?"

Nicholas and Elena hung their heads low. "You're right," they said together.

"He *is?*" Ari asked, sounding stunned that they'd caved so easily.

So was he.

"It's true," Sam said as she yanked on Quinn's sleeve. "Nicholas said if I stole again he'd lock me in the monkey's cage." Then she turned to Ari. "I'm so glad to see you!" Despite the fact that Ari had just ratted Sam out to Quinn, the teen ran to hug Ari tight.

Quinn wanted to pull Ari into his arms, too, but he could see from her posture and taut expression that not much had changed. Being alone had merely let her pull further away.

"I'm glad to see you, too, Squirt. I needed to talk to you all, but I didn't realize you had company." Ari glanced at Quinn through lowered lashes, her cool tone all but telling him that unlike the rest of the family, she resented his presence.

Though Quinn hurt looking at her, there was nothing he could do to help her. She had ghosts in this house that she needed to come to terms with on her own. In the meantime he had a job to do and couldn't afford any distractions. Even if the biggest distraction was the ache in his gut that would follow him no matter where he went.

"I'll call to set up a meeting," he told Elena and Nicholas. "I want the whole family here for a talk. Do you understand?"

They nodded. "We will be here," Nicholas promised. "All of us."

Sam clapped her hands. "Cool! We can have a party!"

Quinn didn't bother correcting her. Instead he shot one quick glance at Ari, who was ignoring him, before he strode out the door.

Ari watched Quinn go and her heart squeezed tight in her chest, but she couldn't call him back. She'd stood in the doorway in silence, listening to him lecture her family on their conning ways, watching as they accepted his words and advice without question. The same words and advice she'd been trying to give them for years, to no avail.

Then there was Sam. Ari didn't begrudge Sam a home. She adored the young girl and wanted to be her big sister. It was the situation Ari couldn't reconcile. For Sam, Ari's parents were willing to turn their beliefs and their lives upside down and change their ways. Yet Ari had had to leave town to get away from the eccentricity and the cons.

All of which led Ari to wonder why she was always the odd man out in her family. Why two newcomers could extract promises from her family that she couldn't.

"So, Ari, what did you want to talk about?" Sam asked. She glanced at Ari with huge, trusting eyes.

Ari suddenly wished she'd asked Quinn to stay as backup. "Let's all sit down," she said, and picked a solitary club chair while her mother and father chose the couch. Sam sat Indian style on the floor beside Spank's cage.

"Here's the story. I did some research on the Internet," Ari said.

"About?" her father asked.

"About Spank. Monkeys in particular." She sighed. "Look, in New Jersey, they can't be kept as pets."

"She's not a pet, she's a—"

"Member of the family," Sam said, her voice rising. "Like me."

Ari looked to her mother for help and Elena rose, grabbing Sam's hand. "We got Spank before we brought you into our home. We didn't look into the legalities. But now we have to." She squeezed the young girl tighter. "Go on, Ari."

Ari drew a deep breath and dug through her purse, pulling out the papers she'd printed early this morning. "Well, I'm not a lawyer, but from what I gather, Spank is classified as a potentially dangerous species under the law."

"That's ridiculous," Nicholas said. "Look at her. Does she look dangerous to you?" He jingled the change can and the monkey blew him a kiss.

Ari sighed. "All I know is that we have to deal with reality. And there are criteria for owning a monkey." She scanned the pages in front of her. "They include things like extensive education on the breed, housing facilities far from public access, and the worst thing is that the law specifically states wild animals shall not be kept as pets. It goes on, but essentially Spank's not a legal alien," she said in a pathetic attempt at humor.

Sam released the lock on the cage and the monkey dove into her lap. "She can't go away."

Ari glanced heavenward. She taught college-age

kids, not thirteen-year-olds, and she wasn't sure how to deal with Sam. Except from the heart. "Look, I'm fond of Spank, too. I don't want to send her away any more than you do. But isn't it better if we place her somewhere she'll be safe and happy before she gets taken away from us and then it's out of our control?"

In response, Sam ran from the room and a door slammed in her wake.

Ari glanced at her parents, feeling helpless and sad. "I'm sorry."

"For being smart enough to do what we should have done from the beginning?" Her father sat down on the arm of her chair.

"You should go after her," Ari said to her mother.

"You're a good girl." Elena gave Ari a kiss on the cheek. "I love you."

"I love you, too."

Her mother took off to find Sam.

Her father put an arm around Ari's shoulders. "You always were the levelheaded one in the family."

She shook her head, suddenly hating the differences between them for very new reasons. "Is that why I never fit in?" she asked, now wanting to feel more like a member of the family than an outsider.

"You are one of us. You always fit in." He grasped her by both shoulders, kissing her on each cheek. "You just never wanted to."

Tears filled her eyes as she was forced to acknowledge the truth in his words. She didn't understand how or why she'd let things get so out of hand, how she'd let herself drift so far from the family she loved. It wasn't even worth discussing why they'd never told her about Zoe's career. Her sister's explanation made sense now.

"Don't worry. Samantha will come around," her father said, misunderstanding the source of her tears.

Ari forced a smile. After all, how could she expect more when she'd kept herself so far away?

She wiped her eyes and smiled at her father. "I hope so," she said about Sam. But from the desperate look in the girl's eyes, Ari wasn't so sure.

"I think Zoe and Sam will get along splendidly, don't you think?"

Ari met her father's gaze. "Yes, yes I do." She swallowed hard. "She'll be home soon, Dad. I can feel it." She hugged her father tight.

"I hope you're right. The one consolation is that I'm sure she knows how to handle herself," he murmured. "In the meantime, let's go bring Spank and her things to your Aunt Dee, okay?" he asked.

Recognizing the change of subject as necessary, she nodded. "Afterwards, I have some ideas about who can take Spank, and I think everyone will be pleased."

Nicholas beamed. "You're the light of my life, Ari. Don't you ever forget it."

But obviously she had forgotten that, along with who she was deep in her heart. Her throat hurt from holding back tears as she realized that in doing so, she had no idea who and what she now wanted to be.

Connor knew he was late as he strode into the diner he

and Quinn had chosen for a quick meeting. He dumped his duffel bag on the floor beneath the table. "Hey," he said to Quinn, sliding into the booth across from him.

Quinn grumbled but didn't glance up.

With a shrug, Connor turned his attention to the menu, studying his choices, whistling while he tried to choose between a burger and a cheeseburger.

"Something's wrong with this picture," Quinn said, speaking at last, a sour tone to his voice.

Connor glanced over the top of his menu. "What the hell's bugging you?"

"Your whistling is annoying the shit out of me," Quinn muttered.

"Like I care," Connor said, rolling his eyes at his friend's attitude, hoping to push him into revealing what was really bothering him.

But Quinn didn't react, merely leaned back in his seat and groaned.

With the case close to being wrapped up, he would normally be intense, but this don't-mess-with-me tone and his fierce expression were over the top, even for him. Connor studied his best friend and an idea finally dawned, making him burst out laughing. "Oh, I get it. You haven't gotten laid lately. That being the case, I can see why you'd be in a foul mood."

Quinn narrowed his gaze. "When I get laid and with whom is none of your goddamn business. Though by that stupid whistle and ridiculous grin, you've obviously been getting enough for both of us."

Connor shook his head, chuckling. "Last I heard,

two people needed alone time to get any action." He wiped his napkin over the tabletop, sliding the crumbs to an out-of-the-way corner. "Maria and I have been a threesome since this whole thing started."

Not only hadn't he gotten lucky with Maria, but as much as he wanted her, he was content to move at her speed. Which shocked the hell out of Connor.

Quinn signaled for a waitress and ordered a black coffee. Connor asked for the same.

"Let me get this straight," Quinn said when the waitress had gone. "McDonald's, carnivals, and hanging out in front of the television with a kid, and you aren't spooked?" Quinn stared at him as if he'd lost his mind.

Connor merely shrugged. Maybe he'd found his mind instead. "It's better than just having myself for company. And it's a damn sight better than walking around sulking like you are," he said. Seeing as he hadn't had the urge to bail on Maria or her kid in the days since their first date, Connor considered it progress.

The waitress stopped by to pour their coffee and take their orders.

"Is Ari giving you trouble?" Connor asked when she'd left.

"You could say that," Quinn replied, staring into his cup. Though Connor had asked a valid question, he wasn't going to get an accurate answer. "Or you could say I'm giving trouble to myself." But Quinn wasn't about to mention his disastrous trip with Ari to the safe house. Not even to his best friend.

"Have you ever considered giving up undercover work?" Quinn asked, opting for a subject change guaranteed to take Connor's mind off women. A subject that Quinn had been mulling in the back of his mind for some time now, but one he hadn't been ready to express out loud.

He expected Connor to look shocked, but instead he received silence that only seemed to grow.

Finally Connor nodded slowly. "Sometimes I lie in bed at night and wonder what it would be like to wake up and not have to run through my cover and the lies that keep me alive," he admitted.

"Yeah," Quinn agreed. "A nice transfer to Detective Division might work."

"Mmm," Connor said.

They mulled over their thoughts in private. Both Quinn and Connor had been undercover since graduation from the Academy. Other than each other, the two men had no family. Too often they were so deep undercover, their real lives were barely recognizable. The FBI had had no trouble putting them on special assignment for the Bureau. They'd already done the groundwork to establish their cover within Damon's operation. And thank God it was almost over, which meant Quinn could begin to focus on the future.

Right now he knew Ari's crazy family had served as the catalyst for facing the thoughts he'd buried for so long. He'd never had a family, and never thought he'd want to. But watching Sam settle in so easily, and seeing how even he could enjoy the normal type of things he'd missed out on growing up, showed him that maybe he was ready to give it a try.

Quinn missed having a life. But he also wondered what kind of life awaited him if he gave up undercover work. And what kind of role the woman he loved would play in that life, when odds were she wouldn't be around to reap the benefits of his decision.

CHAPTER SIXTEEN

Quinn stood alone in Damon's office with a bank of screens in front of him. It was almost over. He'd turned over a week's worth of tapes from the counting room, and government men were working around the clock to find the discrepancies that would lead to Damon's arrest and a warrant to search further. His head buzzed with the anticipation of a job almost completed. So much so that when his cell phone rang, he almost didn't hear it.

He picked up just in time. "Donovan."

"Quinn, I can't find Sam, and Dee said Spank's gone, too," Elena said, in an obvious panic.

His stomach churned. "You're kidding?" he asked, but he knew she wasn't. "Okay, sit tight. I'll find her." He hung up and groaned, then called down to the bar and asked Connor to send Ari to see him.

Five minutes later, she burst into the room. "What's wrong?" she asked, out of breath, concern on her beautiful face.

"Sam and Spank have gone AWOL."

She narrowed her gaze. "Missing?"

He nodded. "And it's not like I can put out an APB on a blonde teenager and her sidekick monkey. Hell, it's not even like I can leave here."

She walked over and pulled him into an embrace. "I'll handle it," she promised him.

He inhaled deep, the scent of her fragrant hair and her bodily warmth reassuring him. "I know you will."

"Does she know where you live?" Ari asked.

"Yeah, so that's one place you can check. The rec center's another." Beyond that, he didn't want to think of the places a young girl could get lost. The only saving grace in this situation was that a teenager traveling with a monkey as a companion couldn't get far without being noticed.

"I'll call you as soon as I know something," Ari promised, and started to dig through her bag, which she'd placed on a countertop. "Yep. I have my cell." As she turned, the bag fell to the floor, contents spilling all over. "Darn it."

She knelt and he helped her pile everything back inside. "It's because you're nervous. Try to remain calm while you're looking, okay?" he said as they rose to their feet.

Her gaze met his and quickly, almost as if she didn't want to give herself time to think, she leaned close and covered his lips with hers. Knowing he had mere seconds, he laced his arms around her waist, deepened the kiss, and pulled her close. He intended to take advantage of what she'd offered.

Tipping her head backwards, she let her tongue slip effortlessly into his mouth and tangle with his. Her body went slack, molding against him, and as her nipples puckered beneath her T-shirt, his body tensed with desire and longing.

She must have felt it, because her legs parted, letting the hard ridge of his erection slip between. Clothing provided a frustrating barrier, but one that allowed him needed time to think.

"Sam," he muttered, pulling back.

She nodded, wiping the back of her hand over her damp lips. "I have to go." Regret tinged her voice and she didn't jump to fix her rumpled shirt or reapply her lipstick to her well-kissed mouth.

"Don't forget to keep your cell on," he said.

"I'll call." Seconds later, she was gone.

Prior to Sam's disappearing act, Ari had spent a long night on her feet. She'd been filled with anxiety, knowing Quinn was getting ready to wrap up his case and end his association with Damon—she didn't know the details of how things would go down. Worry for his safety consumed her, and though she'd promised herself she'd let him do his job, she couldn't help peeking around corners, hoping for a glimpse of his handsome face. She needed Quinn's smile or a quick nod of his head to reassure her everything would be okay.

Once Quinn had called her into his office, she'd been so relieved to see him, she'd dropped the reserve she'd been building between them. She had counted on that reserve to enable her to return to her uncomplicated life in Vermont.

Between her earlier concern over Quinn and the new worry about Sam, she couldn't help but seek reassurance and comfort in Quinn's arms. Or so she wanted to believe.

Finally the rec center came into sight, changing her focus. She'd chosen to check here first since it was open and there would be people around. She'd locked up Quinn's house earlier, so the likelihood of finding Samantha there wasn't as great.

Full of hope, Ari pulled into the parking lot, but ten minutes later she walked out frustrated and no closer to finding the teen. She'd questioned Al Wolf along with most of the kids. They'd all spread out to help her look, though none had seen or heard from Sam at all that day.

Instead of calling Quinn with no news, she decided to wait until she'd checked his house. Once she made the twenty-minute drive, she stepped out of the car once more, this time struck by the drop in temperature. In her hurry to find Sam, she'd left her jacket at the casino, and in her short sleeves, she had no protection against the cold. If Sam had come here, Ari hoped she'd been smart enough to bring a jacket of some kind.

She checked both the front and garage entrances to the house, but both remained locked and alarmed. Next she headed out back, where Dozer had a doghouse and a lead. Quinn had instructed her to leave the dog outside as long as the temperatures weren't too cold.

261

The spotlights shone out back but it was still dark and hard to see anything besides shaded figures of trees. But sure enough, as soon as she rounded the back, she heard the dog's distinctive bark.

She'd quickly learned that he answered to simple commands. "Dozer," she called. "Come."

The dog came toward her—at least she thought it was the dog, but with the dim lighting, she was uncertain. Especially since he seemed to have something large on his back. Ari blinked. She thought she knew what that something was, but the idea was so absurd she had to come closer to be certain.

She took two steps, then another. And then the vision became clear. Spank sat atop Dozer's back as he walked, the monkey holding herself up with pride like the grand marshal at the circus.

Amusement warred with anger. Anger won out and Ari sucked in a deep breath, then counted to ten. When that didn't work to calm her down, she let loose with a loud yell. "Samantha, get your runaway behind out here now!"

At the same time, Ari flipped open her cell phone and dialed Quinn, speaking to him only long enough to reassure him that Sam was okay and to promise that she'd return the girl to Elena and Nicholas before rejoining him at the hotel. For Quinn's part, he'd have to wait his turn to yell and discipline Sam until he could afford a distraction from the case.

But Ari could take her turn now. She strode across the grass and called out Sam's name again.

"I'm here, so you can quit screaming before you

wake the neighbors," Sam said in a sulky voice.

Ari reminded herself that Sam had had a hard time lately. That she'd had more upheaval than most adults endure in a lifetime and that in all probability she had what she thought was a good reason for this particular disappearing act. But the anger and fear still collided inside her, and only the fact that the young girl was whole and in one piece gave Ari a small measure of comfort.

She reached out and yanked Sam by the hand, pulling her into her arms and hugging her tight. "I was worried sick. Quinn was worried sick. And my parents are pacing the floor of the house, both worried sick!" Ari squeezed her tighter.

"Mmmmbrrgggggbbbb," Sam mumbled into Ari's shirt.

"What?"

Sam pushed and wriggled her way free. "I said I can't breathe!"

Ari swallowed hard. "And I can't think when I'm freezing."

She grabbed Sam's hand, then pulled the monkey into her arms and headed for the car. Once she'd settled Spank in the back, she and Sam sat in the front. Ari turned toward the young girl.

"Think you can get me one of those tight shirts?" Sam asked, pointing to Ari's "Damon's" tee.

"Tell me something. Do you not understand the concept of somebody worrying about you?" she asked, letting out a frustrated breath of air.

"Why should I? It's not like anybody's cared

before," Sam muttered. She wrapped her arms around herself and huddled into a ball.

Her profound words took some of the anger out of Ari, replacing it with a deep sense of sadness instead. When Zoe was presumed missing, the entire Costas household had turned themselves inside out with concern and fear. Even as they pushed on with life and business as usual, the love and concern for Zoe never diminished. Which, Ari figured, would land Zoe in deep, deep trouble when the truth was revealed.

But that wasn't important right now. Sam didn't believe anyone could care enough to worry. The sadness in that one statement was overwhelming.

"My parents called Quinn. They were frantic," Ari said.

"Yeah, well, Felice and Aaron called Quinn, too. So did the family before that and the one before that. Even the guy with the paddle in the closet called the cops if a kid went missing. They're just worried about themselves. If they lose a kid, they lose their monthly money from the state or they could even go to jail. So don't try and say that it's me they're worried about."

Ari opened her mouth, then closed it again. This child had been exposed to more than Ari could even imagine, and the sheer pain of her life hit Ariana hard. "Do you believe the same thing's true for my parents? For Elena and Nicholas?"

Sam shrugged. "How should I know?"

Ari tipped her head to one side. "Good point. How *should* you know? Maybe you were testing them?" she asked softly. The idea, once it sprang to life, took hold and wouldn't let go.

Sam didn't answer. From the back seat, Spank clapped her hands, and a quick glance over her shoulder told Ari she was playing with her feet.

Well, as long as she was busy, Ari didn't care. "Let me ask you something. You already decided Elena and Nicholas would call Quinn, since it's what all foster parents do when a child runs away." Ari gripped the steering wheel tight, trying to formulate her question in a way that made sense to a thirteen-year-old girl. "So what are you looking for? Best-case scenario, what can they do to prove themselves?" Ari asked, truly curious about Sam's answer. If she even had one.

"I dunno."

"What did the other parents do?"

"Nothing," Sam said, squirming in her seat. "Maybe a missed meal or something. Well, not Felice. She just said 'Thank goodness this will all be over soon.'"

Ari nodded. Suddenly, she understood. Undertaking the foster-care process wasn't enough to convince Sam she was safe and loved. And for all the talk of adoption, the finalization was a long way off. Too long for a teenager who'd been shuffled around to believe it. For Elena and Nicholas to pass this test, they had to react. They needed to act like parents, Ari thought.

While turning the key in the ignition, she thought back to her childhood. Beyond the pranks and the cons, there was always plenty of love and understanding. Reprimanding, too, when the occasion warranted it. She hoped they could come through now, when Sam needed it most.

The ride home passed in silence, Ari not wanting to push Sam and unsure what to say anyway. It wasn't until they pulled up in front of the Costas house that Sam turned toward Ari and spoke.

"What's gonna happen to Spank?"

Absorbed in thinking about Sam's life, Ari hadn't given much thought to the monkey that night, and the question took her by surprise. "Well, I've been looking online and making some calls. Because she's been well treated and her medical care is all up to date, she's an easy placement. I just don't want her in a zoo or someplace like that." Ari shuddered.

"I don't want her to go," Sam said, stubbornness written all over her face.

With that particular trait, she'd fit into the family well, Ari thought. "Believe it or not, I've been taking that into consideration. What would you think about giving her to an animal trainer? Someone who lives close enough that you could visit, but also someone with good credentials and who treats animals with kindness, not punishment?"

"You're *asking* me?" Sam said, her eyes wide and incredulous. As if her opinion had never counted for anything before.

"Well, seeing as how you love her, and considering you're a member of this family, of course I'm asking you." Ari reached out to rub Sam's shoulder, but the girl jerked away and opened the car door instead.

"Spank's a member of the family, too. Elena always said so and you're giving her away. How do I know they won't give me away next?" With those words,

Sam jumped out of the car and ran for the front porch.

She'd revealed her biggest fear at last. One Ari knew her parents would find much more difficult to assuage than anything else on her mind.

Ari followed Sam into the house, then sat through the session between her parents and Sam, in which Elena and Nicholas laid down the laws in their home. Respect for one another was paramount. By taking off without letting anyone know, Sam had violated the rule. She'd worried the family and had to be punished.

Shockingly, Sam had taken the punishment well, reinforcing what Ari already thought—the young girl was looking for proof that Elena and Nicholas wouldn't abandon her. By including her in the family rules and punishing her for disobeying, her parents had come through for her.

Thanks to that night's revelations, Ari could suddenly relate to Sam more than ever. It wasn't that Ari feared being sent away, but she had always feared being on the outside looking in. Being the twin nobody understood. Being the one who wasn't a real member of the family because she was too different.

The difference was, Ari had had the support system all along. She'd just been too stubborn, too convinced her way was the best, too high and mighty in her ideals to consider anyone else's way. And in doing so, she'd closed her family out of her life and out of her heart. And she'd shut herself off from fun, spontaneity, and anything that even remotely resembled Costas chaos. Like Sam, she'd pushed away those who loved her most—her parents, her sister, and now

Quinn. But understanding didn't guarantee that a lifetime's worth of feelings and habits could change.

Or did it?

Quinn let Ari into his room, unsure of why she was there. Sam was safe, and as far as Quinn was concerned, Ari had no reason to visit him now. He shut the door behind her, then leaned against the wall, arms folded, and waited. The ball was in her court.

"Sam's grounded for the next month." She shifted on her feet uncomfortably.

"She's lucky it isn't the rest of her life," Quinn muttered.

He'd obviously relaxed her because Ari laughed. "That'll come if she attempts a stunt like this again. My father's a huge believer in respect for family, and making them worry the way she did . . ." Ari treated him to a mock shiver and his gaze was drawn to her breasts in her tight tee.

He groaned. Focusing on what he couldn't have was pointless. He'd learned that early on in life. What was it about Ari that made him forget all his hard-learned lessons?

"Sam needed them to react and thank God they came through," Ari continued, oblivious to his inner thoughts. "They acted in Sam's best interest, not theirs. She must be the first kid in the world who welcomed punishment as a sign of love."

Quinn nodded. Because he'd been raised in the same type of environment, he understood the teenager's way of thinking. "If your parents can figure out how to keep her in line, more power to them. I really do think they'll be good for her."

He knew this in his gut because he, too, had looked for signs of being cared for. He'd just never found them. Not even with this woman who knew all the right things to say and do, but was too afraid to take the risk and be herself.

Ari shook her head. "For a teenager, Sam said something so profound, it floored me. She said that since my parents always called Spank part of the family and they were giving her away, what if they gave her away next?"

"So this was a test."

Ari nodded. "One her other foster parents failed."

He pushed off the wall and strode to the center of the room. "Then bless Elena and Nicholas."

Ari followed him, getting into his space. "I was so scared before I found her. I'm still scared," she admitted in a soft, husky voice.

She met his gaze with relief and more in her eyes. But he didn't know what she wanted from him now. He only knew he sensed a turning point. An honest admission she hadn't planned in advance and one he wasn't about to let pass.

"Scared of what?" he asked, his hands clenched at his sides. All his self-control went into not touching her, not reaching out, not pulling her into his arms.

He refused to make that kind of move, which to him was the equivalent of a commitment, before he could trust her more.

"I was worried that something would happen to you

during this whole . . . Damon mess," she whispered, waving her hand around the room, obviously not convinced she could trust that the place had been debugged.

Smart girl, he thought, respecting her intelligence. But it was her heart he was more interested in at the moment.

He stepped closer, closing the already small space between them. "Why?" he asked, prepared to push her hard. "Why are you so worried about me?"

His heart beat a rapid beat inside his chest, and the fear she spoke about threatened to suffocate him. Inside he was still a little boy craving love and acceptance. He'd never allowed himself to expect it, never trusted another human being to give it unconditionally, without reservation. And most of all, he'd never believed anyone would ever invest in Quinn Donovan for the long haul. But despite his well-built walls, Ari had breached them, and he hoped like hell she didn't let him down now.

She stared at him defiantly, obviously fighting some inner turmoil she kept well hidden. "Because I care about you and you damn well know it," she said, then clamped her jaw shut tight. Her eyes opened wide as she realized what she'd just admitted.

Quinn would have liked more. But for now it was enough. He pulled her against him and closed his mouth over hers.

She didn't argue, didn't fight her feelings; instead he felt the moment she relaxed and gave in to what her body wanted. And Quinn was smart enough to know he only had this one time to convince her she couldn't leave him behind and go on with her life as if *they* had never been.

Ari awoke with a renewed spirit. Quinn slept beside her and she found comfort in his body heat and the knowledge that she lay safe in his bed. So much had seemed to tilt and shift in such a short time. She had Sam to thank for testing and proving the power of her family's love. Though Ari had a long way to go before she understood them completely, her heart was now open to trying harder.

But most importantly, she had Quinn to thank for expressing a love of an entirely different kind. Not in words but in gestures and emotions and in a distinctive way she couldn't mistake. He'd made love to her, so she couldn't help but feel the connection between them. One she desperately wanted to believe in.

But fears and questions remained. She couldn't forget how easily he'd blended in and accepted her family. A family she wasn't anything like. Yet Quinn had tried to bring out that more outgoing, sexy, and fun woman he called Ari. But what of Professor Costas? Even without the suits, Ariana was still a part of her personality. Her soul. Could Quinn accept all of her?

Or once again would she be the outsider with a broken heart, longing for something she didn't understand and couldn't have?

The sound of her cell phone pulled her away from her thoughts. She leaned over and pulled it out of her purse, hoping not to wake Quinn. "Hello?" she asked softly.

"Good morning, Ariana. It's Bill Riley," said a deep, familiar voice.

"Well, hello yourself," Ari said to the chairman of the Psychology Department at her school. Despite her thoughts, she wasn't ready to talk to anyone from Vermont. His voice brought stressful tension she didn't welcome.

"I called your parents' house. I'm so sorry to hear there's been no word on your twin. It's dreadful, it really is."

"Thank you," she murmured, the guilt rising in her chest.

"I'm calling because I need to know if and when you plan on returning. Not only because we all miss you, but because I need to work on your replacement's schedule. Of course I understand it's a difficult decision and I'm sorry to put you on the spot," he said with his characteristic mix of academia and caring.

Ari swallowed hard. She knew she'd have to face this decision sometime. "I need some more time here." She pushed herself up in bed and found Quinn staring at her, his expression closed but curiosity evident in his compelling gaze.

"But you'll finish the semester yourself? The kids miss you and there's nobody who teaches with the same flair."

Ari licked her suddenly dry lips. Since when did Professor Costas, in her dark suits and pulled-back hair, do anything with *flair?* "Of course I'll be back," she said, eager to end this conversation.

When she had come home, she'd planned on returning to Vermont as soon as she found her sister. Now the thought of leaving her family—and Quinn—behind wasn't as appealing. "I'll call you when I know more," she promised Bill. "Probably the middle of next week."

By then Zoe would have returned and she would have had more time with her family. Deciding about her permanent future would have to wait until she was more sure herself of where she wanted to be. Where she was welcome and wanted—as the complete combination of both Ari and Ariana, she thought.

Quinn watched as Ari turned off the phone and replaced it in her purse by the side of the bed. He'd awakened to the sweet sound of her voice, remembered the intimacy between them last night, and then had his heated memories and hopes shattered by her words. *Of course I'll be back,* she'd said. He had no doubt she was talking about Vermont.

Which meant she'd be leaving again. Just like he thought. Just like he should have known all along. Didn't everybody in his life walk sooner or later?

"Who was that?" he asked, his voice sounding calmer than he felt.

"Bill Riley. He heads the Psych Department at the university." Ari brushed her hair out of her eyes.

He tried not to be affected by her full lips and disheveled, I-just-had-sex look, but failed. "Must be important for him to call so early."

She glanced at the clock and laughed. "It's nearly

eleven. Actually it was important. He's got a colleague subbing for me and he wanted to know how long I'd be gone so he could arrange the schedule."

"And you told him you'd be back." Needing distance, he rose from the bed.

"Well, I have to finish the semester . . ." Her voice trailed off.

"Of course you do. Just like I have to be downstairs." So far this case was falling into place, but he never assumed anything was complete until it was time to walk away.

Being back on the job now would give him something to focus on other than the fact that he'd nearly let himself be suckered into believing he had a future with Ariana.

She didn't say a word when, seconds later, he closed himself in the bathroom for a quick shower, all the while instructing himself to ignore the confused expression on her face and the wounded look in her eyes.

He was the one who'd taken a sucker punch this morning, not her. He'd put everything on the line for a woman and a future, in an ultimate gamble he was obviously destined to lose.

Alone in Quinn's hotel room, Ari sat stunned by Quinn's abrupt shift in mood from when they'd gone to bed last night to when they'd woken up this morning. She supposed he was shaken by her phone conversation, but so was she. When Ari was with Quinn, Vermont was the last thing on her mind, and that was a notion she knew she had to explore further. But first he had to finish this situation with Damon, just as Ari had unresolved family issues waiting for her when her sister came home.

Which reminded her, she needed to contact the man who was interested in taking Spank. Though she'd found him via the Internet, she'd called an old friend from high school who'd become a private investigator and he'd looked into the man's background. Michael Peters was an animal trainer who specialized in monkeys. He was based in New Jersey and met all the requirements for owning an exotic pet—which meant he met most of Ari's requirements. He lived close enough that Sam could visit. His resumé even said he'd owned the monkey on the television show *Friends* before moving from L.A. If his references checked out, he'd make a good parent for Spank, and Ari felt responsible not just for Sam's emotional well-being but also for the monkey's future.

She dug through her purse but couldn't find the page she'd printed with Peters's information. When, after her shower, she looked for her lip gloss and couldn't find that either, she remembered dropping her purse in Damon's office, and headed downstairs to reclaim her things. After the chilly reception this morning, she only hoped she didn't run into Quinn.

CHAPTER SEVENTEEN

Quinn had a splitting headache and he was in a foul mood. Putting Ari out of his mind wasn't as easy as he'd hoped. She popped into his head when Quinn was checking on the restaurants, when he fired a hotel employee for stealing bath soap, and now again while he studied the monitors in Damon's office.

The one bright spot was that his superiors on this job had just called in with the news—on consecutive Thursdays, the balance of the money from the counting-room tapes didn't match the books. They had enough evidence to take Damon in and enough to obtain a warrant to search the office and seize its contents. As long as they had Damon in custody first.

Otherwise they feared someone on the inside would tip him off and he'd disappear, something they couldn't afford. They needed Damon to roll over on the boys whose money he was laundering, the drug dealers whose cash he turned into legitimate dough. Then they'd not only take Damon down but take drugs off the streets and away from kids. Susceptible kids, like Sam. And before Quinn left undercover work behind for good, he wanted to know he'd had a hand in something that big.

He strode into the offices for what he hoped was one of the last times, and a sense of déjà vu hit him hard.

A dark-haired woman was standing by Damon's desk, confidential information in her hand. Last time it had been casino financials; this time it was information on Zoe. Quinn had pulled the files from the safe earlier. Files chock-full of the information gleaned from whatever digging Damon had done on Ari's sister. The only reason those pages would be incriminating for Damon was because it showed his interest in a supposedly missing woman, but Quinn had planned to give the papers to the feds in order to protect Zoe's identity from prying eyes.

Last time it had been Zoe snooping around; this time it was Ari. At least Damon hadn't discovered her here. Quinn didn't care how close to finished this case was, she had no right to be in this office when he wasn't around and no reason to be sticking her pretty nose into his business.

"What the hell do you think you're doing?" Quinn asked.

Ari turned around fast. Obviously stunned, her eyes opened wide, her cheeks flushed, and her hand flew to her chest. "You startled me."

"Answer my question. What the hell are you doing in here, with private papers in your hands, no less?" He stepped closer, meaning to scare her.

"I'd like an answer to that as well."

This time Quinn was startled as Damon walked into the room, his early return taking Quinn off guard.

Ari opened and then closed her mouth, probably unsure which angry man to deal with first. In her eyes, he saw how petrified she was by Damon's return.

She had every right to be scared, Quinn thought, turning to his boss. "What are you doing back so early? Lover's quarrel?" he asked.

Damon wasn't amused and his lips pulled into a thin, narrow line. "I cut my trip short because a smart man trusts no one."

Though Quinn had heard that line many times before, never had it sounded so ominous. "Trouble in paradise?" Quinn asked, still attempting to keep things light as he figured out the other man's agenda.

Damon shrugged. "Cynthia wanted to see where I worked."

"I thought you went with Roxanne?"

"She had a family emergency and had to fly home. Cynthia wanted to see my family jewels." Damon gestured around the casino but the double entendre was obvious.

"I see," Quinn said. "And once you got here, you gave her some cash to play with and told her you'd see her later?" he said, using Damon's standard M.O. He obviously hadn't given the woman a tour or someone would have informed Quinn he was back. Over the weekend, the influx of new guests had included undercover federal agents.

"Exactly. And then I came here to check on you, and what do I find? That one twin is no better than the other." He shook his head. "You disappoint me, Professor Costas. I thought you were smarter."

Ari sucked in a loud breath at the realization that Damon probably hadn't forgotten he'd found her in his private domain.

"You're wrong, boss. This one's just a bored professor." He jerked a thumb toward Ari. "Just look at her pathetic attempt to fit the part of the sexy siren." He snorted in disgust. "She's nothing like her twin."

Quinn struggled not to glance Ari's way, forcing himself to act like he didn't care about her feelings or how he was deliberately playing on her insecurities and weaknesses to save her from Damon's fury. "Hell, she might be a bookworm, but she doesn't have the street smarts to be a fed." He shook his head and forced a laugh. "She couldn't find her way out of a paper bag, let alone get in *your* way."

"Oh, really?" Damon asked, raising his eyebrows in disbelief. "Then why did she have private files in her hand?"

"Natural curiosity," Ari said quickly.

"Stupidity," Quinn muttered at the same time.

She shot him a scathing glare, proving she wasn't too frightened to be offended. Once again he admired her grit. She was more like the sister she claimed not to know than she gave herself credit for.

Quinn decided to go for broke and play Damon for all he could. There was no other way to save Ari. "It's my fault she found the papers. I heard whispers of feds sniffing around and I pulled your file on her sister so I could destroy it," he lied. "I got called to the casino before I could take care of things and left it on the desk in plain view."

"She knows too much," Damon insisted.

It didn't escape Quinn's notice that the man showed no shock at the mention of the FBI.

Quinn shook his head. "Actually she doesn't know a damn thing—unless you tell her now," he said pointedly. They both knew those files did not indicate what Damon thought had happened to Zoe. Nobody reading it, including Ari, could ever use it as proof that Damon had plotted Zoe's demise.

Damon narrowed his gaze, clearly contemplating his options. "How long was she in here alone? Better yet, *why* was she in here alone?"

"Stupidity," Quinn said again.

"Lipstick," Ari said in a hoarse voice. "I dropped my purse earlier when I came to see Quinn. You see, I missed him and wanted . . . a quickie."

Quinn winced at her attempt to explain her actions.

"He told me it had to wait," Ari rambled on. "But not before I tried to distract him." Her voice grew more sultry, more confident as she tried to convince Damon she'd attempted to seduce Quinn earlier. "But he said not while he was working." She forced a pretty pout.

Quinn couldn't help but watch and listen in amusement.

"I'd given it my best shot though, and so I still needed to fix my lipstick before I went back out to the customers. I dropped my bag and the lipstick must have rolled out. See?" She held up the tube of gloss for Damon to see.

"Convenient," he murmured, rubbing a hand over his clean-shaven face. "But I'm not taking any chances. Not with her and not with you," he said, turning to Quinn.

Catching Quinn by surprise, he reached into his jacket and pulled a gun and trained it on Ari.

A startled cry escaped her throat, but Quinn didn't take his gaze from Damon.

Under his breath, Quinn muttered a curse. His gun was in his holster at his side, but reaching for it now would give Damon a chance to fire fast. "Two sisters can't disappear from here without drawing suspicion. You'd be the likely culprit," Quinn said, trying to slow Damon down and make him think.

Warning bells went off in Quinn's head, instead. Reality clicked into place. Damon's surprise return, his lack of shock at federal interest, his sudden distrust of Quinn, and the careless order to take care of Ari told Quinn one thing—someone had tipped off Damon to trouble and now he was running scared, reacting without thinking things through.

Still, Damon obviously didn't know who in his organization was working against him or he'd have put a bullet through Quinn's head by now. The thought provided some comfort. The other man was testing him instead, giving him needed time.

With the gun still pointed at Ari, Damon propped a foot on the desk and withdrew a handgun from a hidden holster. "The entire time I was with Cynthia, something was bothering me and I finally figured out what it was." He leveled the other gun at Quinn. "I violated my cardinal rule."

"What's that?"

"I put you in charge of keeping this beautiful lady busy and you were too happy to oblige. But the more I thought about you and Zoe's twin, the more I thought about Zoe. And I realized I never saw her body. *That* was my mistake. I trusted you, Donovan, and a smart man trusts no one."

Quinn remained silent.

"It's time for some action. Prove yourself." Without warning, Damon tossed the first gun to Quinn. "Get rid of her."

A small squeak sounded from Ari's corner of the room.

"Get rid of her," Damon said again. "Or I'll do it for you."

Until now Quinn's best bet had been to stall and talk Damon through this, all the while hoping Ari remained calm while Quinn waited for the opportunity to overpower the other man. There was always the slim hope that someone on the floor would get wind of Damon's return and head on back here to check things out. But Quinn wasn't counting on it.

He needed another plan and he needed one fast, especially since he was now Damon's target.

Ari glanced from Damon to Quinn, unable to believe this was happening. She let her gaze settle on Quinn, who hadn't broken a sweat, but who also now had a gun pointed directly at her heart.

"I don't think you want a blood trail in your office," Quinn said coolly to Damon.

"What's the difference to me?" Damon asked. "You'll be the one pulling the trigger. You can call it a lover's quarrel, or the three of us can take a ride some-where and you can do the job there. It's all the same to me, but either way, I'm going to see this one's dead body." Damon's voice dropped an octave and turned as cold as his words. "Or you'll be the one on ice."

And Ari had no doubt he meant what he said.

Quinn wasn't going to like what she did next, but to her way of thinking they were out of options. She glanced from Quinn's gun pointed at her, to Damon's gun pointed at Quinn, and she knew she had to take Damon by surprise.

"All I wanted to do was find my sister," Ari said, and both men turned her way. "Or at least I wanted to find out what happened to my sister. But I'm a school-teacher, not an investigator, and now I've gotten myself into a heap of trouble, haven't I?" she asked, deliberately rambling.

Damon groaned. "Shut her up, Quinn."

"You know, I thought you cared about me," she said to Quinn. "But you've never stopped being loyal to him." She jerked her finger at Damon. "Which means I'm really going to die. Even if I don't know any-thing," she said, her voice rising in pitch.

"Ari," Quinn said in warning.

She ignored him. "But aren't I entitled to a last wish? At the very least a last meal?"

"She's stalling and you're letting her," Damon said. "Do it *now.*"

"I don't want to die," Ari wailed and dropped to her knees. "But if I have to, can I at least have a blindfold? Please?" She moved awkwardly closer to Damon, who stared at her as if she'd lost her mind. "Okay, no blindfold. Then how about a drink to numb the pain?"

"Well . . . wait a minute, this is ridiculous," Damon muttered.

"Please let me live," Ari wailed.

"For the love of—"

In the biggest gamble of her life, Ari cut him off, and with a final howl, she wrapped her arms around Damon's knees. Laying her head against his thighs, she pushed against him with all her body weight.

At the same time, she shut her eyes and prayed.

Quinn's blood pressure shot up as Ari begged for her life, her hysteria building with each word she spoke. Though he knew better than to fall for the act, Damon had always surrounded himself with bubbleheaded, whiny, crying women, and he obviously believed she was another hysterical female. And he went on believing it until she pushed his legs in her final supplication.

For a split second, Damon glanced down. Distracted by her caterwauling, he let his gun arm drop down.

In that split second, Quinn fired.

Just like every other case Quinn had worked on, everything that happened next was in a blur of activity. Connor burst in after the gunshot, with the feds on his heels. Damon, wounded in the shoulder, was hauled off, cursing Quinn in one breath and himself in another for being suckered by Quinn for so long. Ari had been brought to another room, where she gave her statement. And while Quinn knew he'd be busy with wrap-up and paperwork for a good long time, right now he was more concerned with his relationship with Ari than he was with this case.

Damon had taken years off his life when he'd tossed the gun at him, demanding he shoot Ari. Ari had taken at least another decade with her hysteria act. So by the time she walked back into the office hours later, he'd worked himself into a good case of impotent fury.

He took one look at her drawn face and saw the exhaustion evidenced by the dark circles under her eyes, made worse by smudged makeup. Relief at seeing her washed over him and he pulled her into his arms, letting himself inhale her familiar scent and feel her warmth. Dipping his head, he kissed her hard, thrusting his tongue into her mouth. She reciprocated, her body melding to his, her lips warm and eager, as if she too needed the affirmation this kiss held.

And though his relief was real, so too was the realization that this was the first time they'd had together without the specter of Damon hanging over them. No case, no missing sister, nothing prevented him from baring his soul to this woman. And though the time might not be ideal, he doubted he'd find a better one.

With regret, he pushed her away. He held her forearms and asked, "What the hell were you thinking, playing such a dangerous game with Damon?"

She treated him to her innocent look. "It worked, didn't it? I didn't see another immediate option. I knew you wouldn't be happy, but you could thank me for saving your butt instead of yelling at me for taking a risk." She couldn't quite hide the smile on her lips.

He shoved his hands into his pockets. "No man likes

to admit he was bested by a smartass woman with a penchant for relying on old movies to save herself when she's in trouble," he said wryly.

"You knew?" she asked. "You really knew what I was doing?"

"Not until you dropped to your knees like Alan Arkin, but yeah. I saw that you were acting out *The In-Laws* again. And this time it was pretty ingenious," he admitted, giving credit where credit was due. "But it was still risky."

She chuckled, obviously pleased with herself.

"Hey, your sister will be proud of you."

Instead of making her happy, his comment dimmed the wattage on her smile.

"Maybe."

Confused, he asked, "What's wrong?"

Ari shook her head. "Nothing. I suppose you plan to move back to your house now?" she asked, changing the subject.

"Just like you plan to go back to Vermont."

She licked her lips, nodding. "I have to. I just can't leave my students."

He drew a deep breath. Apparently even a cop needed courage every now and again. "I admire that about you. Even if I don't want you to go."

She sucked in a breath, visibly shaken by the admission. "You don't know what you're talking about."

"Now, that's insulting. You think I don't know how I feel about you?" He kept his hands in his pockets, refusing to give in to the impulse to shake her until she understood. "I love you. I've been in love with you probably since the moment I laid eyes on you," he said, raising his voice in frustration.

"And that's the problem. From the minute you laid eyes on me, I haven't been *me!*" Her eyes flashed indignant sparks. "First I was a watered-down version of my sister, and then I was pretending to have the hots for you in public, hoping that Maria would see I didn't have designs on Connor, so she'd confide in me about Zoe. And since the feelings were real and you wanted me, too, you seemed to like that side of me. So you took me out and coaxed the sultry side even more. But that woman isn't *me,*" she said, finally finished and out of breath.

He heard her but he didn't believe the bull she was dishing out. Quinn ran a hand through his hair. The harder he tried to reach her, the deeper into her old self she withdrew. Obviously the fear of being Ari, of being like her family, was stronger and more over-whelming than her feelings for him.

History had a way of repeating itself, and his mother had chosen drugs over him, all the while claiming to love him. So he knew too well that once something stronger than love had a hold on a person, it was nearly impossible to break.

But Ari and the life and the future they could share was worth one more try. "I understand the distinction between Ariana and Ari," he said slowly. "Ariana is the woman I met on the beach in the conservative suit, the woman who 'serpentined' last week and the woman who saved my ass today. *She's* the woman I love."

Ari shook her head, finding his words impossible to believe. How could he make the distinction between the two parts of her when she couldn't? How could he claim to know her when she'd yet to completely find and understand herself?

She pushed aside the voice in her head that begged her to listen to Quinn, to listen to her heart. Because if she accepted his words as truth, if she embraced Ari, it would be the same thing as admitting she'd willingly given up five whole years of her life, spending it in Vermont far from family and friends in order to be someone entirely different from them.

It would mean not that she was afraid to see them more clearly, but that she was afraid to let them see the real her. Afraid that even if she tried to fit in, she wouldn't be able to do it. And where would that leave her now?

"I have to go." She turned and started for the door, but he stopped her with a simple touch on the shoulder.

"If you care about me, don't run anymore."

She faced him, her entire body trembling. "That isn't what I'm doing. I'm just being realistic. I'm saving you the disappointment of seeing the real me later on." Tears filled her eyes, confusion and fear still holding her back. "I'm sorry."

"No, I am. Because I figured you for many things, a beautiful woman with many facets to her personality, one I could spend the rest of my life getting to know. But I never once figured you for a coward."

Then I guess you figured wrong, Detective Donovan,

Ari thought as she pivoted and ran for the exit.

Maybe it had something to do with the fact that he'd completed the job and had put in for a department transfer, or maybe it had more to do with Maria and the unsettled state of his relationship. But for many reasons, Connor was antsy. He'd come to Quinn's beach house to hang out, but his friend was withdrawn and morose, not providing much in the way of help or company. So while Quinn sat on the couch and stared out the window, Connor paced the floor, unable to sit still.

"What is it with women?" Connor asked at last. "They say they want truthfulness and honesty, yet when you give it to them, they want nothing to do with you." He still cringed every time he thought about his last talk with Maria, the night the Damon case had gone down.

"Beats me," Quinn muttered.

"For weeks, Maria wanted to know everything about me. All the while we worked on the case, even after we got close, she sensed I was holding back. 'Talk to me,' she said. But I couldn't."

Quinn propped his feet on the table and leaned further back into the cushions. "This job wreaks havoc on any attempt at a social life or an intimate relationship."

"No shit. But the case ended and I finally gave her what she'd been asking for. And I told her everything. That I was a cop. That I'd been undercover too long and I was getting out. Wouldn't you think that would make her happy?" Connor scratched his head.

He sure as hell had thought Maria would be ecstatic at his openness, and since most women bitched about secrecy, he'd figured she'd love not having to deal with undercover work and the hell it brought into his life.

Quinn merely grunted, so Connor went on. "Well hell no, she wasn't happy. She said she liked that I was a simple bartender. Now she says she's got to get used to me all over again and she doesn't know if she can do that." He shook his head, something he'd begun to do too much of lately. "What kind of sense does that make to you?" he asked his friend.

"None," Quinn said, without meeting his gaze, the waves in the ocean holding him captive.

Connor didn't care. He needed a sounding board and Quinn was only too happy to pretend to listen.

"If you ask me, she's goddamned scared," Quinn said, finally addressing the crux of the issue.

Connor cocked his head and stopped his pacing. Quinn's words actually made a dent in his confusion, and he wanted to hear more. "What do you mean?"

"I mean that she's obviously scared of a committed relationship. Want to know why?" Quinn continued before Connor could reply. "Because if she admits she's in love, then she's got to face herself, faults and all."

Hell, Connor thought. Who'd mentioned *love?* But the notion of Maria being scared, now that made sense, and Connor mulled over the possibility.

Sure, it was easy for her to let him into the fringes

of her life. It was even easier for her to take the baby steps of allowing him to spend time with her kid. She could tell herself she was making a start in a relationship. After all, that was what Connor had been telling himself, too. But he'd found himself falling for the dark-haired beauty and her son, and the simple life they lived. He even found himself wanting to experience the idea of family.

His fears of doing to them what his father had done to him were beginning to evaporate. Slowly but surely, Connor was trusting himself to do right by them. He even understood why. He'd been in foster care for years, and understood dysfunction and abandonment better than most. The more time he spent with Maria, the easier Connor found it to do the opposite of what was done to him. He liked giving. He enjoyed seeing the light in Joey's eyes when he tossed a ball and the boy caught it in Connor's old glove. And Connor wanted to come back for more.

But once he'd started discussing his life with Maria in the hopes of starting a deeper relationship, *she'd* made up excuses to run.

Damned if Quinn wasn't right. "You got a point, man. Maria is scared."

Quinn looked at him as if he'd lost his mind. "Who's talking about Maria?" he asked. "I'm telling you about Ari."

Connor burst out laughing. So they were both lost in their own thoughts. "They're both women, what's the difference?"

Quinn laughed for the first time all night. "Apparently none."

But at least Connor now had a handle on Maria, which gave him an edge in dealing with her fears and insecurities. All things he ought to understand, since he had plenty of his own. As far as the love thing Quinn mentioned, well, there was time to deal with that once Maria started thinking like a rational human being and not . . . well . . . not like a woman, he thought wryly.

Long after Connor left, Quinn couldn't sleep because his bed smelled of Ari. He couldn't relax over a beer because Ari had rearranged his kitchen. And he couldn't figure out how to turn on ESPN because the cable company had changed stations while he'd been gone. Instead of the box being programmed to show the sports channel when he first turned it on, like it was when he lived alone, Ari had left the television on the History Channel.

Nothing was the same. Everything in his once private domain reminded him of Ari, and when he closed his eyes, she was even in his dreams.

The only place Ari wasn't, was in Quinn's life. And that was something he had to accept. Along with the fact that he was intricately involved in her life—or at least her family's lives—thanks to Sam.

Which reminded him, he had a family meeting to conduct in order to make sure the Costas clan gave up their conning ways so that they could be approved as Sam's guardians. He couldn't allow Ari's crazy relatives to take any unnecessary risks or plot any ridiculous schemes. He owed that to Sam even if it meant facing Ari again.

Assuming she hadn't taken off for Vermont by now.

CHAPTER EIGHTEEN

Nicholas Costas had gone to sleep early, the drama of Zoe's homecoming obviously wearing him out. Ari understood. She was drained herself, both physically and emotionally. But she was also elated her family was back together and whole, Zoe and now Sam included. So while her father slept, the women of the house sat around the kitchen table. Spank included.

Her mother had insisted Aunt Dee sneak the monkey over to be included in the family gathering. To Ari's shock, Zoe and Spank didn't seem to get along. When Zoe turned her back, Spank stuck out her tongue. And when Zoe tried to speak, Spank made loud, rude noises just to be the one that got attention. Ari had never seen anything like it.

"It's so good to have all my girls home," Elena said, echoing what their father had said earlier.

"It's good to be home. You can't imagine what it was like to be stuck in that house for weeks on end," Zoe said, but as soon as she spoke, Spank began to bang a spoon on the table. Loudly.

Elena sighed. "She's just jealous. She always felt she had to compete for attention when Zoe's around because—"

"Zoe likes to talk?" Sam asked, giggling.

Zoe grabbed a napkin, rolled it into a ball, and tossed it at Sam. "Can it, Squirt."

Sam wrinkled her nose at Zoe, but the love and longing in the young girl's eyes would have been painful were it not unconditionally guaranteed to be reciprocated by anyone and everyone in the Costas house. Even Zoe, who'd only been home a few hours. At least those two would get along just fine, Ari thought, smiling.

"Did I say I was sorry?" Zoe asked, glancing around the table. "Because I am. Truly, horribly sorry for making all of you worry about me and think I was . . . dead," she said, nearly choking on the word.

"You apologized too many times," Ari said. "We understand why you had to do it." Actually Ari understood so much more, having had to lie to the family, too, in order to keep Zoe's secret and their parents safe.

Elena strode over to Zoe and hugged her tight. "It's my fault for putting this whole sordid mess into action. I never should have tried to set you up with Damon. Never should have brought you into the casino in the first place. So we both shoulder some responsibility." She kissed the top of her daughter's head. "And now it's over. We put it behind us and move on, yes?"

"Yes," Aunt Dee chimed in. "And Zoe, wait until you see the plans for the spa. I know we mentioned things to you before you disappeared, but the actual plans are incredible," Aunt Dee said, light dancing in her eyes as she began to talk about the project.

Ari watched from a distance. Not as an outsider looking in, but as someone appreciating the scene before her and the family she had as if for the very first time. Warmth filled her as she studied the interaction and accepted that she was in fact a part of this family and its dynamics.

She might not understand it all, but with age came wisdom and with distance had come the realization of all she'd missed out on by running away.

"Eeew! Would you stop playing with your feet at the table?" Zoe yelled, interrupting Ari's serene moment as she smacked the monkey's hand.

Spank in turn pulled a lock of Zoe's hair.

"Children, stop!" Elena clapped her hands.

Spank laid her head on the table, while Zoe turned to her mother. "This is mortifying."

"She doesn't live here anymore, so cut her some slack," Elena whispered, ostensibly so Spank wouldn't overhear and have her feelings hurt.

Ari couldn't help it. She giggled. Giggling turned to laughter and from laughter came tears. A huge family hug ensued that engulfed Ari in love and comfort and understanding—all things she'd missed over the last few years.

And if she still had an empty hole in her chest, well, nobody else had to know it was because she already missed Quinn.

Ari's bags were packed. She'd been back home in her old room in her parents' house for the past three days. Blessedly, the loudest part of the construction had ended, and since she no longer needed to sleep days, she had no noise issues to deal with. She and Zoe had had some late night catch-up talks, and Ari was certain Sam would adapt well to living with her family. All in all, life had returned to normal. Costas normal.

Yet Ari hadn't returned to Vermont. Instead, she was dressing and putting on makeup for a family party. A three-part family party, consisting of a welcome-home bash for Zoe, a welcome-to-the-family party for Sam, and a going-away party for Spank.

The monkey had won a starring role on Broadway in *Doctor Dolittle.* Spank was destined for stardom.

"Knock knock." Zoe peeked into the doorway. "Care for company?"

"Sure."

Although she and Zoe had talked often, there was still a wariness on Zoe's part, as if she didn't quite trust in their sisterly bond. Only time would undo the rift that Ari had created. Wanting to breach the chasm was part of the reason she didn't want to leave just yet. The other part was Quinn, the man she'd turned away yet couldn't stop thinking about, day and night.

Zoe sat on her bed and crossed her legs, eyeing Ari with a grin on her face. "I like the skirt."

Ari glanced down at the black mini. "Oops. I forgot to return it," she said, caught at stealing her sister's clothes.

"Reminds me of when we were younger."

Zoe laughed while Ari was suddenly trapped in a time warp. "We *did* share clothing, didn't we?" And not the prissy tops and trousers Ari had been favoring for too long now.

Her twin nodded. "For a while we shared everything. Until you put up a wall and pulled away from the family."

Ari swallowed hard. "I hated that our family was so different from everyone else's," she admitted. "I wanted to blend in and not stand out, and to me that started with the way I dressed."

"It wasn't . . . isn't just the clothes. It was the attitude. You changed. You condemned us and our choices. And as a kid, I could understand it more than I did over the last few years."

Ari nodded. "I wish I could say it wasn't intentional." She settled in beside her sister. "But in the beginning I wanted to create distance and later it had become a habit. If I told myself I didn't understand you, then I couldn't be like you." She sighed.

"There's nothing wrong with embracing individuality," Zoe said. "For you or for me. But that overwhelming need not to be one of us . . ." She shook her head. "That I never understood."

Looking back, Ari couldn't comprehend it either. "What started out as adolescent embarrassment ended up changing me." She held her hands out in front of her, trying to explain and apologize at the same time. "And then the disastrous affair with Jeffrey just topped it all off and I needed to get away."

"And now you're going back." Zoe pointed across

the room to the fully packed suitcases that lay open on the floor.

"I have this semester and next to finish." But the excuse sounded lame to Ari's ears. Yes, she had a job and a commitment, but many teachers took unexpected leaves and the school and the students survived. In her case, the substitute was a talented young professor seeking tenure. She'd be happy to take over and finish Ari's class.

She blinked. *What was she thinking?*

"Do you enjoy teaching?" Zoe asked.

"I *love* it. I really do, but—"

Zoe nudged her leg. "But what?" she prompted, a knowing smile on her lips. "But you enjoyed the excitement here, too?"

Ari laughed, almost reluctant to admit her twin had a point. "Yeah. I did."

"I thought so, especially after I heard how you pulled off the ultimate Costas con."

As Quinn had predicted, pride suffused Zoe's voice, but all Ari could think about was her twin's choice of words. "What do you mean I pulled off a con?" Her throat seemed to close as she spoke the word.

"When they released me from protective custody, Marco said Quinn had raved about how you'd distracted Damon with your rendition of *The In-Laws*." Her eyes glittered with amused laughter. "Dropping to your knees, crying, howling, begging for your life, all so Quinn could catch Damon off guard. And all without being preplanned."

Ari felt herself blush, a heat rising to her cheeks as

her federal-agent sister went on about her amateurish attempt at saving the day. "It was a gamble. A gimmick. All I could think of on the spur of the moment."

"That's right. You thought on your feet and you did it just like any Costas would. You pulled off the ultimate con on that dirtbag Damon. After all the bimbos he dated, the man finally got his comeuppance by a woman. It's sweet justice." Zoe grinned. "But for you, it was absolute proof."

"Of?" Ari asked, but she had a hunch she already knew.

"That you're one of us," Zoe said. "It's in your blood, it's in your genes, but most of all it's in your heart." She spoke the words Ari had already accepted that night in the kitchen.

Reaching over, Zoe pulled her into a warm hug. "Welcome home, Ari."

Ari's eyes filled with tears and she embraced her sister in return.

"Marco said Quinn had to be damn quick on his feet to get what you were doing." Zoe eased back, still not finished regaling Ari with Marco's version of events. "Either that or you two must have had some kind of mental telepathy or connection." Her twin's voice trailed off as the truth obviously dawned. "So what exactly is going on between the two of you?"

"Nothing," Ari said. "Not anymore."

Zoe narrowed her gaze. "But something did. I knew it the second I saw you two at the safe house. If he did anything to hurt you, I'm going to kill him," she said, and from her protective tone, Ari knew she meant it.

"Quinn's a good guy. He's been through a lot in his life and he deserves someone who'll be there for him."

"And you won't?" Zoe scoffed at the notion. "I can tell you that even if you finish the semester in Vermont, you'll be back."

"What makes you say that?" Ari asked, but a smile tugged at her lips. The thought of coming home for good opened the vise around her heart and she breathed easier.

Zoe rolled her eyes. "Didn't we just cover all that? You're one of us. You can't go back to that boring life in Vermont any more than you can button up your collars again." She pointed to Ari's lace camisole, which she'd sneaked out of Zoe's drawer to pair with her already pilfered miniskirt.

"I've been telling myself that I don't know who I am. But I do," Ari said softly. "It's just so hard to admit it out loud."

"Why?" Zoe asked.

"Because it means I lost five years of my life living in Vermont, away from you, from Mom, Dad, and the rest of the family." Admitting her faults wasn't easy but it was the first step toward making her way back.

"It helped you grow. It helped *us* grow and change and come to understand you better, too," her sister said. "And now it's in the past, right?" Zoe looked anxious as she awaited an answer.

"Right," Ari said. "I really did have some good times in Vermont and met some good people and friends. It just isn't right for me anymore. It hasn't been for some time." She'd just been too stubborn, too entrenched in the conservative world she'd created for herself to admit it.

"It took my missing-person stunt to prove to you what you knew all along. In here." Zoe tapped her chest, right above her heart. "But I'm so sorry about the pain I caused all of you."

Ari nodded. "I know. And you can stop apologizing for it."

"Now that you're facing your family and your past, I have one more question for you," Zoe said.

Ari shrugged. "Might as well get it over with all at once, so shoot," she said, laughing.

Zoe sobered as she said, "You wasted five years away from your family. How many are you going to waste away from Quinn? The man you obviously love?"

As Ari glanced at her twin and contemplated the question, she wasn't laughing anymore. Because Zoe was right. She *did* love Quinn and had for some time. Voicing the truth she'd been fighting made her light-headed and giddy.

She loved him.

She loved his tough-guy exterior and the softness inside he didn't let many people see. She loved the way he'd created his own family out of Connor and Sam, all the while denying he had anyone in his life he cared about or who cared for him. And she loved how he'd put her before his job, first by admitting her sister was alive and then by taking her to the safe house and risking his career. But she hadn't repaid him well.

Quinn Donovan was a man with a difficult history behind him, and one who didn't trust or give of himself easily. He'd given Ari his heart, but not once had she admitted she felt the same. She'd pushed him away, the fear of finding and accepting herself too overwhelming.

She'd let him down and he had every reason to withdraw into himself and keep her at a distance now. Just as she had no choice but to confront him and see if they could try to create a future together.

She glanced up to tell Zoe she was right, but her twin had disappeared, leaving Ari alone with her thoughts. Ari hoped it wasn't an omen of things to come.

Connor led Maria into the Costas house, his hand on her back. An unfamiliar feeling of pride swelled inside him, that he had this woman and her son by his side.

"Connor!" Zoe called out, coming up beside him. "Maria! I'm so glad you could make it." She knelt down to the boy's level. "And this handsome guy must be Joseph. Your mommy told me all about you when we worked at the same place." Zoe held out her hand and the boy took it. "I have the best surprise for you," she told him.

Remembering what Quinn had said about the reasons for this party, Connor laughed. "You're gonna like this one, Joe." He and the boy had settled on the more grown-up name of Joe to replace the childish Joey his mother insisted upon.

"Can I take him to see Spank?" Zoe asked Maria as she rose to her feet. "Just down in the basement. You can catch up with us there."

Maria nodded. "It's fine with me."

"Want to go see a monkey?" Zoe asked.

"Heck yeah!" He took off at a run, Maria calling after him.

"Behave," she yelled, too late for him to hear.

Connor laughed. "He'll be fine." He squeezed her hand in reassurance.

She was so used to handling Joe alone that it was difficult for her to let him out of her sight or cede control unless she was working. Now that Connor's last undercover stint was over and he'd taken on regular shift work, he intended to change all that.

"Let's go get a drink." He motioned to the bar set up in the corner of the room.

"What are they constructing?" Maria asked as she waited for her drink.

Connor shrugged. "Quinn mentioned something about a day spa."

Maria's eyes lit up. "Oh, I'd love to have a place to come to after a long night of work. Maybe I can even afford it one day."

The bartender handed her a drink and she let out a long sigh as she sipped the cola. Another thing he'd noticed about Maria, she didn't drink liquor or beer when her son was around, and as a result, neither did Connor.

"I guess you don't know what a detective earns, do you?" he asked.

She raised an eyebrow. "My mother taught me it's rude to discuss religion, politics, and money."

"Unless you're with a person who's looking to make a long-term commitment and needs to know we're on the same page."

She choked on her soda and began coughing. "Connor—"

"No. No more avoiding, no more jokes, no more anything except the truth." He grabbed her hand and held on tight. "I care about you." He more than cared, but he wasn't looking to scare her off. If she agreed, he had time to convince her. "And all I want for you to tell me is whether you feel the same. If so, I think we can build something. You, me, and Joe."

She blinked, tears filling her eyes. "I care but I'm scared. And I hate you for making me admit that," she said, trying to turn away.

"Good." He pulled her back. "Hating me is a start. Besides, I'm scared, too." Going out on a limb, he admitted his deepest fears to Maria. It was something else they had in common. "Did you know they say there's a fine line between love and hate?" he asked her.

She glared at him, but he saw the beginnings of a smile on her lips. Her smile warmed the coldest places inside him. Like he'd told Maria. It was a start.

From the festive sounds downstairs, the party was in full swing, and Ari was finally ready to face her family and resume her place within it. She walked to the top of the stairs and paused at the wall of shame. As she viewed the pictures from a new, adult perspective, she saw a remarkable collage of family photos. A history few people could claim and one Ari was now proud to be a part of.

She couldn't erase the years she'd distanced herself, but she could make up for them now and enjoy the present. As she made her way to the bottom step, she noticed the newest addition to the wall, a picture of Sam and Spank in matching dresses. What struck Ari most was how the young girl's blonde hair fell around her shoulders, no baseball cap in sight, no attempt to hide from herself or blend into the scenery.

To Ari, the irony was clear—while Ari had lived here, she'd run from herself. As soon as Sam moved in, she'd done the opposite. In the Costas house, Sam had finally found the sense of security that enabled her to be herself. It had taken Ari much longer, but she'd finally come full circle.

A smile on her face, Ari strode into the room to join the party. She'd been told only family would be present, and so when she caught sight of Connor, Maria, and Quinn, she felt as if she'd been sucker punched by the unexpected guests. In Ari's mind, there were two possible explanations.

The first was her gut reaction: the family had blind-sided her by bringing Quinn here. But her mother had sworn she'd learned her lesson trying to matchmake with Zoe and Damon, and so the second explanation that came to Ari's mind was the more plausible one. Even if it was more twisted in logic.

This was a family party. Sam was now family.

Quinn was Sam's family, which made him part of the Costas extended family. Since Connor was like family to Quinn, that explained his presence, and he'd brought Maria. All in all, a typical Costas type of gathering, Ari thought.

If she weren't so stunned, she'd thank her family, since they'd saved her from having to seek Quinn out on her own. But with no warning and no time to plan how to handle him, she felt trapped, and her stomach bunched into tight, nervous knots. Just because they occupied the same breathing space by no means guaranteed the outcome Ari wanted.

Quinn watched Ari's entrance. The sense of longing he felt upon seeing her warred with anger because she hadn't been able to get past her damn fears and walls. Hell, nobody had bigger walls than he had, and he'd torn them down for her. Man, he didn't want to be here, and as soon as they got past the celebration stage and he could lecture the family all at once about ending their con-artist ways, he was out of here.

"So glad you could make it," Nicholas said, coming up to Quinn and pulling him into a bear hug. "I even forgive your . . . how do you say? Deception for not telling me Zoe was alive. You saved her and that's all that matters." The older man hugged him again. "You will always be part of this family."

Without warning, a lump rose in Quinn's throat as Ari's father offered him the acceptance he'd never had. "Thank you, sir."

Quinn felt the heat of a stare at his back. He didn't

have to turn to know Ari was watching the entire exchange. Ari, in the black miniskirt she'd worn on her first trip to the casino and a flesh-colored lace top that made him want to drool.

Ari was still dressing as if she'd accepted her freer, more sensual side. But Quinn knew better than anyone, Ariana Costas knew how to use clothing to her advantage. Whether she was covering her Costas roots with conservative clothes or, as now, dressing to fit in with her relatives, nothing with Ari was ever as it seemed. How could it be? Inside she was still running, and nothing, not even his declaration of love, could change that.

He'd given her his heart, something no one had ever received from him before, nor would they again.

Nicholas shook a finger in front of his face. "It's a good thing you paid more attention during this case of yours or both my daughters would be gone."

Quinn forced a laugh, since the older man seemed to think he was hysterically funny. "Sorry. I got distracted."

Nicholas nodded. "Well, I was just reminding you there are no formalities among family. So no more calling me 'sir,'" he admonished. "Oh, look. Kassie's here." The older man headed to welcome his sister and her brood.

"I don't know what to make of them," Connor said, coming up beside him.

"If you mean the family, I understand. They can have that effect on you." Quinn chuckled, recalling his first meeting with the relatives when he'd been pick-pocketed by the monkey.

Connor slapped him on the shoulder. "You can handle them."

"For Sam, I'll manage," Quinn said wryly.

"But I was talking about handling them for Ari."

Quinn rolled his eyes. "Not everyone's finding love as simple and as easy as you. The woman wants nothing to do with me, or haven't you noticed?" Quinn asked, since Connor already knew Ari had run from him and he also knew why.

"I know she hasn't stopped staring at you since she walked into the room."

And that could be explained by lust, Quinn thought. God knew their chemistry was explosive. And in the past, with any other woman, that would have been enough for Quinn. But from Ari he'd wanted more.

Connor didn't comment further and was soon distracted by Maria's return from the basement.

The rest of the evening passed with toasts and thanks and hugs and kisses. Not surprisingly, Ari avoided him the entire time.

Quinn glanced at his watch. Enough time had passed and he clapped his hands, calling the entire family to attention. It was time to make sure they knew that with a child in the house, their conning future had come to an end.

And then he was going home.

Ari wasn't surprised her entire family stopped to listen when Quinn demanded the floor. He had that commanding presence, something she'd noticed from the moment he'd tackled her on the beach.

"I need to say a few things and then you can all get back to your party," Quinn said.

"About what?" Cousin Daphne, the nosy one, asked.

"About Sam's future and everyone's behavior from now on."

Sam let out a loud, adolescent-sounding groan. "Don't say anything to embarrass me, Quinn," she called from the back of the room.

Ari chuckled. "If you're going to live with this family, you'd better get used to being embarrassed. As well as being the center of attention," she told the girl. But surprisingly, the thought no longer held the bitter memories it once had.

Quinn glanced her way. For the first time all night, their gazes met and held and a wealth of under-standing passed between them. A wave of warmth and security swept through Ari as she realized how lucky she was to have found this man who understood her feelings about herself and her family and accepted her anyway.

What he didn't know about was her acceptance of herself. And because she'd pushed him ,so far away, she didn't know if her revelations had come in time for *them*. She needed to get him alone, and there just hadn't been an opportunity during the party. Not when everyone wanted to thank him for helping Zoe and to get to know him. Ari had given her family the time they needed, since she planned to steal him away later.

"I noticed the monkey's not up here," Quinn said, breaking the silent connection between them.

309

"She's in the basement," Aunt Dee said. "With her trainer."

"New owner," Sam chimed in. "Did you hear? Spank's got a new job."

Quinn raised an eyebrow. "She's not mooning in exchange for spare change, is she?"

Apparently Quinn hadn't been privy to the recent developments involving the monkey.

"Spank's gonna be a star!" Sam said, her excitement tangible. "You see, Ari found a man who's allowed to own monkeys. Because she didn't want my case-worker to make me leave here. At first I was so pissed." She shook her head, obviously catching Quinn's glare. "I mean I was so *mad*."

"Better," Quinn muttered. "Go on."

"But then Zoe came back, and she told me that Ari's the conscience of the family. She wants everyone to do the right thing. And giving Spank away is the right thing to do if I want to live here forever. And I do, Quinn. I really do."

Ari watched as the dialogue between Quinn and Sam took center stage, his planned lecture giving way to something far different. His expression softened as he listened to Sam's heartfelt plea. The rest of the family remained silent, taking it all in, too.

"I agree that Ari wants what's best for everyone," Quinn said, surprising her. "Except herself. Then she's too afraid to stand up for what she really wants."

The room was awash with loud gasps.

Ari raised an eyebrow, her hands coming to her hips. "Of all the unmitigated gall," she muttered. It was one thing to yell at her in private, but to condemn her in front of her family was something else entirely and she wasn't about to let him get away with it.

"Are you telling me I'm wrong?" Quinn asked, obviously challenging her.

"Ooh, I sense a good argument," Nicholas said.

"It's like one of ours," Elena agreed.

Nicholas let out a loud growl. "But ours end up in the bedroom and they aren't married," he said in protective-father mode.

Zoe placed her hands over Sam's ears.

Ari cringed. She'd wanted to wait until the party ended to talk to Quinn, but he was obviously spoiling for a fight. And no matter what her father said, Ari refused to discuss her future in front of her entire family.

"Apparently you forgot you were about to lecture everyone here on morals and upstanding behavior?"

He glanced at her family. "No more cons, no more games. I'm a cop and if I catch you red-handed, you won't leave me with a choice but to turn you in. Plus if a caseworker gets wind of anything other than a respectable business going on here, she'll pull Sam faster than Spank can pick my pocket. Got it?" he asked.

They all nodded and murmured their assent. It was a miracle, but somehow Ari believed they understood.

Then Quinn turned his glittering eyes back to her. "I'm finished."

"Good."

She'd learned more than she realized from watching

her mother deal with her father over the years, and now Ari decided to take control of the situation and Quinn. "If you have something to say to me, you can do it in private. *Now.*" She turned and walked out of the room, not looking back, ignoring the stares of her relatives, the laughter, the knowing looks.

She'd just executed a typical Costas-woman move by making a scene. Well, Quinn had started the spectacle, and if he wanted to talk, he'd just have to damn well follow her and accept that the family thought *she* had complete power over him.

In reality, Ari knew better. Even if he followed, the man had the power to break her heart.

Quinn didn't know what had possessed him to provoke Ari in front of her family, but he was furious at her and when the opening presented itself, his frustration and anger had spilled over. Now he had to pay in the form of humiliation in front of all her relatives.

Ignoring Connor, who stood in a corner trying not to laugh, Quinn glanced around the room at the expectant faces, especially Nicholas's.

Finally he merely shrugged. "You said it yourself." He spoke directly to Ari's father. "It's the best part of making up."

"When you are married."

Quinn groaned. "Then tell your daughter to stop running away."

"I heard that," Ari called from the doorway.

Quinn had had enough. He strode through the crowd, grabbed her hand, and pulled her through the entryway and out the front door.

"Where are we going?" she asked, outraged, as he opened the door to his truck and nudged her inside.

"Somewhere we can be alone." But somewhere he could get to quickly, which didn't leave him with many options.

Minutes later, he'd parked near Islet Pier. Once again, he grabbed her hand and led her to the vacant snack shack where they'd first officially met. She didn't have a coat and neither did he, which suited him fine. It would force her to talk fast and openly or freeze to death.

No sooner had he pulled her into the shack and slammed the door and the cold wind behind them, than Ari cupped his face in her palms and kissed him. A quick, hard, determined kiss.

"What was that for?" he asked, stunned at her complete reversal in behavior.

"For being you. For loving Sam enough to put yourself out for her. For being a master at handling my family. For putting them in their place. For gaining their respect and mine." As she spoke, she rubbed her hands together to keep warm.

He knew she was cold but Quinn wasn't ready to pull her into his arms and provide body heat. "I'm so glad you approve of my actions." He wasn't anywhere close to understanding where this crazy female's mind or heart was, and he refused to let Ari trample him again.

"You need to understand a few things." She paced the floor, an obvious attempt to keep moving and stay warm. "You think that I should get the concept of family because I'm so lucky to have one."

Quinn shook his head. "Honey, I know exactly what it was like for you." And he'd offered her as much understanding as possible. "Maybe you need to hear what it was like for me. My mother was a drug addict and a hooker. My father was any one of hundreds of guys who paid for the right to her body. I don't know and I don't care. Neither did she as long as she had the money for her next fix. Food wasn't as important as drugs and because of that, she OD'd one day and I found her."

Ari winced. "Go on," she said, apparently knowing not to offer sympathy.

Smart girl, he thought. He hated talking about where he'd come from. Now *he* started pacing the floor, trying as always to outrun what was always there, inside him.

Ari remained silent, frozen in place, waiting for him to continue.

"From there it was one foster home after the next. I've been on my own for longer than I can remember, and I always lived by rules that I understood. Nobody watches out for you except yourself, and everybody will take off one day if given the chance. Including you. Hell, especially you. I told myself over and over that not only would you leave, but you wouldn't want anything to do with me long-term. And man, you proved me right."

He refused to meet her gaze. "So whatever game you're playing now, dressing and talking like *Ari,* I'm completely prepared for you to morph back into your prissy Ariana mode. I'm through trying to convince you I love all parts of you. Hell," he said, running a hand through his hair. "I'm just through."

"Good," she said, coming up beside him. "Because I'm just getting started. Everything you ever said about me was right. I was running. I've always been running. Growing up is a scary thing for anyone. Some more than others. I never realized how good I had it. The truth is, you get the notion of family a lot more than I ever did."

He shot her a disbelieving glance. "Now, that's a laugh."

"You didn't have a family and you created one out of Connor and Sam. You met my parents and my wacky relatives and you didn't judge or condemn. Instead you fit right in and a part of me resented you for it." She shook her head. "It was just so easy for you, when it never was for me."

Though he warned himself not to, he reached out and touched her arm. "To fit in anywhere, all you need to do is accept yourself."

She blinked, tears forming in her eyes. "I know that now. From the minute I heard Zoe was missing until right this minute, I've had to really look inside myself." She bit down on her lower lip.

The uncertainty in that small gesture tugged at his heart. "I've seen inside you all along."

She smiled. "I know that, too. You helped teach me to accept myself."

"Is this your way of telling me you're leaving for

Vermont, Ariana?" He used her full name for the first time, hating the feel of it on his tongue because it signaled the end.

"I can understand why you'd think that, but no. I'm trying to tell you that I'm staying. I love my family and I miss them and I want to come home. Well, not to their house. That would be too much for any partially sane person. But home to New Jersey," she said, her words rambling, coming as fast as her thoughts. "It has to be after I finish the semester, because I really do owe the school and the students that much. Unless of course they don't need me after all. We'll see."

"That's all great." His head spun from the unexpected revelation.

She met his gaze. "And I'm so grateful to you for helping me reach this point in my life." She grabbed his hands and held on tight.

He remained silent.

"Don't you have anything else to say?" she asked, hope and something more in those huge green eyes.

What did she want from him? "I'm thrilled that your family has you back. I am. But I can't exactly say I'm overjoyed I'll have to run into you when I come to visit Sam."

Without warning, Ari burst out laughing. "Oh, Quinn, I'm sorry. I just replayed that whole conversation in my head and in all my soul-baring I forgot the most important thing." Her expression sobered, her eyes grew wide and imploring.

He almost allowed himself to hope, but that flame had already been extinguished.

"I love you. Whether or not I blew my chances with you, I'm coming home to stay. But you have to know that I do love you. I may have spent my life running away from everything that was good, but I'm stopping here. Now. And I want to walk out of this frozen snack shop knowing I'm heading toward a future. With you."

Quinn felt as if time had stopped. He'd given up hope and stopped believing. Even when she said she was staying, a part of him clung to the past and the little boy who felt he didn't deserve the family all the other, *good* kids had. He was certain Ari was letting him know that although she'd be in town, they wouldn't be together. He couldn't allow himself to think she'd want him and to suffer the unbelievable pain she'd inflicted the first time she'd walked away.

Until now. Until she said those three words that nobody in his life had ever said to him. Ever.

He pulled her close. "Do you mean it?" He asked because he had to, but he already knew. He felt the warmth, the caring, the love he knew had always been there between them. She'd dug deep enough to cause herself inner pain and had come out the other side whole.

She nodded. "I mean it. I love you with every fiber of my being. And though I wouldn't blame you if you turned and walked away, I wouldn't let you. I'd just have to tackle you on the beach and take your breath away. Like you did to me that first time. Like I want you to do to me now."

Quinn was only too happy to oblige. He lowered his

lips to hers and kissed her like there was no tomorrow.

Ari threaded her fingers through his hair and pulled him close, although with the barrier of clothing, she couldn't satisfy the desire to feel skin against skin and lose herself in him.

But that was okay for now. They had all the time in the world together. And only the rest of their lives would do.

Epilogue

The Islet Pier News
Monkey Business Disrupts Broadway Premier

The much anticipated Broadway premiere of *Doctor Dolittle*, starring hometown heroine Spank Costas, a monkey of questionable family lineage, was marred by rude gestures and crude remarks. The histrionics didn't come from a boorish audience member but from the star of the show when a cast member forgot to empty his pockets. The actor did a handstand and a penny fell to the floor on the stage. In turn, the monkey dropped her pants and mooned the shocked audience. "Learned behavior is easier to teach than to unteach," said her trainer, the reputable Michael Peters, who blamed her previous owners for the night's catastrophe. The play was postponed indefinitely.

Center Point Publishing
600 Brooks Road • PO Box 1
Thorndike ME 04986-0001 USA

(207) 568-3717

US & Canada:
1 800 929-9108